Readers love
CHEYENNE MEADOWS

Feline Persuasion

"…a short, fun read with some super-hot and caring shape-shifting men! What more can you ask for?"
—Crystal's Many Reviewers

"…a very hot, very well written triad story."
—The Kimi-chan Experience

"I would recommend *Feline Persuasion* for anyone who likes their shifters hot, Alpha, and sexy as all hell."
—The Novel Approach

Friends With Benefits

"…a lovely book, with a catchy storyline."
—Sinfully

"…I have to say this is one very entertaining read and I got quite a few laughs."
—The Romance Reviews

Shadowing Mace

"The sex was off the charts… and sex doesn't usually sell a book for me, but this was so well written that I needed to add it to my review."
—The Blogger Girls

"This is just one hot, steamy read that is also quite a bit of fun."
—MM Good Book Reviews

By CHEYENNE MEADOWS

Feline Persuasion
Friends With Benefits
Shadowing Mace
Relentless

Published by DREAMSPINNER PRESS
www.dreamspinnerpress.com

RELENTLESS

CHEYENNE MEADOWS

Published by
DREAMSPINNER PRESS

5032 Capital Circle SW, Suite 2, PMB# 279, Tallahassee, FL 32305-7886 USA
www.dreamspinnerpress.com

ISBN: 978-1-63476-871-9
Digital ISBN: 978-1-63476-872-6
Library of Congress Control Number: 2015917574
Published February 2016
v. 1.0

Printed in the United States of America

This paper meets the requirements of
ANSI/NISO Z39.48-1992 (Permanence of Paper).

A huge thank you to Edward. His insights and suggestions are always right on the mark and very much appreciated.

Prologue

ANOTHER BEAD of sweat trailed down the side of Jag's face, his already saturated headband unable to hold any more. The sun's stifling heat and blazing brightness caused several more drops to follow similar paths. His shirt clung to him due to the dampness. More than anything, Jag wanted a hot shower. That wasn't happening, at least not soon. He could get cleaned up when, and only when, he completed his mission—this endless mission in the bowels of the deadliest acreage in Afghanistan. Three weeks had passed as he'd holed up in one cave crevice or another, tracking Sandman, the most violent, cruelest bastard to walk the earth in a long time.

If he could have moved Sandman faster, Jag would have. Instead, they were stuck following a vague trail of bodies from one end of the noxious place to another. Sandman never showed himself and proved worthy of all the rumors. In essence, he was a sniper of the highest caliber—smart, talented, and fucking psychotic, with an obsession for carving up his victims like pieces of morbid artwork.

"Damn it. Where is he?" Mark, Jag's spotter, grumbled as he raked the area with his high-powered binoculars.

Jag held steady, constantly watching through his specialized scope that allowed him to see an ant crawling on the sand over a mile away. "He's out there. I feel him. Just be patient," he whispered, low enough so that only Mark could hear him. In Korangal Valley, otherwise known as the Valley of Death, voices carried and echoed in the mountains. In order for a sniper to stay alive, he had to be still, quiet, and lethal with his aim, something Jag excelled at.

Mark scooted a bit farther away, grabbed his canteen, and took a long drink. "If I had to be out here with anyone else, I'd have gone mad by now."

The sentiment worked in both directions. Jag glanced over at Mark and offered up a smile. "Ditto. Even up to our armpits in tangos and sand in places it shouldn't be, at least we're together."

A grin appeared on Mark's face. "Love is crazy, huh?"

"Yeah." Jag saw the concern written on his lover and husband's face. After five years together, he could read Mark like a book. Right now, Mark itched to be free, to return home and pick up where they had left off, as a happily married couple. "And I do love you."

Mark's muscles relaxed for a split second before he became sober and tightened once more. "There's something...."

The whine of a bullet split the air. An explosion sounded right next to Jag's ear. Immediately, he returned fire, his training demanding he protect his position, even from an unseen threat. A spray of sand blew across his face and body. He ignored it, centered on his scope, and blasted away in the direction the shot came from.

A few seconds later, he stopped, came off his scope for a split second, and froze at the sight.

Mark lay lifeless, face down next to him. He appeared to be sleeping, except for the hole in his helmet and the much larger one on the other side. Body fluids oozed from the large wound, seeping into the sand and congealing.

Jag wiped at his face, then looked at his fingers. Not sand. Blood and brain matter. Mark's. All Mark's.

Mark. Oh, God. Mark!

Fury and overwhelming grief hit him like a locomotive. Inside, he screamed in horror, rage, and unbelievable pain. This wasn't supposed to happen. They were supposed to have the rest of their lives together. Not cut short in such a horrific fashion. *No. It can't be real.* One more glance at Mark cut through his denial. He reached over and checked a pulse, even as he already knew the answer. Nothing. He choked and gagged, physically sick at what had been done to his husband. His heart raced even as it shattered with emotional agony.

Another shot rang out, ricocheting off the boulder he used for cover.

Methodically he shoved everything into his kill box and forced himself to think of a plan. Mark was gone. There was no doubt now with the size and location of his wound. Jag's position compromised, he needed to move, to stay one step ahead, before Sandman came over the rise and gunned him down in a flurry of bullets.

Survival instincts and years of training took over. He glanced at the sun nearly on the horizon as he started packing up. Task done, he pulled out his satellite phone and called for an emergency medevac. When the voice on the other end asked how bad, it took everything he had to blurt out the fact that Mark was dead. The operator's whispered cuss came across loud and clear as well as his promise to get there first thing as soon as the strong crosswinds died down after dark. Judging from the sky that would be two or three hours. For the deepest part of the night to happen would be much longer. Jag swallowed hard and memorized the pickup location and time.

He checked his black-faced digital watch and cringed. He had seven hours to make the rendezvous site.

Glancing down once more, he blinked back tears as he shouldered both his ruck and Mark's. The heavy load didn't mean anything except that he could feel and Mark no longer could. Using all his strength, he bent down, levered Mark's body over his shoulder, grabbed his rifle with one hand, wrapped the other around Mark's legs, and started down the back trail.

A large lump formed in his throat. He could barely swallow as he hurried down the steep incline, sticking to the cliff walls whenever possible in order to stay in the shadows. Insurgents abounded and he wasn't about to be cut down by one of them. Time and fatigue no longer registered. Not now. Not when his destination mattered above all.

His life didn't mean much right now, but he wasn't ready to throw in the towel. Despite his oppressive burden, two facts kept him hurrying down steep slopes, over rocky outcroppings, and through a harrowing high brushy area typically filled with insurgents. First, he had to make the rendezvous with the chopper and get Mark's body to safety. No way in hell would he leave it behind for Sandman to cut up like a dissected frog. Secondly, he had a hunt to finish.

Sandman would pay. Maybe not today or tomorrow, but he would die by Jag's hand and beg for mercy from the devil himself before Jag returned to home base. Then, and only then, would he allow himself to grieve the loss of his life's love.

THERE YOU are, you son of a bitch.

Jag eased forward another inch. He'd been snaking across a flat grassland for the past week and a half. Each day he progressed perhaps fifteen feet closer, yet not near enough to ensure an accurate shot. Twice, patrols of Sandman's motley crew had nearly stepped on him as they moved from their temporary camp to scout for unsuspecting soldiers close by. Each time, Jag held his breath, praying he wouldn't have to give away his location by creating a scuffle and killing the men. That would draw attention and sign his death warrant as the odds were certainly in their favor.

Finally he'd moved within range, then waited out another two days for Sandman to appear with his small band of local rebels. Odd that Sandman took on some youngbloods, but not totally surprising. Sandman typically worked alone, but surrounded by military coalitions, he drew in some other men for distractions and to harass the allies at any given opportunity.

Revenge became the fuel for Jag's constant hunt. He'd taken a short break in order to bury his husband, say good-bye for once and for all. It was the hardest thing he'd ever done. He'd alternated between crying and cursing Sandman. Nothing helped, though. Nothing short of blowing that bastard's head off would.

So, as soon as he buried Mark, Jag had taken the first military transport back to Afghanistan, trying to pick up Sandman's trail. He'd spent weeks searching, night and day, alone. Five weeks had passed before he came across a sign of Sandman, in the form of a shoeprint and a lingering scent. His gut told him to stay the course, and it had never been wrong before.

Now he'd cornered the motherfucker. *Too bad Sandman had let his guard down. It's going to cost him his life.* A sense of anticipation leaped to the fore at his sarcastic thoughts. Keeping his cool, he methodically went about his preparations.

One shot, one kill.

Jag peered through his scope, lined up his aim, centering Sandman's chest in the crosshairs. With no Kevlar vest, the torso became the better target. More area to hit and less of a chance of missing than going for a headshot or even one to the hip. Jag didn't want to get greedy. He just wanted the most lethal way to take Sandman out in the blink of an eye.

He blew out his breath, slowed his pulse, and waited for the space between one heartbeat and the next. At that moment, he squeezed the trigger.

Sandman's chest erupted with a spray of blood. He crumpled to the ground as the other men grabbed their weapons and took off toward nearby brush for cover or began searching for him, Jag didn't know which, nor did he care.

He saw the gift he'd been given and started back the way he'd come, gradually and without the slightest jerk or rush to give himself away.

That was for Mark, you son of a bitch. I hope you rot in hell.

With that thought, he crept toward his home base, aiming for the setting sun, and safety. Alone, his mission complete. Now his husband and the other victims and their families could finally rest in peace.

Chapter 1

Three years later.

JAG DRAPED his washcloth over the side of the bathtub, stretched out his legs, and reclined back into the steaming hot water. Rarely did he have time to simply relax and pass the time soaking. Today he made an exception because he'd earned some downtime, weeks of it, considering what he'd just been through. Hell would have been a vacation compared to the east side of Belize. At least he'd been successful on his mission and had returned home a couple of hours ago for some much-needed R and R.

He rested his head back on the edge of the porcelain tub, adjusted for comfort, then closed his eyes in sweet pleasure. His skin might resemble a dehydrated prune before long but he didn't give a damn. For once he was going to indulge in a few small luxuries in life, ones he appreciated probably more than almost everyone else. After all, he'd come from nothing, clawed his way through life to attain his present standing. Not something he bragged about, no. Yet in the right circles, his moniker, Jaguar, sparked varied reactions, anything from fear to respect and several emotions in between.

Rolling his shoulders, he ignored the resulting burning twinge, left over from his last mission. A bullet had torn through hide, muscle, and a couple of tendons before he could take out the other guy. Thankfully, he healed quickly or it might have been his last.

Refusing to dwell on the past, he sank a bit deeper into the soothing water, felt the tension slowly ebbing from his body, and blew out a weary sigh of relief. Pushed way too hard lately, he needed a break in order to recover.

A familiar scent carried to his nose, quickly followed by the sound of hard footfalls and the door closing solidly. Recognizing the visitor long before he appeared, Jag didn't bother to budge from his comfortable position. Instead, he waited for his cousin Ronnie to step into the bathroom before drolly saying, "You don't have to stomp around and slam the doors. I might be older than you but I'm not deaf." A decade and a half separated them in age. Jag had always seen Ronnie like a younger brother, one who insisted on tagging along and pestering him. Still, he couldn't help but like the kid who had the gumption to stick to him like glue no matter how hard Jag tried to convince him to pick another new best friend and leave him alone.

Now, at nineteen, Ronnie had grown tall and lanky. He still had a few years to fill out, but already he showed promise. Jag wasn't the only one who noticed. The colonel and his ragtag team of former military shifter specialists had recruited Ronnie last year, welcoming him into their fold. He might have lacked formal training, but he'd learned from Jag and had a natural ability when it came to digging up information on anyone and everyone. Ronnie might not make it to the front lines, and Jag hoped that would be the case, but he could make a huge difference at the base office.

"It never hurts to be careful."

"Uh-huh." Jag read concern and determination on Ronnie's face. "Why are you bothering me?"

Ronnie shifted his weight from one foot to the other. His gaze flicked across the room, to Jag, then to the floor.

Jag didn't miss the body language or nervousness from his normally fairly laid-back cousin. Nor did he really want to hear what Ronnie had to say. After all, the way Ronnie was acting, he had nothing but bad news to impart.

"The colonel called. They need you."

"Tough shit. I just got home." Jag had the luxury of picking and choosing his assignments so he could easily turn this one down.

"He said it's important."

"He always says that. He can find someone else to be bait this time." Jag picked up the shampoo bottle, squirted some into his hand, then rubbed the liquid into his hair. He took his time rinsing. After nearly a week since a decent bath, cleanliness took precedence.

Ronnie's shoulders slumped but he stood his ground.

Jag's gut began to churn. Quickly he rinsed his head, picked up the nearby towel, and wiped his face. Only then did he stare at his cousin. "Spill it already."

"It has to be you."

"Why?"

Ronnie looked to the ceiling as if seeking divine inspiration before meeting Jag's eyes. "It's Sandman."

Jag's breath caught as his heart sped. Immediately he pulled the plug on the tub, stood up, and started drying off. "When? Where?"

"The colonel said he'd give you details when you showed up at headquarters." Ronnie's voice took on a relieved tone.

"I shot that bastard three fucking years ago. Are you sure it's not a ploy to just get me there?" Jag's near-paranoid nature popped out. After all, that's what had kept him alive this long as a sniper extraordinaire and assassin.

Ronnie shook his head. "The colonel wouldn't use his trump card unless he had to. Besides, he sent something."

Intrigued, Jag paused with the towel over his shoulders. "What?"

"This." Ronnie dug something out of his pocket, held his hand out, and opened his palm.

Jag glanced at the bullet casing, saw the impressed seal, and stopped breathing. The S-shaped mark could easily be duplicated, but no one else in the world forged sand into a casing as a decorative adjunct. These weren't the bullets he used to kill; this was his personal trademark, one Jag knew all too well.

"How? I killed that bastard. Back then. Why now?" His stomach clenched at the knowledge that he'd failed in his last attempt to eradicate the living embodiment of evil otherwise known as Sandman.

"We don't know. His body was never found or identified. The colonel thinks he survived and is back with a vengeance. The latest victim...." Ronnie cringed and turned his head.

Jag could imagine. He'd seen more than enough of the Sandman's cruelty in the past. The victims went through a torture so vile even the most seasoned veteran became sick at seeing the results.

"Shit." Jag threw his towel aside and strode toward his bedroom, Ronnie in his wake. He dressed in a record time, pulled his black duffel bag from under his bed, and started checking all his equipment. He needed anything and everything he had, from ammo, to his two sniper rifles, to makeup and clothing for camouflage. His life and success depended on blending into the surroundings in order to get close enough to take a shot. Once he pulled the trigger, he knew the target was dead. Because he never missed and his kill rate hovered right at 100 percent.

Yet the evidence in Ronnie's hand proved him wrong.

His imperfection—his apparent lack of success with the most important kill of his career—set loose a deadly monster. The realization chilled him to the bone.

Finished with his preparations, Jag zipped his bag, slipped on his boots, and slung the duffel over his shoulder. "I'm going hunting."

Ronnie nodded, worry written all over his face. "Take care of yourself, Cole."

Very few people on this earth knew his given name. He wanted to keep it that way. Too personal otherwise and he'd made a habit of keeping people at arm's length throughout life. His recent loss had only strengthened that resolve.

To everyone else he was Jaguar, or Jag for short, the kind of beast that existed as part of him. This generic moniker revolved around his abilities and skill rather than his broken heart and soul.

Jag squeezed his shoulder. "Thanks for taking care of the place while I'm gone."

"Sure." Ronnie stared at him for a long moment, then pulled him into a strong hug, one Jag returned with true affection.

As soon as they released each other, Jag appraised his cousin who was quickly becoming a man. "You were a good kid. Now you're a pretty damn good man." He offered up a small smile. "Keep an eye on things. I'll be back as soon as I can."

"Will do." Ronnie stood up straighter and grinned with pride.

Jag inclined his head before strolling out the door.

Destiny awaited in the form of his greatest adversary back to kill with glee, screw up his life, and make him pay.

"How could that bastard be back?" Jag sat down in an old wooden chair, which squeaked under the addition of his weight.

Colonel Derrick "Mac" MacPherson stared at him from the opposite side of his huge wooden desk. His salt-and-pepper hair had been recently trimmed, a nice change from the wild locks he'd been sporting last time Jag saw him. Big and burly, the bear shifter had been around awhile and had the wisdom and scars to prove it. His face alone carried deep crags and lines, a testimony to age and a rough life full of stress. At that moment Mac's black eyes broadcasted banked anger and disgust. "Who the hell knows? But the evidence doesn't lie."

Jag replayed the memory of taking down the Sandman, just like he'd done a dozen times since Ronnie interrupted his bath. Nothing stood out as wrong and he knew he'd hit the man. Hell, he'd seen the blood splatter, the body jerk and fall, the enormous wound in the chest. "I put a .30 caliber bullet through the fucker's heart. Men don't get back up from that."

"I know. Shit." Mac blew out a breath and opened a folder. "Take one look at this and you'll be convinced he's back from the dead. Or maybe his ghost." He turned the documents around and laid them on the desk in front of Jag.

After a quick glance, Jag growled low in his throat, his inner jaguar furious and more than ready to tear that son of a bitch apart with his claws. "It's his MO all right." Regret washed over Jag. He should have checked the Sandman's body before, ensured the bastard was truly dead. *And been blown to pieces for my efforts.*

"Maybe it wasn't him you killed?"

Jag shook his head. "It was him. Right down to the scar on his left cheek."

"Copycat?" Mac pulled the folder back toward him. "I can't see anyone being psychotic enough to mimic his kills."

"Neither can I." A particularly painful memory flashed through his mind. Jag forced it aside.

"Maybe we had the wrong guy all along," Mac grumbled.

"I don't think so." Jag had tracked the bastard for months, learning his preferences and abilities. No way could they have totally missed the mark with this one. "Obviously it doesn't matter. He's back or there's someone following in his footsteps. Either way, there's no choice." He paused a second. "Just give me the coordinates and I'll track down his ass."

"Kunar Province."

Jag sighed. What better place for a serial killer to hole up than in the middle of an all-out war zone. As in past times, battles drew in people who were out to kill, not for a cause or for their country, but for the joy of snuffing out life. Nothing new except for one thing: Sandman had a mean streak wider than Jag had ever seen, as evidenced by the tortured bodies of his captured victims.

Unfortunately a normal person couldn't stop Sandman. Only Jag could. "Get me transport and I'll get started."

"You need a couple of days' rest first." Mac never let a man get in over his head. He believed those in charge should be able to do the job he asked his men to do and ended up on the front lines now and again fighting with his unit. Caring and honest, Mac bent over backward to make sure his men had the best of everything and all their needs were looked after, including the basic ones.

"Tell that to the bastard as he carves up another soldier." Jag picked up his bag and stood.

"Wait a blasted minute. You can't go haring off like a hothead."

"Time's a wasting, Colonel," Jag answered almost flippantly. He knew the score and the sooner he was back in his element, the sooner he could slay that bastard once and for all.

"Fine. I'll spell it out for you. You're too important to lose, so you'll find a spotter waiting to join you on this mission when you reach the base."

Jag's heart stuttered as a tendril of fear shot through him. "The hell you say!" He glared down at his commander. "I work alone and you know it."

Mac's jaw ticked. "Not this time."

Jag saw red. After losing Mark—his best friend, husband, and former spotter—just over three years ago, he swore never to take one on again. He couldn't protect them and refused to carry the responsibility of their loss on his shoulders. Mac had never insisted. Until now. "I'll decline the mission." Not about to budge, he stepped up to the game of hardball.

"Then I'll send someone else."

To their deaths.

The words hung in the air unsaid between them.

Jag swore viciously. The squeeze of being between a rock and a hard place stung. He countered with reason. "I'm your only shot. So leave it to me. Alone."

"Not happening. I'm not about to sacrifice the best sniper we've ever had because you're too stubborn to face facts and admit you can't do it by yourself."

Ire rose. Jag growled low in his throat. "You know damned well why I never want another spotter again." A hint of pain carried in his frustrated tone.

"I understand, but I also know this. Without a spotter, you're a proverbial sitting duck. You need two sets of eyes and you can't watch your back all the time. Not in that hot zone and not with Sandman around. If anyone on this earth can take down Sandman, it's you. But you can't do it alone."

"I did it before," he gritted out.

"And he's back again."

The stark reality shut Jag's mouth. His arguments dried up even as his annoyance remained. He'd never win this battle with Mac. And Mac pulled all the strings to get him to where he needed to be. "Fine."

Mac stared at him for a long moment as if appraising his truthfulness and acceptance before bobbing his head just once. "You'll meet up with Sonar at the base. The commanding officer there has strict orders to keep you on lockdown for twenty-four hours before turning you loose."

A full day to get to know his new right-hand man, to eat, to rest up, and to plan. As much as he hated the wait, he knew the time together was an essential. Spotters and snipers didn't immediately bond, and they had to have almost a like mind when it came to surviving in the middle of a brutal war zone surrounded by enemies who wanted nothing better than to kill them, drag them in, and claim the huge bounty on the head of each and every sniper in the region.

"Set it up." Jag spun around and started for the door.

"Cole?"

He stopped and turned to face Mac, another one of the few who knew his real name. Rarely had he used it, which meant he had something personal to say.

"Be careful out there."

With a quick nod, Jag walked out the door.

Chapter 2

JAG STEPPED out of the chopper presently resting on the tarmac and scanned the area. Not much had changed since he'd last been there a few months ago. Tents made of camouflage fabric dotted the area surrounded by razor wire, a decent deterrent to any enemies wanting to come in too close. Men walked here and there, presumably going about their routine activities until it was time to go out on another mission, which might be in two minutes or two weeks. In a war zone, no one worked a typical nine to five.

"Captain Mallow?"

Jag turned to find a young man staring at him with a mix of curiosity and devout respect. Several inches taller, Jag easily looked down at the soldier, noted the youth in the man's face, and once more wondered why those who barely had a start on life ended up in the ranks on the front lines.

Age didn't necessarily mean inability or lack of courage. Jag himself stood as an example. "Yeah."

"We've been expecting you." The man gestured toward the right, turned, and started walking.

Jag dutifully followed at his own pace. He took in each and every building, defense fortification, and soldier. Survival strategies learned long ago had him calculating strengths, weaknesses, and potential safe ground in case of an attack. While the open desert all around might allow for easy visibility of incoming planes, choppers, and vehicles, it also left the back of his neck itchy.

The sooner he could get out of the nest of humanity and back into his element, the more comfortable he'd feel. *Even if I have to be leg shackled to a damn spotter.*

He wore desert fatigues similar to the other soldiers he noticed, yet different. His were specially made, had ample pockets, and room for a Kevlar vest or two, along with some backup emergency supplies—a typical sniper's stock with a couple of extra goodies, including the ability to change color like a chameleon.

As a shifter living with humans, Jag had learned long ago to keep his specific DNA composition all to himself. Mac and the other guys on the team were in the same boat, all shifters with remarkable talents that the military drooled over. Thus, they always had work, earned hefty paychecks, and were able to use their talents at a top level. The downside was they had to be overly cautious around others. Humans didn't know of their existence and he, for one, didn't trust any of them enough to share the secret. Endless possibilities existed if that guy blabbed to the wrong person. He'd worked way too hard over the years just surviving to end up locked up in some research facility as a lab rat. Death would come first. He'd ensure it.

Their small group expanded now and again when Mac recruited another potential skilled player. Otherwise they pretty much kept to themselves, hung around the base, and didn't venture into the masses of humanity unless searching for a quick hookup, entertainment, or were on the trail of a target.

Oddly enough, the team pretty much got along, despite the various species involved. Nature normally would have predicted that high-level predators would fight in order to be top dog. Not them. They, for the most part, let bygones be bygones. Besides, Mac ran the show and no one had enough balls to challenge him. Jag wasn't dumb enough nor would he want the position. Best to stick with what he knew: sniping.

Opening his senses, he detected the typical scents of a military station in the desert. Sand, sweat, fuel, and fear permeated the air. His acute hearing picked up on tidbits of conversations along with the occasional click of a weapon being stripped down for cleaning.

Yeah, not much had changed since he'd left. *Damn it anyway.*

"Sir?" The corporal paused and waited for him.

Jag resigned himself to another meeting with a bigwig, a hard night learning the ways of his new spotter, and hours of sleeplessness, compliments of anticipation and nightmares. *Joy for me.*

He followed his guide into an average-size tent near the center of the base. His eyes immediately adjusted to the lowered light, allowing him to see a gray-haired man standing by a large corkboard studying a map. As they neared, he twisted around, locked gazes with Jag, then motioned toward the chairs. "Take a seat. Corporal, you're dismissed."

The corporal hurriedly left as Jag plopped down, stretching his long legs out in front of him. Definitely not proper protocol when meeting a higher-ranking officer, but Jag didn't care much for rules and policies. He'd been raised on the streets and in the jungles. Respect was earned and fancy metal stars didn't automatically give someone that status.

Jag stared at the all too familiar map for a moment, noted the lines, pins, and markings, then snorted.

The general frowned. "Something funny?"

"Yeah. Unless you've taken the western end of Korengal Valley, including the subterranean caves, I wouldn't mark it as a safe road to travel."

Brigadier General Clomp, according to his stars and the name on his shirt, glared at him a moment before turning back to the area in question. A second later he returned his attention to Jag. "How do you know?"

"I helped clear out that patch of bad guys last time I was here. Temporarily, I might add. Those tangos like to hang out in the underground too much to stay away. The cool temps draw them in just like the snakes that they are."

"Jaguar," General Clomp uttered under his breath, the single word filled with amazement and respect.

Jag didn't validate the general in any way. He simply sat there and waited.

The general looked him over, then took his seat. "I see. Your commanding officer said you were a bit of a hard sell, but well worth the effort."

After readjusting his pack, Jag sat perfectly still; only his eyes moved from time to time. He didn't wiggle his toes or tap his fingers in nervousness or just to pass the time. Those habits could get a sniper killed in a jiffy.

"Let me spell it out for you. Sandman is back. I don't know how, but he's left hints and signs."

"When was the last time and where?"

"Travelers Pass almost a week ago."

Jag cussed to himself. "He's gone."

Clomp shook his head. "I don't think so."

"Sandman has a real bad addiction to cutting people up. He's not going to sit on top of a rock getting all suntanned for a week in between kills. Not his style."

"Where would he go? The action is here."

"And that's the million-dollar question." Jag wanted to slap some sense into the older man. Instead, he reined in his frustration and opted to learn what he could before heading to a bunk for the night.

"We'll find out soon enough. It's not like he hides the bodies to make them hard to find."

Jag knew that for a fact. He'd seen too many of the poor bastards, including a friend, sliced up like roast beef. Rage and sorrow stirred in his gut. He ignored both.

"Here's what we have so far." The general tossed a manila envelope to Jag.

Jag opened it, scanned the contents, and replaced them. While some information might prove enlightening, most of it fell into the category of old news and hearsay.

"I'll have the corporal show you to your quarters for the next twenty-four hours. Your spotter is already there and will meet up with you soon." He stood. "Thanks for coming on such short notice, Captain. I know your services will be exemplary."

Jag regained his feet, inclined his head in lieu of a salute, and left the tent, envelope and duffel in hand.

A few minutes later, he stood before yet another tent. The corporal didn't bother to come in, instead, left him at the entrance without a word. Jag watched him go for a second before turning back to the makeshift doorway. He sniffed, caught a vague scent, and tilted his head in bewilderment. Intrigued, he pushed the door open and stepped inside.

STEEL, A.K.A. Sonar, heard the footfalls right outside his door, lifted his nose to the air, and drew in a deep breath. Scents intermingled and then dispersed, leaving one tangy, potent brew behind. Hot, spicy, and definitely a big cat shifter. Jaguar, if he didn't miss his guess. He'd scented more than his fair share over the years, especially since they tended to occupy the same territories, much like their wild cousins in Central and South America.

He licked his lips and grinned to himself. Seemed his sniper buddy and new BFF had just arrived.

The owner of the intoxicating aroma stepped through the door and stared at him for a long moment before lifting his lip to expose a fang.

In human form the eyeteeth were just a bit more prominent but not out of the realm of typical human variations. Still, the gesture spoke volumes to shifters.

Sonar arched an eyebrow and peered up at the new guy drolly from his sitting position on a chair. "Let me guess. You must be Jaguar."

"Yeah."

Sonar rolled his eyes. Nice to know the guy had a stick up his butt and didn't get high marks for playing well with others. Not completely surprising as most big cat shifters tended to be loners, just like their wild kin. "Considering what you are, seems to me your boot camp buddies had a definite lack of imagination when it came to call signs."

Jag's eyebrows furrowed as he frowned. "They didn't come up with the moniker. I did."

"Well, that explains it."

Jag shot him a glare before walking over to the far bunk and placing the large duffel bag on the floor beside it.

Sonar took the opportunity to check out the guy. Big and strong came to mind. Built and prime soon followed. Though in fatigues, Jag radiated power. Wide shoulders drifted down to a strong back, narrower waist, and a damn fine ass that would make anyone drool. Sonar could almost see the muscles snapping and flexing with each movement under the fairly loose fatigues. Strip the man down and he would be lean, chiseled, and have ample ability to get the job done, no matter what the job might happen to be. From hand-to-hand combat, to sniping, to fucking, Sonar knew Jag would be a force to be reckoned with.

No doubt his new bunkmate was an alpha. The way he moved, the straightness to his back, the carriage and pride, which showed with every motion all shouted top kitty. Jag was more than Special Forces. He was the apex predator.

The short black hair appeared freshly trimmed, barely brushing his collar. Obviously Jag didn't favor the buzz cut any more than Sonar did, a plus in Sonar's book. He respected the military lifestyle and those in the service, but sometimes the best soldiers were the ones who didn't follow the herd in all matters. Haircuts were one of those deciding factors.

He recalled Jag's unusual eyes: amber, piercing, and full of intelligence. They reminded him of a wild predator, feral and calculating. Certainly they'd put off lesser men. However, Sonar found the intensity to be compelling, intriguing, and oh, so sexy.

What the shit? I just met the guy and I'm already lusting after him like a cat in heat. He chided himself and shoved down his libido but couldn't bring himself to ignore the man sharing his small living quarters.

"Anyone here know what you are?" Jag's baritone voice whispered across the space, too quiet for anyone passing by to hear.

"Nope. And I ain't telling. I'm not real smart sometimes, but I'm not a dumbass either."

Jag nodded once. "Then I'll spell this out for you, nice and simple. I work alone. Don't want or need a spotter. But I'll do whatever it takes to have another chance to personally send Sandman to a fiery hell. Stay out of my way, follow orders without question, and we might just survive this ordeal."

Sonar blinked at the brash frankness. His inner cat bristled at the commanding tone and dictator-like attitude. His brief thought of bedding the guy quickly turned to one of kicking his ass. Irritated, Sonar took to his feet and stormed over to stop inches from Jag. He pinned the other man's gaze and let him have it with both barrels. "Listen up, you pompous prick. I'm a Green Beret, not some fresh-out-of-boot-camp private. From what I understand about the bastard, it's going to take two of us to take him out. Not to mention there's one hell of a war going on around us. Alone in the hot zone makes you a dead man walking. My job is to watch your back, be your right-hand man, and assist you to nail as many bad guys as you can. I don't care for direct orders, am not afraid of anything, and refuse to back down because you have a piss-poor attitude about this mission. I've never failed before and I'm not about to start because you're in a snit and flashing fangs."

They glared at each other for a long moment before Sonar decided he'd gotten his point across. Stepping back, he put some much-needed space between them while never taking his eyes off Jag. He knew better than to turn his back on a pissed-off cat.

Just as the tension grew to a fevered pitch, a loud voice outside carried through the thin walls of the canvas tent. "Blue Squadron calling for QRF, quick reaction force, in the dead zone. Gold Squadron to the tarmac. On the double."

Sonar saw Jag's eyes narrow before he turned around, grabbed his bag, and rushed for the door. Not to be left behind, Sonar snagged his backpack and rifle, nearly stepping on Jag's heels the whole way.

They came to a stop at the loading area where a first lieutenant held up his hand. "Gold Squadron only."

"Do they have a sniper attached to the unit?" Jag asked.

The first lieutenant's face pinched. "No."

"One in the combat zone?"

"Not right now."

"Then I'm going." Jag stepped up into the chopper with ease of practice.

Sonar hopped in right after his new partner. He inclined his head to the other guys lining the walls and squatted down beside Jag just as the door shut and the helo elevated.

"Do you know the area?" Sonar asked, needing to figure out a plan, where to set up, and what Jag's preferences might be in the next three minutes.

"Yeah."

Sonar's eyebrows shot up. "I wasn't told you've been to BFE before."

Jag shot him a glance at Sonar's mention of bum-fuck Egypt, military slang for the middle of nowhere. "Spent three tours in this hellhole before being pulled to another."

Sonar noted the subtle dulling of Jag's eyes as if a particularly painful memory emerged. Just as quickly, Jag slipped a determined mask back over his face.

Whatever happened before had left a mark on Jag, a particularly savage one. Sonar would bet his stripes.

A hint of uncertainty crept in, causing Sonar's gut to churn. His partner had just reentered the area after months away. Things changed. Buildings and territories were destroyed or unrecognizable. Jag obviously had had some bad days fighting over this barren land and his pride would force him to keep up the pace, the endless battle, without knowing when to call a halt for some much-needed rest.

Sonar's new partner might be the best sniper in the world, but he could just as easily be his own worst enemy.

Chapter 3

"YOU'RE LOW. Bring it up about three feet and to the left one and a half," Sonar rattled off, still peering through his spotting scope at the scrawny dirt road between buildings nearly in rubble.

Another explosion rocked the area. Gunshots rang out, voices carried. Jag didn't bother to look up, break his concentration, or make a single sound.

He saw the dust kick up from his bullet landing short without the commentary from his assigned spotter. Immediately he dialed another mil on his scope to compensate for the almost one-mile distance and light wind. Afterward, he waited patiently, watched a man peek around the corner, the strap of a weapon lashed across his chest. As he leaned in more, Jag caught the glint of sunlight on metal, aimed, blew out a breath, and slowed his heart rate. The man started his dash across the street. Jag lightly pulled the trigger, sending a bullet through an open area in a low cement wall approximately eight feet in front of their position on top of an old school building. A second later, the dark-haired man carrying a grenade launcher crumpled to the ground. His exploding chest and blood splatter told them he wouldn't be getting back up.

Jag clicked another shell into the chamber, his eyes locked on his scope as he cradled his M40 sniper weapon in steady hands.

They'd been at this for nearly eight hours straight. Not once had Jag taken a break for more than a couple of seconds to guzzle some much-needed water. Every thirty to forty-five minutes, he was supposed to come off the scope, give his eyes a break. Another ideal situation taught in sniper school that didn't carry over into the real world.

Sweat poured, mixing with the constant dust blowing in the light breeze and covering him in pasty grit. Despite the specially fitted earplugs, his ears still rang. His shoulder ached from recoil and holding a position for such a long time, but all of that barely registered. He was a sniper and had long ago learned to ignore discomfort in order to hone in on his target. Those abilities allowed him to stay alive in the middle of some pretty dangerous places. To move, even a flinch, alerted others of his presence.

Survival trumped everything, including hunger, thirst, and the need to empty his bladder.

Twenty men had fallen to Jag's bullets so far. Despite the number, more always came. An endless supply it seemed, even though they saw their comrades cut down before them for trying the exact same thing. They either didn't take the hint or were dumb enough to stay the course. Each one waited and watched before attempting to sprint across the street to deliver guns and ammo to their counterparts. Those he ambushed with his aim, cutting them down in midstride.

One shot, one kill: the sniper's motto.

He thought of nothing else except clearing as many of the insurgents as he possibly could, relieving the foot soldiers from constant threat of gunfire while buying them more and more area to spread out. With almost a mile range, Jag continued to hammer at the enemy, pushing them back, creating a safe zone for the others to return to when the fighting became too hot to handle. He took advantage of every opportunity, even when men tried to dash over to drag their fallen to safety. Taliban forces were just that: the enemy who would love nothing more than taking out American and Allied forces each chance they had. Jag decimated their numbers. By doing so, fewer good guys would end up in the crosshairs of an insurgent's rifle.

The sun had started to set, limiting the light. No matter. Jag could see nearly as well in the darkness, thanks to his shifter genetics. If all else failed, he had night-vision goggles and a night scope in his bag.

Several minutes passed where no one else appeared in his view. The noise died down with the waning light. Darkness didn't always mean the city went to sleep, so Jag couldn't simply put down his gun and call it a day. War raged 24-7. The battle ended when it did and not before.

"Commander is pulling the front-line troops back so fresh ones can take the lead for nightfall." Sonar stood up slowly, stretching his back as he swiveled and swept the area with his gaze. "Looks like we can settle in for a while."

Jag hesitantly lifted from his scope and opened all his senses, then gave a quick nod of agreement. They needed to pack up and move while things remained fairly calm. One rule of being a sniper was to never stay in the same place for long. Enemies could and often did zero in to a guy's location, especially if his feet started to grow roots. That meant he needed to find a new nest long before dawn or be out of the city entirely and back on the trail of the all too elusive Sandman.

For a second, he appraised his spotter, grudgingly noting that Sonar had stayed with him the whole time. Didn't bother with silly questions, just pointed to this rooftop, got them all set up, fed him ammo when he needed it, and accurately guided his shots. With Sonar's help, he'd managed to clear an area covering nearly a mile around his present position. His gun's top limit.

Sonar packed up his equipment, quietly going about his task, glancing up now and again, alert and searching for potential danger.

Jag liked that about the guy. Always vigilant. Always looking. Just the kind of man he'd like to have at his back. Except he wanted to work alone. Needed a solitary hunt. Never again would he put another friend in jeopardy. He'd learned that lesson the hard way.

Shoving aside the bitter memories, he turned his attention once more to Sonar. An ocelot shifter, judging by his scent and coloring. His short brown hair carried almost a reddish hue, similar to the spots on the fur of his wild cousins. Blue eyes made for a nice contrast, as did the square jaw that promised stubbornness and determination. Perhaps a couple inches shorter, Sonar didn't lack for strength in the form of thick muscles, revealed each time the fatigues pulled snug over his arms, back, torso, or thighs. The Kevlar vest only added to Sonar's strength and appeal. He certainly filled out the uniform well, a fact Jag hadn't missed from his first glimpse of the man back at base.

Sonar possessed some traits native to his inner beast, as evidenced by his actions earlier. Jag couldn't remember the last time someone dared to get in his face and take him to task for his in-charge attitude. The fact that Sonar had done so impressed him. He knew ocelots were territorial and quite aggressive, especially the males, but he hadn't expected an ocelot shifter to go toe-to-toe with him.

Interesting. Damn interesting.

Add in that primed male body just made for fucking and Jag would give up his daily rations for a week to have enough downtime to bend Sonar over and plunge balls deep. Or would have if it had been a few years back. Now he had little interest in sex at all. Not since Mark.

Before he could take a stroll through the past, Sonar spoke.

"Do you want to hang out here for a while longer, catch a ride back to the base, or find another campsite for the night?" Sonar met Jag's gaze, then arched an eyebrow in curiosity as if he could read Jag's thoughts.

"Let's move." Jag busily gathered up his supplies, packing each item with extreme care.

Get your mind back in the game, sniper. Distractions lead to death.

Chiding himself, Jag closed his bag and checked his clip, then pulled his handgun from its holder on his ankle. Close up, the smaller weapon worked better.

Sonar did the same.

Together they skirted from one relatively safe spot to another, finally exiting the city completely under the cover of darkness.

A while later Jag held up his hand, calling for a halt. He'd made his way back to the hills surrounding the city, heading to a former safe place to hang out for a few hours before deciding where to take his hunt from there.

Jag approached slowly and cautiously, using his other feline senses to verify what his eyes told him. Sure enough, the small cave covered by thick brush remained empty and mostly hidden from view, a definite relief. The cave branched off and led deep into the mountain where few would tread even if they knew about the place. They'd be safe enough for a while.

"We're covered here." He whispered the words, knowing Sonar would be able to hear him with his exceptional shifter ears.

Tired, but nowhere near his limits of endurance, Jag walked a few feet inside the darkness before stopping near an intersection. The place allowed him to watch the entrance while staying in the shadows, even in the brightest sunlight. They could immerse themselves deeper into the mountain, but he preferred to be able to spot his enemy as they headed in his direction, rather than wait for a surprise attack in a blind-ended cave.

He stored his backpack against the wall right behind him and dug out a couple of MREs. One he passed over to Sonar before sitting down.

Sonar made his own small nest, securing his supplies for the night. He accepted the pre-prepared meal with a nod, tore open the package, and started to eat with obvious hunger.

While nowhere near a home-cooked Thanksgiving dinner, the food wasn't bad. Of course, anything tasted good when one was starving.

"You're damn good, Jag. Best I've ever seen." Sonar uttered the praise between bites of food.

Jag shrugged, not bothering to complain about Sonar shortening his nickname. Most people had done so in the past as well. However, he didn't care for compliments especially since he had obviously missed the most important target of his life. For that, others had paid and would continue to pay dearly until he got Sandman in his sights once more. "What do you know about Sandman?"

Sonar lifted a shoulder. "He's a particularly cruel bastard in a particularly cruel war."

Jag snorted. "That's not the half of it."

"Heard he's into torture and is able to come back from the dead too." Sonar met Jag's gaze.

"Yeah." He chewed slowly, not really tasting his food. How Sandman managed to get up from a sure kill strike he had yet to figure out. And the mystery ate at him. Immensely.

"Is he a shifter?"

Jag shook his head. "He doesn't carry the scent of one if he is. But he's too good to be human. Brass would love to get him under a microscope, but there's no way he's going in alive. Even if he surrendered to me, I'm not dumb enough to believe it. He's dead as soon as I get him in my sights, this time for good."

SONAR HEARD the steely vow in Jag's voice and understood his reasoning. If what he'd been told was true, Jag's beef with Sandman was personal. Considering how much the bastard loved to cut up his victims, he could easily understand why Jag made Sandman his number one priority. Anyone who caught a glimpse of his handiwork wanted to get their hands on the bastard.

He only hoped that in the resulting confrontation, Jag could pull off another miracle shot, because no one else had the ability to take down such an evil giant. If so, they would have long since eradicated the biggest blight on the map already.

"You're not regular military." Sonar opted to change the subject and learn a bit more about his new partner. Questions boggled his mind and he found their isolated hideout a great place to voice them, in a whisper, where no one else could overhear.

"No."

"Yet you're on loan to the regular grunts?"

Jag glanced up at Sonar. "I'll share just because of what you are. You must be able to keep your mouth closed or you'd be in a research lab instead of on the front lines." He stabbed another bite of food. "I work for a group of private-sector Special Forces. We're all shifters, led by a shifter, and contracted out when the military finds themselves in over their heads."

Sonar absorbed the words, finding them sound and truly not a surprise. With the extra abilities shifters carried, they made for great assets in the age-old game of war. Perfect soldiers able to shift, track, sniff out enemies, and heal quickly even from the worst wounds. What government didn't want those kinds of men on their payrolls?

Too bad he hadn't known about this unique group before now. He'd have joined up with them instead of selling his soul to the US Army for the next few months. "Think they'd be interested in one more member?"

Jag paused with the fork halfway to his mouth. "Want to join up?"

"Maybe. I'd want to read the fine print first. But it sounds like a better deal than being surrounded by humans day and night, unable to shift for weeks for fear someone will see."

"When I get back, I'll pass your name along to the colonel."

If we get back.

The unsaid words hung in the air.

Sonar drank from his powder packet of instant juice, finding the taste not too terrible. Much better than the last one he tried.

"Bat ears."

He lowered the cup to stare at Jag. "What?"

"Your call sign. The guys thought you had bat ears."

Sonar grinned sheepishly. "Yeah. I could hear so well, they thought it would be a good nickname."

"Little do they know you really do have bat ears in your animal form." A ghost of a smile hovered on Jag's lips.

"Funny. I might have big ears compared to the rest of me, but ocelots are cool."

"If you say so." Jag inflicted a hint of boredom into his voice.

"If you don't care for Sonar, you can call me by my real name, Steel."

Jag kept eating, not bothering to reply.

Undeterred, Sonar tried again. "Got a real name?"

"Yeah."

"Gonna share?"

"Nope."

Befuddled, Sonar tilted his head and studied Jag's face. He'd never met a man so tight-lipped and stubborn about giving up basic information. "Why not?"

"I don't share that with *anyone*."

A bit stunned, Sonar processed that tidbit of knowledge, easily reading between the lines. The statement said it all. From what he'd picked up from Jag, he could easily label him a loner, an alpha predator, and someone who pushed himself beyond reason. He recalled the glimpse of tremendous pain and sorrow that had flashed in Jag's eyes earlier in the day. Whatever had happened must have been fucking bad because not much could rattle a man like Jag for long and cause him to shut down his emotions completely. Most men were serious when they had to be and relaxed when they could. The Jag he'd seen thus far stayed on strict alert every moment. He'd seen the situation before, though not with shifters. Those men who held it all in seemed to suffer the most post-traumatic stress and ended up falling apart. A handful even committed suicide because they were unable to cope any longer.

The thought sent a wave of ice through his veins.

Though they'd just met, he couldn't stand by and let such a man, a hero in every sense of the word, crumble under the extreme pressure he put on himself. It might not happen today, next month, or in the next few years. But sure as snow comes in winter, Jag would eventually break under the constant strain.

With newfound insight, Sonar drew in a deep breath and braced himself for the nearly impossible task at hand: keep Jag sane, healthy, and alive while he hunted one of the vilest serial killers in the history of man.

Chapter 4

JAG AWOKE instantly. He fully opened his senses without a single tiny movement to give his location away. Pulling on all his inbred abilities, he searched for anything off or unnatural near the hillside cave he'd chosen for the night. Slowly he blinked, his cat eyes more than capable of seeing details despite the dim light of predawn.

A tiny scuffing sound caught his attention. He sought the source, quickly locating a small goat herd over one hundred yards away. For a second, he considered remaining in his big cat form, stalking one of the animals, and fetching his own breakfast. He'd done just that numerous times in the past. The ability to live off the land allowed him to disappear off the grid and stretch his limited resources out for an extended period of time. Just as quickly, he discarded the idea. While he could easily survive on his own devices for weeks if necessary, he didn't want to waste time or deal with the outcome if someone came across the remains of his kill. Since no large felines called that particular corner of the Middle East home, there would be way too many questions brought up. Sure, most humans might attribute the goat's death to a wild dog, but he couldn't guarantee that.

Better safe than sorry.

Another one of the mottos he lived by.

Glancing over, he found Sonar curled up against the stone wall, also in his animal form, the ringed spots of his coat blending into the shadows well. While he and the ocelot might find more natural camouflage in the jungles of South America, their fur still offered nearly as much hiding potential in a dark portion of the desert. Not to mention their senses were definitely sharper in this form, giving them a decided advantage over humans if someone happened to stumble across their hideout for the night.

The fact that Sonar had morphed into his ocelot form first only mildly surprised Jag. In the war zone, only the smart, careful, and lucky survived. Men took advantage of every gift and skill they had to get through their time and return home in one piece. Shifters were no different in that respect.

With no threats looming nearby, Jag took the opportunity to check out his temporary partner. Sonar's spotted body might be quite a bit smaller than his, but it didn't lack for muscles or strength. Conditioned and compact, Sonar probably could dart and pounce with the best of his wild cousins. Maybe outhunt them as well. Large pointy ears flickered back and forth, catching his attention. *Bat ears.* Jag grinned to himself at the moniker. He'd give Sonar kudos for having the biggest ears he'd ever seen on a cat. Probably gave him an edge over Jag in the hearing department too. Jag bested him in most other features, though. Size, power, probably even stealth. One of the benefits of being the apex predator in a habitat.

Idly, he wondered if ocelots possessed a close family unit or favored a looser one like most shifters. In his experience, shifter families were created. DNA might drive a couple to pair up, but that didn't always result in offspring, a community, or a pack. That's where shifters really differed from their wild cousins. Shifters chose to live alone or to be part of a social group. Individual preferences mattered more than genetic traits in that respect. He'd certainly heard of small groups of shifters who made up neighborhoods, villages, or even sections of cities. Their influence and reputation extended beyond their physical borders. Yet they passed as humans, never once rousing suspicion that they might be otherwise, as far as Jag knew. If anyone uttered a single rumor otherwise, they would have been dealt with. For the secrecy of shifters hung above all their heads. If ever lost, they'd be hunted until death. All of them.

He swept the area with his gaze once more and shook off the morose reality of his kind.

He might not have a large pack to call his own, but he had his team, and a bit of family. That was enough. Or he used to believe so. Lately, he'd been growing more restless. Bored. Lonely. As the period of mourning faded, he found himself sizing up other men as possible applicants for the position of boyfriend. Thus far none of them met his standards.

With a big yawn, he stood up, stretched, and sniffed the air. Nothing out of the ordinary. Reassured, he summoned his human form and quickly redressed.

Sonar stirred, eyed him, and extended his front legs complete with claws. He repeated the same motion after standing and arching his back. Short fangs flashed in the dark for a brief moment before he sat on his haunches with a barely audible huff.

Jag arched an eyebrow, a bit amused by the ocelot's less than eager attitude this morning. "Cute."

Sonar lifted his lip once more and added a nearly silent hiss.

He's so not a morning person. Unlike Jag, who loved this time of day, when the world seemed to still in preparation for another busy day. "Yeah, bite me, little kitty." Jag drolly whispered, not the least bit intimidated by the aggressive body language. He finished dressing, strapped on his Kevlar vest, followed by his backpack. Lastly, he picked up his guns, sticking a pistol in his ankle holster, another in his shoulder holster under his shirt. A long knife dropped into his thigh strap for easy reach. The sniper rifle he carried in hand.

Satisfied, he glanced down at his companion to find Sonar back in human form, clothed, and snapping his backpack and belt in place. "Where do you think you're going?"

Sonar spared him a glance. "With you. Where else?"

Jag shook his head. "You might consider heading back to town and rejoining your unit. Where I'm going is no place for man, beast, or the devil himself."

Sonar's eyebrows scrunched together as he frowned. "I will *never* shirk my duty, no matter what."

Jag saw the determination and annoyance written clearly on his spotter's face. He blew out a breath in resignation. "Then be prepared for a journey into hell."

"Been there, done that. Have the badge to prove it," Sonar sneered as he gathered up his gun.

"That was the fairy-tale version of hell. This is the stuff of nightmares." Jag started heading in the direction of Sandman's last known location.

Sonar quickly caught up. "This sick bastard might be one of the worst, but I guarantee he's not the only one into gruesome torture."

Jag lifted his chin and scanned the horizon. "Maybe so, but he's the only one I care about."

"Why?"

Ignoring the question, Jag continued along a goat path leading over the hill and through several more. The terrain proved a bit treacherous due to loose rock, silt, and the great possibility that an enemy insurgent might be lurking or had already left a calling card in the form of an explosive device.

"What's Sandman to you, Jag?"

Jag met Sonar's gaze for a split second. His gut lurched as old memories and emotions threatened to spill over. Stoically, he shoved them all down, forcing himself to focus on the task ahead. Only it, nothing else mattered but redemption. He'd see Sandman dead and buried this time. It's the least he could do, considering.

Sonar could fish all he wanted. Jag wasn't about to give up his innermost secrets, especially not in the middle of a mission. "Keep up. I'm not stopping until I get to the small rise about ten clicks from here. The sooner we arrive, the sooner we figure out where he's gone to ground."

SONAR GRUMBLED under his breath as he watched Jag tirelessly navigate the harsh terrain, pushing to reach his destination come hell or high water. The relentless pace left Sonar scrambling to watch their backs, keep an eye up ahead, and traverse the large rocks that had slid from farther above during one of the last rainstorms weeks ago. Dust covered his boots and clothing. It hung thick in the air, clogged his nose, and interfered with his acute sense of smell. The result left him more than antsy. He needed all his senses functioning perfectly in order to keep them both safe on this dangerous trek. To have one of his major ones impaired could easily affect their outcome. In a majorly negative way.

Jag seemingly didn't suffer any of the same problems. He simply kept moving, looked around now and again, and rarely slackened the pace even for a brief break or to take a sip of water.

Give the guy credit for intensity and dedication.

Too bad Sonar would rather kick him in the ass instead.

Each time he tried to dig a little deeper into Jag's reasoning, the sniper shut him down. Cold. Whatever ate at him or made this one mission of utmost importance remained a mystery to Sonar. And that only added to Sonar's uneasiness.

At first Sonar had been excited about working with Jaguar, the ghostly figure who traveled the world as a freelance top-of-the-line sniper. Clouded in myths and stories of amazing deeds, Jag carried his accomplishments on his sleeve, was rumored to possess more than his fair share of arrogance, and didn't take shit off anyone. A legend already, to hear others whisper about his prowess, his skills. The ability to take out the worst of the worst with a single shot from unheard-of distances.

Now, the brightness that surrounded Jag had dulled, leaving Sonar to glimpse the real man within. Jag hurt. He bled. He kept his mouth shut, fixated on the job, and refused to let anything stand in his way.

Respect for Jag grew as did an innate sense of frustration. The guy just didn't know how to let go, not even for a day. Not to mention, he walked around tall and sure, as if daring anyone to take a potshot at him.

While his carriage might add to the tales and to the bounty presently on Jag's head, it also served to demoralize the enemy. If someone as famous as he could just jog around the countryside without being killed, he either floated under a lucky star or had stored up enough good karma to be kept safe.

The idea didn't settle well with Sonar. To him, Jag just taunted the insurgents, taking an unnecessary risk.

"Why don't you silhouette yourself against the skyline next time?" Sonar bit out.

Jag turned to face him. "Got a problem with it?"

"Yeah. It's a good way to get shot."

"Or bring out the boogey man."

Sonar shook his head. "From everything I've heard about Sandman, he's not stupid enough to stick around and wait for you to come get him."

"True." Jag lifted his nose to the wind. "Which is why I'm not too concerned with staying low. There's no one nearby and I'm almost 100 percent positive that Sandman has long since packed up and moved."

"To another town? Another battle zone?"

Jag shrugged. "No telling. But, like any good sniper, he doesn't stick to the same place long."

Sonar paused in midstride, the telltale scent of old blood and death carrying on the breeze. He latched on and hurried that way, Jag right on his heels.

Several paces later, he stared down at a soldier, a dead one at that. The man's nude body was riddled with slash marks. Sonar looked closer, noted the intricate designs resembling an ancient medallion, and knew for a fact the man had been tortured before he finally died from blood loss.

Bile rose in Sonar's throat. He forced it back, clenched his teeth, and turned away from the gruesome sight.

Jag stared at the body as if searching for evidence with a professional eye. His jaw ticked and his fists clenched, the only real physical signs that he'd been affected.

Sonar drew in a couple of deep breaths and regained control of himself. "I get why your sole goal is to eliminate this bastard. *Now*."

Jag glimpsed his way. "It doesn't get any easier."

"I'd expect not." Obviously Jag had seen the results of Sandman's work before. Sonar prayed he never would again. However, he didn't put much confidence in that hope. Until they found and eliminated that son of a bitch, he would continue to play his sick game.

The glint of light off metal caught his eye. Sonar bent down, picked up what appeared to be a shell casing, and stood. The embellishment on the metal drew his attention. While most casings were devoid of even a maker's mark, this one had an *S* on one side, made with a different element than the rest of the piece. He rolled it until a set of etched numbers showed. "What's this?"

Jag strode over, took the item from him, and studied it. "His hallmark, but the numbers are new."

Perplexed, Sonar raked the ground with his gaze, searching for more clues. Finding none, he focused once more on Jag. "Any clue what they might mean?"

"Hold this." Jag handed the casing back to Sonar before digging through his pack. He pulled out his GPS tracker and punched buttons. "Well, I'll be damned."

"What?"

"Sandman left us a clue all right. He left us the coordinates of his next location."

Sonar blinked, trying to absorb this latest development. "Why in the hell would he do that?"

Jag met his gaze. "Because he knows I'm tracking him and has decided to have a little fun."

"By giving away his location?" Sonar thought for a second. "It's a setup. It has to be."

"Yep." Jag stared at his device once more. "We don't have a choice but to take the bait."

"Are you insane?" Sonar's mouth fell open.

Jag narrowed his eyes and pinned Sonar with a glare of such intensity the hairs on Sonar's neck stood on end. "Take another look at that dead man and tell me you're willing to ignore the only lead we have to Sandman's location. I guarantee you there'll be dozens more if we don't join the devil in his own game."

Sonar glanced to his side, then back to Jag. Resolve solidified in his mind. "Just tell me where in the hell we're going."

"Brazil."

"Why there?"

"Your guess is as good as mine."

Chapter 5

TWENTY-FOUR HOURS later, Jag walked down a street, his mind in turmoil. He truly believed in his gut, which clamored loudly, that Sandman had drawn him into a sick game, one he couldn't decline. The tip and idea proved sound. Why? He didn't have a clue. Sure, he'd shot the bastard and paybacks were hell. Did Sandman know it was Jag who had shot him? Did he single him out as a challenge?

Answers remained out of reach and all too silent, forcing Jag to simply go with his instincts. No matter what they found, even an ambush, he'd have to go along. With eyes and ears wide open.

A call back to base updated the colonel on their travels, lined up a plane ride, and cleared the authorization for Sonar to tag along. After all, he had been assigned to Jag's six for the duration of the hunt. However annoyed that order made Jag.

Jag checked the numbers on his GPS tracker once more, glanced up at the sign on the building, and shook his head. "This is it. Whatever that's worth."

"A bar? Why in the hell would Sandman lead you here? It's not like he can hide a body in the middle of the dance floor." Sonar scowled.

"No clue what that wily bastard is up to. Only one way to find out." Jag led the way and they walked in.

Jag's eyes took a second to adjust to the lower lighting before making out more details.

Although it was only late afternoon, the establishment was starting to pick up business for the night. A handful of customers sipped beers at tables while the barkeep stared with boredom across the room. Another man collected empty bottles and cleaned tables, looking like he'd rather be anywhere but there. His age put him in his teens while his facial features resembled the barkeep's. More than likely family members, which meant the kid had no choice in where he worked.

Loud music thumped, the decibels hurting Jag's sensitive ears. A couple hit the dance floor, moving to the beat.

Most wore casual attire, similar to what he and Sonar had pulled on before their jet ride. As comfortable as he was in his camos, he needed to blend in. So, jeans and button-down shirts were the choices of the day.

"I'll have a look around on this side of the room. You take the other." Sonar headed to the back of the room, leaving Jag with the front section.

With no idea what to look for, Jag searched the area, both people and objects, trying to locate anything that would remind him of Sandman.

"Took you long enough."

Jag spun around, spied a young man with medium-length light hair and an arrogant sneer on his face. He also read a mixture of anticipation and nervousness on the man's face. Certainly not native, judging by his complexion, his English words, and American accent. "Who are you?"

"The guy you're looking for."

Jag blew out a frustrated breath and turned away. "Not interested."

The blond shoved in front of him, blocking his path. "You should be. If you want Sandman."

Now that got his interest. Jag studied the man with newfound intrigue. "What's he to you?"

The guy shrugged. "I'm just a messenger. You can call me Tony."

His patience waning, Jag glared at Tony. "Then tell me already so I can be on my way."

Tony smiled wickedly, his gaze traveled over Jag's body, lingered on his groin, and finally returned to meet his eyes. "Oh, I don't think so. Nothing comes free."

Jag bit back the urge to grab Tony by the neck and shake him. "What's the price?"

Tony licked his lips and tilted his head, once more checking out Jag's endowment. The unmistakable scent of lust carried to Jag's nose. He could see the wheels turning in Tony's head and braced himself for the answer he was sure to hate.

"Fuck me," Tony said softly while reaching out to boldly cup Jag's crotch and give his genitals a squeeze.

Jag narrowed his eyes and resisted the urge to tear the man's arm from his body.

Sonar approached, noted the location of Tony's hand, and his eyes widened. "What the hell?"

Tony ignored him. "The new boyfriend?"

"No."

"Pity." Tony trailed his fingers up Jag's body. When he tried to touch Jag's face, Jag pulled back. "Fuck me like you used to fuck your dead lover and I'll tell you the next location. Refuse and you fall out of the game. Sandman goes free."

Sonar tensed. Jag felt the anger coming off his partner in waves. He shoved his emotions into his kill box and lifted his chin. "One fuck. I top. You give up the information and I walk away, no strings attached."

Tony chewed his lip before giving a slight nod. "Deal." He gestured toward the bathroom. "A bit clichéd, but it's close."

"Lead the way." Jag started to follow when Sonar grabbed his arm. "You can't be serious."

Jag spared him a glance. "I need that next location."

"Not like this."

"If it means getting closer to Sandman and slitting his throat, I'll screw the devil himself." Jag tugged his arm free and strode straight to the far corner of the establishment, turned down a short hall, and found the door already open. Tony waited for him with a lopsided grin that might have been sexy if he wasn't such a prick. The small bathroom had two stalls and appeared reasonably clean compared to some of the dumps he'd visited. The door had no lock, but he didn't give a shit. He shoved it closed anyway, more than ready to get this over with.

"Have you screwed anyone since Mark's death?"

Jag forced down the growl of rage and blanked his face. Just because he had to suffer this indignation and fresh salt in the wound didn't mean he had to speak about it. To anyone.

Mark's memory wouldn't be tainted by this event. Jag refused to allow it. This was filthy sex for the sole purpose of getting closer to Sandman. Nothing about gentleness, love, or sensitivity would be involved. They couldn't be. He'd locked those feelings away years ago. He was a sniper, a shooter, a hunter. Never again would he be a lover in the true sense of the word. Forever. Or so he'd thought. Until recently.

Time heals all wounds.

He ignored the inner voice and returned to the distasteful situation. "Drop those pants and bend over the sink so I can drill your ass."

Tony snorted. "One-track mind." He unzipped Jag's jeans and tugged them down.

Jag's cock sprang free.

Tony reached for it.

Jag stayed his hand and spun him around. "I said to drop trou and bend over," he ordered with a low growl.

Tony obeyed, wiggling around before his pants fell to his ankles. He rested his forearms on the porcelain sink, lifted his head, and stared at Jag in the mirror.

The sight did little to turn Jag on. He stroked himself roughly until his cock hardened enough to perform. For a second he thought about spitting in his hand to add a bit of lube, then quickly rejected the idea. This wasn't about comfort; this was about tapping Tony's ass and getting the hell out of Dodge.

He set the tip of his dick against Tony's hole, grabbed the man's hips, and surged for home. Tightness prevented him from bottoming out on the first try.

Tony squealed and jerked.

"Tell me Sandman's real name." When no answer came forth, he thrust hard.

"Shit." Tony's legs buckled for a second before he managed to regain his balance. "I don't know, man. Seriously. He just paid me to do this."

Jag stilled. "Then tell me a reason I should believe you."

Tony blew out a breath. "The man has a scar on his left cheek in the shape of an *L*. He showed me a picture of you and warned me that you'd be uncooperative."

Detecting Tony told the truth only added to Jag's strangling level of frustration. He fed the emotion into his strokes, setting a brutal, punishing pace.

Tony whimpered, whined, and arched his back in response. His face screwed up, whether in pain or pleasure, Jag didn't know, nor did he care. Instead, he ignored Tony's reactions and pumped for all he was worth. He didn't even worry about tearing the guy's ass open. All he wanted was to finish as soon as possible and get on with his mission.

He grunted and plunged in hard and deep, Tony's body alternating between dipping and lifting in front of him. He knew Tony attempted to get the angle just right in order to hit his hot spot. Jag couldn't give a damn. In fact, he purposely tried to aim high, selfishly unwilling to give the bastard a single moment of pleasure from this carnal rooting.

"Fuck, yes." Tony groaned, his eyes closed as he threw his head back.

"Tell me the message."

Tony met his gaze in the mirror. "So you can pull out and leave? I'm not that much of an idiot."

Jag closed his eyes, focused on his cock, and ran a few erotic images through his mind to help him leap toward the peak. Neither the act itself nor the man bent over did much for his libido, but the snippets of fantasy did.

He grasped Tony's hips harder, sank that much deeper, and sprinted for home. The welcome tingling along his backbone announced his imminent climax. He reached for it with all his being.

Tony whined as his ass clamped down on Jag's shaft, rhythmic milking motions that announced his own orgasm had arrived.

He pulled out, ran his hand up and down his length, then moaned when the first pulse streamed from the flared head and out onto Tony's upraised rear. A couple more followed before Jag drew in a deep breath, grabbed a couple of paper towels, and cleaned himself before wiping the cum off Tony, not because he hated for Tony to be covered in stickiness after such a carnal act. Instead, he worried about anyone having access to his body fluids, analyzing it, and discovering his secret.

"The message. Now." He gritted out.

"In my… right jean pocket." The breathless words came out as a hushed whisper.

Jag heard well enough.

Only when he was satisfied not a single drop remained did he shove the used towels into his pocket, refasten his pants, and delve into the place Tony indicated. He found a piece of paper wrapped around a shell casing. The decoration and size fit into Sandman's pattern. He opened the folded paper, saw a list of numbers, and frowned. "Some numbers are missing."

Tony nodded. "He said you'd notice that. The last two digits are Mark's birthday. April first."

Jag's breath caught. Sandman had it out for him, definitely, using each and every trick possible to twist that knife lodged in his heart along the way. At this rate, he'd be on the edge before he even got close to Sandman. His superhuman efforts to contain his pain would last only so long. If this dragged out much longer, he'd snap.

Which is exactly what Sandman wants. To break me. The only question remained why.

Stoically, he folded the paper back up and stuffed it into his other jacket pocket. He walked out of the room, leaving Tony still panting and leaning over the sink.

Catching sight of Sonar, he inclined his head and shoved through the side door, more than eager to get the hell out of there.

"Did you get it?"

"Yeah."

"You okay?"

Jag didn't bother with an answer. Instead, he focused on his following step: hitching a plane to the next destination and taking time for a long, hot shower with plenty of lye soap.

SONAR WALKED beside Jag, his thoughts in turmoil after picking up bits and pieces of the conversation back at the bar. Jag was gay, had a boyfriend, and was more than willing to fuck some bastard's ass in order to get needed information. The whole thing took Sonar aback.

Sonar's gut clenched. Jag wasn't the kind of man to be manipulated. Yet he stood there and let that bastard do just that. Everything from feeling him up in public to dragging him off to the restroom for a quick pump and dump. None of that meshed with what Sonar had picked up about Jag to date.

The fact that Jag was gay, or at least bi, didn't truly surprise Sonar. With his looks, Jag could have either gender at his beck and call.

Still, he couldn't believe Jag went through with the ridiculous deal. The fact that he did so told Sonar so much. Namely, that he'd do anything to find Sandman, be it travel all over the world, tear a room apart or, in his words, "screw the devil himself." If that wasn't revelation enough into Jag's obsession, the other tidbit added fuel to the fire.

Jag's dead lover.

While not a betting man, Sonar would wager the clothes off his back that Sandman had had something to do with the death of Jag's boyfriend. That puzzle piece clicked in solidly and explained a few things. Namely why Jag would sacrifice anything and everything to get Sandman once and for all.

"Going to tell me what happened?"

"No."

Sonar's shoulders dropped. He really didn't expect Jag to just plop down on a park bench and confess a painful past. Still, they were partners and he needed to understand some things in order to make this work and keep Jag alive. "He killed your lover." Sonar made it a statement.

Jag's jaw ticked, the only sign that he'd heard Sonar's remark. His steps remained consistent, leading them back to the SUV they'd left a couple of blocks away.

They arrived at the vehicle and slid into their seats. Jag yanked out his satellite phone, pushed a button, and began speaking rapid fire.

Sonar watched him for a moment, still baffled by the man he'd been teamed up with for the duration.

Jag clicked off, stored his phone back in his pocket, and started the engine. After checking the mirrors, he pulled easily out into the road and ramped up the speed.

"Where to now?" Sonar asked.

"Paris."

Sonar sighed. "That bastard gets around."

"Yeah."

He took a moment to appraise Jag. While he might look calm, cool, and collected, Sonar sensed a building volcano underneath. Jag might have his emotions and expressions down to a calculated science, but Sonar's senses picked up more than the typical human could ever dream of. Namely, the subtle aroma of rage coming from Jag.

He could empathize. While he might not have been in the mix, he still felt the outflow shocks. Hell, he'd wanted to punch Tony in the face for daring to touch Jag like that, then again when he threw out the bargain. Extremely offended, Sonar could only stand by and watch Jag reduced to the level of a whore.

Protective instincts came out of nowhere, nearly blinding him with anger. Jag could handle himself; that was a fact. Still, that didn't stop Sonar from wanting to shove that bastard away from Jag, to demand another way to obtain the information, to spare Jag such indignation.

Fury rose once more. He shook off the useless emotion and focused on Jag.

If his belief was true that Sandman had killed Jag's lover, how could the man bury his feelings, go through so much humiliation, and keep going? *Revenge.* That had to be what Jag lived for these days. The goal made him hard, determined, and was the only reason Sonar could see that Jag would willingly lower himself to such a base level for a clue. That kind of dedication took guts.

Sonar knew he was watching a legend at work.

His resolve firmed. One way or another, Jag would rid the world of Sandman and live to tell the tale. Even if Sonar had to tie him down and make him decompress along the way.

Chapter 6

"JET LAG sucks." Sonar muttered under his breath as he and Jag walked slowly away from the plane terminal and toward a hotel. They'd caught a late transport out of Rio and landed in Paris just after dawn.

Worn out, yet keyed up, Sonar walked alongside Jag toward their destination. "A hot shower sounds like heaven."

Jag nodded. "We'll get some shut-eye and a hot meal, then hit the trail this afternoon."

Sonar read the tiredness in Jag's eyes but knew he'd never consent to do much more than take care of his basic body needs on this mission. He pushed himself hard. *Too hard.*

"It's been nonstop for the past few days. Why don't we take a break?"

Jag glared over at him. "The longer we take to find Sandman, the more people die. I don't know about you, but I don't want *that* on my conscience any more than what I've already got."

Sonar bristled. "He's dragging you all over the world and sapping your energy. Playing with you. When the time comes, you won't be at your best. Exhaustion leads to mistakes. Even the best warrior needs downtime."

Jag stopped and faced Sonar, his eyes sparking with anger. "Do whatever you want, but I'm not slowing down until I have that bastard in the crosshairs. Nothing else matters."

He walked away, his long strides eating up the distance.

Sonar followed at a more sedate pace.

An hour later he stepped from the shower, finding Jag standing by the window, looking out. His straight back and stiff carriage told Sonar that Jag might be clean, but he wasn't any closer to relaxing and sleep than he was when they first landed in France.

Jag's still-damp black locks held a bit of curl, taking the edge off the chiseled features and intense scowl. His unbuttoned shirt framed a wide chest that flowed into narrower hips and a six-pack abdomen that most athletes would kill for. The muscles of his arms bunched as he pushed himself away from the wall and turned to the bed nearest him.

Sonar's pulse kicked up at the gorgeous male body on display in front of him. More than that, he respected Jag as a man and saw the goodness carefully tucked away within. Those features were even more important than the near-Adonis physique and appearance belonging to Jag.

Too bad Jag had closed himself off to the rest of the world. He had so much to offer if he'd just open up, even slightly.

Sonar finished drying his hair and tossed the towel into a nearby hamper. He tugged at his sweatpants as he crossed over to the other bed. They'd already eaten and bathed. Next up was a few hours of much-needed shut-eye before getting back to work.

Sitting on the edge of his bed, Sonar contemplated the situation. He'd been with Jag for less than a week, but he'd gotten nowhere in the trust department. If they were to continue on and be successful, that had to change, starting with Jag confessing some details of his past.

"I was told Sandman was dead. Then, next thing I know, he's back on the map again."

"I shot the bastard. He's just too fucking mean to die." Jag stretched out on his bed, his long frame taking up nearly the whole length of the mattress.

"Any idea how he survived?" From what Sonar had heard, Jag never missed. Even if he did by an inch, those big rounds would do enough damage to finish anyone off.

"No. I wish I did."

Sonar ran some scenarios through his mind. "Are you sure he's not a shifter? He could've changed forms and healed almost any wound."

"I've worked that angle endlessly. It just doesn't pan out. He doesn't smell like a shifter, nor act like one. I'll give you that he has to be more than an ordinary human, but what, I have no clue."

Sonar picked up on the annoyance in Jag's tone. Poor guy probably had driven himself half-mad trying to figure out Sandman, all to no avail. "Okay. Let's try looking at it from another direction. What does he have against you?"

Jag put his hands behind his head and stared at the ceiling.

"It's easy to see he's leaving clues for you and you alone. So why you? Why not someone else? What is your history with the guy?"

Jag slowly turned his head to look at Sonar. His eyes snapped in warning.

Sonar didn't back down in the least. "I need to know what's between you and Sandman."

Jag snarled. "You don't need to know jack shit."

Sonar pulled on his restraint and tried reason. "This is personal for you, I get that. But we're in this together, and I can't help you if I don't see or understand what the issues or ramifications might be. If you tell me what happened, what's driving you, we can work out how to get past the obstacles and use it to our advantage."

Jag glared at him before lifting a lip to expose one of his fangs. "I told you all you need to know. Just stay out of my fucking way."

His patience at an end, Sonar sat down on the edge of Jag's bed, close enough where he could demand Jag's attention. "Listen up, tough guy. This mission involves me. I'm not just going to stand back and jack off while you run the show. Nor am I willing to be a tethered goat just waiting for Sandman to set his sights on me. The way I see it, it's going to take both of us to do this so start talking."

Jag scowled and growled.

Sonar gave it right back. "I'm not dumb or suicidal. There's something personal about this mission and it revolves around your dead boyfriend."

Jag's breath hitched as his eyes flashed fire.

Sonar seized the train of thought and ran with it. "And there it is. Chances are Sandman had something to do with his death."

Jag sat up in a rush, jumped off the bed, and started pacing the room, his steps stiff and agitated. "You want to hear it? All of it?"

Sonar spun around to keep Jag in his line of vision. "Yes. Just spill it already."

"Sandman killed Mark. He was my spotter, working at my side. I had Sandman nearly in my sights. So close. But before I could squeeze the trigger, he took out Mark next to me. I sat there, coated in Mark's blood and brain matter, until Sandman retreated into the bushes. The next seven hours, I carried Mark's body on my back, dodging insurgents while praying Sandman wouldn't find me before I could return Mark's body to a safe enough place for a chopper pickup." Jag lowered his head. "I promised to take care of him. Told his parents that I'd keep him safe. After all, he was human and not as strong as a shifter."

Sonar stopped breathing. "He knew what you are?"

Jag stopped in his tracks and lifted agony-filled eyes to meet his gaze. "Yes." Jag started to say more, then closed his mouth. He drew in air and his eyes glazed over. "For nearly an entire day, I wore his body fluids, long since dried to my skin, as I carried him along those damn goat trails until a lift could be arranged. I didn't want to give him up even then, but I had to."

"So he could be sent back home to his family," Sonar finished.

Jag lifted his chin once more. "So I could hunt that son of a bitch and blow him to pieces for what he did to Mark."

The emotion in that one sentence stunned Sonar. Controlled rage mixed with deep suffering. "How long did it take?"

"Too fucking long. Months." He picked at his camo pants. "Each time he'd best me, carve up another poor bastard, taunting me with his whereabouts. I finally caught up to him and put a gaping hole in his chest. It was over. Until a couple of weeks ago when he left me another calling card." Jag's voice trailed off.

For a long time, Sonar said nothing, just absorbing Jag's story, his heart clenching for the guy who had been through so much. No downtime. No opportunity to decompress or work through what had happened. Just endless days with a single goal to keep him going. He didn't know if he could have held up nearly as well as Jag had.

"How long ago?"

"Three fucking years. He was dead, gone, for three fucking years." He rubbed his thighs and arched his neck to stare at the ceiling before meeting Sonar's gaze. "He killed the man I loved. I hunted Sandman down. Finished it. Said my piece. Now the bastard is back to haunt me again."

"Wow." Sonar ached to reach out, to touch Jag, draw him into a hug. Something told him Jag wouldn't be pleased with the compassionate act.

"I can't protect my spotter. I learned that. No matter what I am, I'm not able to keep anyone else alive." He stared at Sonar as he spoke, his words soft and flat. His face returned to the familiar mask Sonar had come to recognize. "I know you're here to help, but it's only making things that much harder."

"Your job isn't to protect me. I take care of myself. Remember that."

Jag started to protest, but Sonar spoke over him. "Like I said, this is going to take both of us, working together, to nail the son of a bitch.

That means we watch out for each other, don't dash off on a rabbit trail alone, and use our brains instead of just gut reaction."

Jag's eyebrows scrunched, but he remained mute.

"Give me a chance to be your right-hand man. We did well as a team back on the front."

"I work alone." Steely determination carried in Jag's tone.

Sonar shook his head. "Not anymore. You're our only chance of taking out Sandman. If you fall before then...." Purposely, Sonar let that thought play out in Jag's mind.

Jag turned away and drew in a deep breath.

Deciding he'd gotten his point across, Sonar switched gears. "How long were you and Mark together?"

"Five years." The words turned hollow as if Jag were reading mindlessly from an article instead of talking about the tragedy of his personal life.

Sonar realized that Jag had released his emotions for a brief moment before compartmentalizing them once again. He was shutting down, burying his grief deep inside. Not a good move in Sonar's opinion. To keep the pain in was to let an abscess begin to fester. At some point it would worsen, sicken Jag, and erupt. Most likely at an important, pivotal moment. He might have had three years to deal with the horrific loss, but that didn't mean all his memories wouldn't fly back with such potent reminders left by their adversary. "I know why it's personal for you. But why is Sandman targeting you? Do you know the bastard?"

Jag shook his head. "Not that I know of. No one knows his real name and as far as I know, there's only one picture of him out there."

"He's a fine sniper, so he's had to have some training. If not in the US, then in other countries."

"That's an endless road as well. Intelligence came up with nothing on the guy. Nothing at all. As far as they're concerned, he just appeared out of the blue, started creating havoc, and is fucking impossible to kill."

Sonar heard the weariness in Jag's voice. To carry such a massive load for so long. No wonder Jag's attitude was pretty pissy. His would be too, if he'd experienced not even half of what Jag did. Having such a sick bastard rise from the dead would rattle and irritate just about anyone. "So, he's a serial killer, a highly trained assassin, so to speak, running loose around the world. He's engaged you in a game of tag, for some unknown reason, and has the ability to survive mortal wounds." Sonar ran one hand through his short hair. "Sounds like a deranged immortal out to play a game of who's the best sniper in all the land."

Jag snorted. "That part I figured out a while back."

Something nagged at Sonar. "You said the guy in Brazil called Mark by name. How did he know that?"

"From Sandman. Supposedly he told Tony the last two numbers on the GPS were Mark's birthday. April first."

"How would Sandman know that about Mark? I can see where he might get Mark's name, either from some sort of reconnaissance or even a list of those killed in action. But his birthday?"

Jag drew in a breath. "It wouldn't be a big leap to find the information. Any search engine would give you that, especially with links to the local papers and obituaries."

"Still...." Sonar couldn't shake the feeling that they'd only scratched the surface on this particular mystery. "A sniper might go after another sniper for the bounty or for the challenge of ruling the roost. But he wouldn't drag you all over the world for that. He'd stick to his territory and make you come to him." Sonar tapped his lips. "This is personal for him too. But why?"

Jag shrugged. "If you figure that out, let me know. I've been racking my brain along with others who are a damned sight smarter than me. We have nothing."

"Mark has to be the key."

Jag's chin lifted. "Why do you say that?"

Sonar met his gaze steadily. "If you don't know Sandman, have never been around him, then there's no reason for him to single you out except as a sniper duel. This is so much more than that. Which brings us back to Mark."

"Forget it," Jag snapped with renewed anger. "Mark was as loyal they come. He'd never sell us out. *Never.*"

"Whoa." Sonar held up his hands. "I wasn't going there." Although the idea had some merit. He stored it away for later. "I was just wondering if Mark knew Sandman."

Jag tilted his head and glanced away. "He never said he did."

"Did you ask him?"

"No."

"There just might be our first clue."

Jag sighed. "I hate to say it, but you might be right."

Sonar inclined his head in acknowledgment, relieved that Jag had simmered down and opened up to him. It was a start, a good one. "There's not much we can do about it right now. So, let's get some sleep and work on this more later." Sonar returned to his bed, checked to make sure his pistol was still under his pillow, then pulled the covers over him. He rested on his side and watched Jag return to his bed. He stretched out and stared at the ceiling, probably too worked up to drift off to sleep. Sonar regretted adding to Jag's burden and getting him all ramped up, but he didn't regret needling the truth out of his partner. He could now draw on his instincts and training in order to know how to deal with and defuse Jag along the way.

One way or another, we'll get your revenge, Jag. I promise you.

Chapter 7

FIVE HOURS later, they stepped out of a taxi, dressed like ordinary tourists, with backpacks strapped to their backs. Jag had broken down his rifle and stowed it away in his ruck, but still felt a bit naked without it. Unfortunately, traipsing around the small city outside Paris with a gun in hand would garner more attention than he wanted. He and Sonar settled for stashing their handguns and knives in holsters against their skin. The loose clothing covered everything well, giving no hint that they were armed to the teeth.

Jag checked his GPS tracker. "This way."

Sunset was upon them, the brilliantly colored sky aiding in both cloaking them as well as giving them enough light to see readily, especially with their advanced eyesight, compliments of their feline DNA.

They entered a park area where a few people lingered, most strolling along a walking path that took them in a circle around the ponds, flower gardens, and an open grassy area.

Jag slowed his steps, checked the reading once more, then gazed straight ahead. "In the thicket."

Sonar's eyes narrowed. "The scent...."

Jag inhaled, detecting the unmistakable aroma of blood and death. "Shit." Resisting the urge to run, he strode straight ahead, found a small opening in the thick brush, then pushed through. Several paces later, he halted as the unseeing eyes of a man looked up at him.

Rustling noises announced Sonar's arrival, right on his heels. "Oh, hell."

Jag heard Sonar swallowing and trying to take deep breaths in an effort to work through queasiness. He could relate. The gruesome sight, a nude young man, with deep gouges cut into his entire body. An artistic pattern drawn out on a once-living man. Jag could only hope the poor guy had been dead before the torture began. Judging by the amount of blood, he wouldn't lay odds on the fact.

His stomach churned, not with nausea, but with rage. Once again an innocent man had paid a horrible price all because he missed his shot and allowed Sandman to recover and start his game all over again. He cussed himself and his lack of perfection when most needed.

Sonar tilted his head. "He looks like the last one. Same dark hair, clean-shaven, oval face. Even the nose is pretty close. It's odd they look so much alike."

"Not really."

"What do you mean?"

Jag sighed, his shoulders slumping in defeat. The past blurred into the present. Like a déjà-vu horror. "They all look like Mark."

Sonar's gaze flew to Jag's face. "That's downright cruel." He eyed the body once more. "When did the victims start resembling Mark?"

Jag shrugged. "Around the time Sandman killed him. It was like he chose to get serious at that moment. Drew a new line in the dirt."

Sonar glanced around. "Why here? What's so special about Brazil and now France?"

"Mark and I vacationed in both places." The words came out full of self-condemnation. The coincidence was too great to miss. Sonar had been right last night; Mark was the key. It wasn't as simple as sniper on sniper. *No. This was deep hatred.*

"At this very spot?"

Jag shook his head. "No. But in this area."

"The bar?"

"Never been there before. We were tourists, not there for a party or a hook-up."

"Well, shit." Sonar scrubbed his face. "You know what this means?"

"That Sandman was stalking us." The facts added up fast. "The creepy bastard followed us all over the world. Now he's recreating those stops in order to prove a point."

"More like stalking Mark. Since you didn't know him before Mark entered your life," Sonar pointed out. "Mark *had* to have known him. To spend so much time and energy dragging you all over the place, it had to be more than a fascination with Mark. It had to be a relationship, albeit an unbalanced one."

Jag had already come to the same conclusion. As much as he hated the idea of Mark and Sandman being lovers, he now saw the truth written on the wall. For whatever insane reason, Mark and Sandman had been close at one point in time. Something happened, which freed up Mark to be with Jag. Sandman obviously hadn't agreed with the breakup and started on the road to psychosis by carving up young men who resembled Mark and by targeting them until he killed Mark. Now he had one more circle to complete. Destroying the man who took Mark away from him—Jag.

"He's pissed and lashing out. Trying to hurt me just like he figures Mark and I hurt him." Jag drew in a deep breath and resigned himself. "This ends now."

Sonar tipped his head in agreement. "His days are numbered. The bastard will punch his ticket straight to hell damn soon."

Scanning the area, Jag discovered another shell casing next to the victim's neck. He reached over, careful not to touch the body, and plucked the clue from the ground. Sure enough, it matched Sandman's individual signature, complete with numbers etched into the side.

Automatically, he entered those same numbers into his GPS unit, waited a few seconds, then glared at the screen.

"Where?"

"The jungles of Argentina."

Sonar met his gaze. "What's there?"

Jag swallowed hard. "The place where Mark and I married and spent our honeymoon."

Sonar's mouth fell open.

Jag forcefully shoved aside any and all emotion. Focusing entirely on his mission, he spun around, left the brushy area, and started back toward the hotel. He would make an anonymous report about finding a dead body and line up a plane to South America.

Soon, Sandman. Soon I'm going to blow your goddamn head off.

HALF AN hour later, Jag walked back into their hotel room, waited for Sonar to follow, and threw his ruck on the floor.

He'd been too late. Again.

Guilt settled on his already weighted-down shoulders as his restlessness peaked. He wanted to wrap his hands around Sandman's neck and squeeze the life out of him. Shoot him. Stab him. Send him to hell in any way, shape, or manner that he could. Instead, he found himself stuck for another few hours in Paris before a chartered flight could pick him and Sonar up and take them to their next destination.

"Shit." He sat on the end of the bed, found stillness unacceptable, promptly stood back up, and began to pace. "Waiting is fucking useless." The image of the youth ran through his mind. Another life snuffed out all because of his screwup. His kill box flew open, allowing all the negative stuff to hit him all at once.

Dammit. Not now. Get a hold of yourself.

Sonar shut the door, locked it, and dumped his backpack next to Jag's. He glanced at Jag. "I'm sure your commander did the best he could."

Jag swung around as he neared the window and glared. "We're sitting here on our hands and Sandman is out there carving up another innocent. That doesn't sit well with me." He couldn't suppress the frustration, the feeling of being caged, the acute inability to do something, anything.

Sonar shook his head. "It's not like any of us can control the world."

Jag snarled.

Sonar stared at him drolly. "I get it. You're pissed. Believe me; I am too. However, snapping at me and complaining about the speed of air service doesn't help matters any."

"I don't need your damn lip right now." Although he realized he was being unfair to Sonar, he couldn't seem to stop. Tension rode him hard, as did the nearly overwhelming guilt. Another family would mourn tonight.

"Listen up, Rambo. I'm just telling you the way it is. Either take it or not. I don't give a fuck. Either way, stop reading me the riot act while crucifying yourself for something out of your control."

Sonar stepped closer, invading Jag's personal space, causing him to cease his pacing. Jag flashed a fang in warning.

"Not working. You might be one stick-up-the-ass bastard, but I'm not about to roll over and beg." Grit entered his voice as he narrowed his eyes and met Jag's stare.

"You don't know anything."

Sonar crossed his arms over his chest. "Wrong again. You're batting zero so far. Let me tell you what I know. You blame yourself for everything. Guess what? Time for a reality check, Jag. You're not God. You don't rule the earth and the sun doesn't revolve around you. Welcome to the world of mortality and limitations. You're a soldier, not a miracle worker."

"It's not good enough." Jag scrubbed his face, his nerves crackling, making him severely edgy and on the brink of losing his hard-won control.

"Is anything ever good enough for you?"

Jag growled louder.

Sonar didn't even flinch.

"I'll show you good enough." Sonar bracketed Jag's head, held him steady, and covered Jag's lips with his own. Hard. Demanding. Intoxicating.

Jag froze for only a second before the flames caught. Anger turned to fiery passion, the likes of which Jag couldn't recall. He groaned low in his throat, nipped Sonar's bottom lip, and thrust his tongue inside on Sonar's gasp. They dueled for dominance for a few seconds before Jag plundered away, tapping Sonar's tongue as he tasted and explored. He tilted his head, realigned their lips, and devoured like a man starving for sustenance. Sonar gave as much as he took, mimicking Jag's tongue action in such near perfection, Jag's full cock began to throb in earnest.

"Need you." Jag tugged at Sonar's shirt. When Sonar stepped back in order to pull it over his head, Jag grasped the zipper on Sonar's pants, yanked it down, and quickly undid the button. He pushed the unwanted denim down until it formed a puddle around Sonar's ankles. Unable to wait a moment longer, he ran his hands over Sonar's chest, testing the muscles, rubbing across warm, smooth flesh before pinching each nipple until it pebbled under his fingers.

Sonar moaned as Jag licked up the column of his throat. "Your turn." He grasped Jag's shirt and lifted.

Too heated for finesse, Jag stripped with practiced ease. Desire lashed him to move faster, to get naked, and to take the whole party to the nearby bed. Kicking free of his pants, he took a moment to stare at Sonar, raking him from head to toe and back again.

Chin up, Sonar stood straight as if for military inspection. Jag grinned at the irony. He was going to inspect him all right. Every single inch until he cried out in a mind-blowing orgasm.

Jag noted the thick, muscular build of Sonar, the sprinkling of dark hairs across his wide chest, the narrow waist, which led down to an impressive erection jutting toward him with just the slightest downturn at the tip. As he watched, a bead of moisture formed at the tip.

"Damn. So damn sexy." He licked his lips, unable to tear his gaze away.

"I could say the same for you." Sonar wrapped his fingers around Jag's dick, squeezed lightly, and ran his hand up and down the entire length. Twice.

Jag bit back a moan. "Shit."

Sonar grinned wickedly. "Gonna blow your load with just a hand job?"

The unveiled challenge leashed Jag's nearly rampant libido. "No fucking way. I'm not coming until I'm balls deep in your ass."

Sonar arched an eyebrow as sensual heat darkened his eyes. "Then do it."

Jag gave the order. "On the bed. Ass in the air." When Sonar moved to do his bidding, he checked out the room for anything he could use for lube. Spying a bottle of hand lotion, he strode over, plucked it from the dresser, and carried it back to the bed. Quickly he spread some over his cock before adding more to his fingers. He set the bottle aside, climbed on the bed behind Sonar, and smeared some of the cool gel against Sonar's opening.

Sonar flinched for a second before wiggling his rear.

"Burn?"

"Cold."

Jag grinned wolfishly, slid two fingers inside, and started readying Sonar for the hard and fast invasion to come. Feeling the snugness, he worked on the sphincter and ran his free hand along Sonar's back and around to Sonar's erection. He tugged a couple of times, learning the feel. Sonar's moan challenged his vow to not rush this part.

The moment Sonar's body loosened to Jag's satisfaction, he lined up his cock, grasped Sonar's hips, and pressed inward.

Sonar arched his back, hissed, then shoved in counterpoint with a powerful move.

Jag slid in, hit bottom, and growled at the great pleasure. "Shit, that's good. So damn tight."

"Fuck me. Fuck my ass." Sonar's words came out gravelly, as if he could barely speak between clenched teeth.

Not waiting for another invitation, Jag set a rapid pace, jabbing short and deep, before adding power with long, precise strokes. He angled downward, strumming Sonar's gland with every penetration.

Sonar bucked, surged backward, and growled.

Slapping sounds filled the room, along with the heady scent of lust. Jag drew it all in. Pure delight followed as he maintained a furious rhythm, spearing in time and again. He couldn't get deep enough, go fast enough. Sonar matched him in intensity, driving up Jag's pleasure tenfold. He ran his hands over Sonar's flanks, down to his big cock, and began to stroke.

"Oh, fuck. You're going to make me come."

"Do it already." Jag grunted as his cock began to swell even as a tingle at the base of his spine warned of impending climax.

Sonar whimpered, moved in counterpoint, and gyrated.

"Jack yourself off." Jag released Sonar's dick and began the surge for home. He went back to short, rapid thrusts aimed at hitting all of Sonar's hot spots along with his own.

Once. Twice. A third time.

Black spots flashed before his eyes. He threw his head back, gave a muted shout, then plowed in as deep as he could go.

Sonar's body clamped around Jag's pulsing dick with hard, rhythmic, clenching motions that added to Jag's moment of rapture while milking his cock for every drop of cum he could give. Going still, Jag absorbed every moment of fleeting bliss possible. Winded and fatigued, Jag rested across Sonar's back, drawing in large gulps of air.

All too soon, he returned to earth. Lifting himself from Sonar, he gently pulled out. Sonar shivered, lay down, and rolled over to peer up at Jag. "Damn."

"Yeah." Jag climbed off the mattress and headed into the bathroom. After washing up, he returned with a towel and started cleaning Sonar. He could have let the other man take care of his own needs, but that didn't set well with him.

Satisfied, he tossed the towel into the corner and returned to the bed. Jag sat down, blew out a long sigh, and met Sonar's gaze.

At a loss for words, he simply stared.

Sonar grinned wickedly. "If I'd known alpha jaguars were that good, I'd have tried one a long time ago."

Jag halfway smiled. Relaxation seeped through his body, replacing the horrible tension of the previous hours, leaving him in a decent mood and up for a little banter. "You might have been disappointed."

Sonar's eyes flashed with amusement. Boldly, he raked Jag's body, lingering on his groin. "Fishing for compliments?"

"No need. I already know the score."

"Which is?"

Jag's grin grew wider. "I scratched your itch pretty damn good."

Sonar laughed. "That you did."

For the first time in days, Jag chuckled.

While their joining was based solely on sexual need and stress release, he'd discovered something more.

Sonar made for a fine friend and a great fuck. The combination didn't go unnoticed.

SONAR LOOKED over at Jag, trying to read his expressionless face. No luck. Jag had shut down after their chat earlier in the day and finding the body only reinforced his stoic features. The fuck session didn't seem to loosen Jag's tongue, even though it did help with some of the accumulated tension, at least for the moment.

He recalled the explosiveness of their coming together, Jag's dominance, his ability to hit each and every one of Sonar's hot spots along the way. Tenderness had no place in their screwing, but Jag didn't hurt Sonar in the least. A bit rough and hard-core, Jag gave Sonar exactly what he wanted: to be fucked thoroughly until he came. Jag met those requirements and then some.

It was just screwing. Not about to happen again.

He warned himself not to make too much of what had occurred back in that hotel room. They were on a mission. They both needed an outlet. The wait provided them with nothing to do for a while. Sex happened. End of story.

Only Sonar didn't want that to be the case. He saw something special in Jag and intended to pursue it. If they ever finished this damn mission.

Sonar sat back in his seat, marveling at the private plane that had arrived around midnight to escort them to the next stop in their venture. Nonmilitary, the small plane resembled something a movie star or a rich popular singer might use for travel all over the world. Aisles of seats took up the majority of the front area, two on each side, a dozen rows front to back. A bathroom and kitchen area, at the tail end. In between were the comfortable seats, large plush recliners that could open up into a makeshift bed. Definitely a step up from coach on a 747.

They'd simply flashed their government security badges, stepped right past the check-in line, and marched directly to the plane, their duffel bags carrying their weapons and other equipment on their shoulders. That was one advantage to being top-level military: no questions asked and no waiting for the X-ray machine or pat downs.

"Tell me again how we rate this particular luxury."

Jag spared him a glance. "We needed to expedite this trip. Thus, private instead of commercial."

"Uh-huh." With the pilots in the cockpit as the only other people on the plane, Sonar felt comfortable asking the question at the front of his mind. "Another benefit of the group you work for?"

"Yeah."

"Must be nice. I *have* to get transferred to that place."

A brief relaxing of Jag's features told Sonar he'd broken through a tiny bit. "I'll give a recommendation for you. But you might want to know exactly what you're getting into first."

"Worse than being stationed in BFE for months at a time, eating sand, and forgetting what real food is?"

"Can be." Jag turned to look out the window. "We go after the big names in the business, the ones even the best Special Forces and CIA operatives can't touch."

Sonar blinked. "Hired assassins?"

Jag met his eyes. "That's a lot of our jobs."

"Damn." To think there existed a group of shifters, all highly trained to kill, contracted by someone higher up to track down and dispose of someone amazed Sonar. Sure, he knew the world had its fair share of assassins. No big secret there. Yet, using shifters to do the deed made for an interesting twist.

Where was I when those guys were recruiting?

In the shifter world, most groups weren't that chatty with others. No solid bond held them all in a loosely tied family. Instead, for the most part, shifters went their own way. They lived by their own code as well. The rules were fairly straightforward: don't let humans know they existed and don't go around killing things that would make humans suspicious. Simple.

DNA proved the only exception. Most of the same species of shifters managed to get along, form connections, and be friends. Even the apex predators. Parents passed down their particular species' DNA to their children, ensuring another generation would continue on. Just like human children, kids resembled their parents, acted like them, and tended to follow in their footsteps. Species stuck together during the tough times, helping one another out. Not solely in some cases, but most knew that others of their own kind had their backs.

Which explained why members of the same species tended to pair off. Proximity, comfort, and that DNA link that spelled similarity, kinship, and understanding. Sonar realized that hybrids did occur, but only knew them to be rare. Not every group accepted them either.

Sonar's immediate family was close. A normal household, by human standards. They just had a few extra abilities, the same for most shifters he knew. They'd found a way to infiltrate human society and live a quiet existence. Probably some shifters fell out of the realm and opted for a different lifestyle, but he couldn't say he'd known any of those.

"We infiltrate, expose, take down, and pretty much everything in between," Jag continued in a whisper. "It's not for everyone."

"Obviously. Still…." Excitement rushed through his blood at the thought. The adventures, the good that could be done. Little oversight and few restrictions too. The fact that Jag could just dial up someone and get a private plane in a couple of hours said something. Luxury. Possibilities. A damn sight better than he had at the moment, waiting for his commander to pass down orders. Free thinking wasn't always appreciated in the traditional military, just another reason he chafed under the uniform some days.

He'd known his career would take a different route once Jag showed up. Now, he realized that all levels of the military existed. Some much better than others. To fall under the special ops heading allowed for luxuries and opportunities Sonar had never really considered before. Same tree but a decidedly different branch. One he wanted to transfer to and check out for himself.

Sonar had been around the block enough to know different levels of security existed in the system. He had a really good idea that Jag was top level and lived off the grid. "Let me guess. You don't officially exist."

A ghost of a smile covered Jag's lips. "Nope."

"Not even to the platoon leaders?" There was always someone in the know. It was just a matter of who.

"I don't fall under their authority. I just check in now and again."

"Nice."

Jag inclined his head. "It's better this way. We're a different breed altogether. I don't know how you've managed to stick with your job immersed with humans, not able to shift at will or make your own way."

Sonar sighed. "It's tough. There's times I'm nearly crazy with the need to let my cat out. Restless and agitated. If we're out on patrol, I try to find a couple of minutes in order to do so. Otherwise, it's a crap shoot back at base. I share a tent, so finding alone time is pretty damn hard."

"Not my cup of tea."

Sonar snorted. "No shit. I can't see you kissing up to commanders. Hell, you'd be in the brig so many times, they'd name the place after you."

Jag grinned slightly. "Probably." He paused for a second. "Now you sound like Mark. He was all the time harassing me about getting away with anything and everything despite my bad attitude."

Sonar noted the change in Jag's face with the soft gesture. The happy memory transformed Jag into someone else. Less deadly assassin and more handsome stud. Jag could put models to shame with his physique. His rugged face told of a hard life, though still captivating and sexy all the same. Primal and sharp, Jag radiated danger, deadliness, and dogged determination.

The combination whetted Sonar's desire all the more.

"Does that bother you?"

"No." Jag scratched his forehead. "It was kind of nice, actually. Remembering the good times. Especially now."

"I'm glad to hear it. That's the sign of healing, I understand. Recalling the good times."

"I made my peace with Mark back then. Moved on because that's all one can do." Jag's lips thinned.

Sonar read between the lines. Jag had worked through everything. Until this latest fiasco. Sonar thought back on the bombshell Jag had unloaded earlier today. He'd been married. The fact had surprised Sonar as well as cleared up quite a few items. No wonder Jag refused to let go and went to any length to see this through. Sandman didn't just kill his friend, spotter, and lover. He'd killed Jag's husband.

The pain had to be enormous. Sonar just couldn't wrap his mind around how agonizing that must have been, seeing his spouse, the one he loved above all others, murdered right in front of Jag's eyes. Then to have to carry his body out of the war zone for hours while small chunks of his body coated and dried on Jag's skin and clothes. *Damn rough.*

He knew Jag blamed himself for Mark's death, believing he had screwed up and Mark paid the ultimate price. Sonar also understood that each death since had added to Jag's burden.

With new insight, he studied Jag, amazed he'd been able to hold it together back then in order to hunt Sandman. Jag lived for revenge. That was obvious. The question became what would he do once his one goal in life was complete.

The answers floating through Sonar's mind rattled him. His gut told him that without such an important reason to continue on, Jag might splinter under this relentless load.

I refuse to let that happen. There's something between us. A friendship. A bond. I'm not about to give up on him, no matter what.

Needing a bit of brightness, Sonar dug his wallet out of his pocket and opened it. A picture of his family stared back at him. He smiled at the happy images.

"Your family?" Jag asked.

"Yeah. My sister and parents."

"No girlfriend?"

Sonar snorted. "Since I'm exclusively gay, no."

"Wondered about that."

"I don't mind which way people's gates swing, even both directions. I just never could get all hot to trot over a woman. Problem is the whole military gay quandary. It's just easier to keep it under wraps than to chance ruffling some homophobe's feathers."

"Isn't that the truth."

"Pretty much makes it tough to date. Can't go off base without a pass, can't ask a fellow in the barracks out. Leaves me hanging."

"Got your eye on a particular man?" Jag eyed him closely.

"Nope. Humans are fine, but not my preference."

Jag pursed his lips but said nothing.

Sonar turned to Jag. "Your team. They have issues with gays?"

"Not in the least. That's one thing I never have to worry about with those guys. They judge people by their actions, not by their genetics or which side of the fence they fall on."

"Must be a relief."

"It is." Jag stood up and stepped over Sonar, heading toward the back. Sonar watched him go with interest and a spark of hope.

Maybe, just maybe, we're getting somewhere.

Chapter 8

AFTER RESTOCKING their provisions and catching a ride to the Iguazu rainforest of Argentina, Jag led Sonar along one of the common hiking trails. Each step took him farther into the jungle and closer to his past.

He'd almost lost his hard-won self-control when the coordinates popped up on his GPS screen. The one place he never wanted to go again due to the abundance of memories. If there was any other way, he'd do it. Unfortunately, Sandman called the shots and unless he showed up, he'd never know where to find the son of a bitch. Half a dozen times on the flight over he considered throwing in the towel or turning the tables and letting Sandman hunt him. Only the realization that Sandman would continue to torture and kill kept him on track. Whether he showed up or not probably wouldn't matter to Sandman. But it would to Jag's conscience.

As it was, he wrote out a list of places he and Mark visited during their time together. Over twenty-five countries ended up on the paper. Too many to go over. Sonar came up with the idea to cut it down to the special places, those with particular sentimental value. Even sorting for the most memorable ones only cut the number down to ten. With no pattern and no way to second guess Sandman's next move, Jag had no choice but to follow the clues given him. Damn him to hell, anyway.

Jag drew in the humid air, listened to the calls of the birds and monkeys, and raked the lush green environment surrounding him. Memories fired hard and fast, each one sweeter than the last. Jag was torn: excited to return to one of his favorite places on earth where he could just be himself, living wild and free, yet gravely saddened at the same time. He could never walk those trails again and not remember his husband, lover, and friend.

For two glorious weeks, he and Mark had camped out in this very forest, exploring and loving, becoming closer than they'd ever been before.

Now, Jag had returned with a heavy heart and vengeance as his agenda.

"It's beautiful, I'll say that," Sonar noted.

Jag remained mute and continued walking along, his inner beast prowling and demanding to be released here, in his natural habitat. *I'll take some time to run free. Just enough to pacify him.* This wasn't a fun trip made for relaxing. Too bad. He could have used some downtime, to just be a jaguar and forget the world's problems for a while.

How many times had he shifted with Mark in attendance? Dozens? He'd never forget the expression of awe and amazement on Mark's face each and every time. Mark made the transformation extra special by looking at Jag as if he were a god. Then he'd turn into a kid again, wrestling with Jag's big cat, enticing him in a game of chase, or splashing water at Jag, thinking his beast hated being wet.

Jag laughed the first time Mark had done just that, and then Mark hollered when Jag jumped right in, sending a wave washing over Mark. The indignation on Mark's face. So classic.

His heart cracked a bit more as the happy times flashed through his mind. They were the best days of Jag's life cut way short.

Three years ago. Bury it in the kill box already, soldier. He sucked in a deep breath and forced himself to leave it all behind. Just like he'd done back then. When Sandman went down under his shot, peace descended over Jag. The circle had closed. Oh, how naïve he'd been.

At least he had a pretty damn good right-hand man at his side in the form of Sonar.

After all this time alone, Sonar had stood toe-to-toe, needled him for answers, and refused to back down when times got tough. He'd been quiet and respectful, supportive, and a damn good listener when he finally drew the details out of Jag. Hell, Jag had to give him credit for a good head on his shoulders too. Sonar had managed to discover missing puzzle pieces and snap them together, making a much clearer picture.

Always preferring to be alone, Jag found most people, even shifters, annoying after a period of time. Thus far, Sonar seemed to be the exception. Ironic, considering how Sonar had stood up to him, nose to nose, more than once. Jag had always leaned toward submissive males, avoiding those with higher status like a huge hailstorm. He'd always believed that his alpha personality needed someone much more agreeable and malleable in order to be happy.

That didn't explain why Sonar, who obviously dipped into the submissive role only now and again, intrigued him so. By all accounts, they should have been at each other's throats way before now. Instead, Jag felt a calmness from Sonar that extended to him. Soothing. Natural. Like a walk in the park on a sunny spring day.

He found himself staring at Sonar and wondering about the man. What made him tick? What was his background? His future plans? His feelings about sticking around once this mission was done? Questions sat on the end of his tongue that he dared not verbalize. Not yet, anyway. Not until he had his head on straight and a few things figured out.

Besides, priorities first. Duty before play.

And, by damn, he wanted to play.

"I smell water," Sonar pointed out from behind him.

Jag wouldn't have wanted to bring another man to this location, except Sonar seemed to belong. Maybe he'd just grown on Jag over the course of the past few days. Maybe Jag had learned to trust him. Hell, maybe their fucking had actually meant more than just a pump and dump. One way or another, Sonar fit the land—and him.

"Another click or so and we'll be at a small waterfall flowing into a pool."

"I'll take it. Sweaty and gritty isn't my favorite way to be."

Jag concurred. After all his trips to Afghanistan, he no longer took bathing for granted. Too many days passed between showers when he was out on an op, hiding in the hills, in order to keep men safe from the ever-present insurgents.

Sonar drew closer, his steps nearly silent despite the uneven trail.

An ocelot. Sonar would be in his element here as well. He could almost feel Sonar's cat begging to be free, to hunt, to run, to finally have time to stretch his legs after being captive way too long.

A kindred spirit.

The thought took him by surprise in how right it sounded.

If he was totally honest, Jag could say that Sonar made each hop on this mission a little easier to take. Sandman had provided a heart-wrenching game plan, one that Jag wasn't quite sure he could have handled all on his own. He would have made do because nothing short of Sandman exploding into tiny pieces would stop Jag from trailing him. Still, with Sonar there to help keep him on track, he could put aside his emotions and move forward.

He recalled their quick fuckfest back in Paris. Sonar instigated the fiercest coupling he'd experienced in a while. He'd not been able to summon the courage to take another man for a test drive. Yet something had snapped in that moment. He and Sonar just clicked. Fire caught and he couldn't have walked away if the entire city crumbled into the sea.

He'd felt closer to Sonar than he had anyone besides his team members. Odd considering how solitary he preferred to live. Still, Sonar's personality, his looks, his wit, and grins invited Jag to open up. To give them a chance.

A chance at being fuck buddies? Romance? Love?

Jag wasn't sure, but one thing stood as a fact. He didn't carry a single regret for tapping Sonar's ass. Hell, truth be told, he wanted to do it again. The sooner the better.

"Do you think he's stalking us now?"

Jag shook his head and pulled his focus back to the present. "He knows I'll follow and has to stay one step ahead. He can't plan, capture, and kill fast enough if he's behind us."

"Makes sense."

They walked a bit longer before Sonar spoke again. "My inner cat is about to rip through my skin feeling he's on home territory."

"Mine too." Jag glanced back at Sonar. "We'll make time to let them out for a while. Being restrained too long only makes them—and us—edgy and antsy."

"So, we're camping for a few days?"

Jag blew out a breath. He didn't want to spend any more time than truly necessary here. Too many memories, too much pain. Still, they'd traveled thousands of miles with little sleep and downtime in between. They needed to be fresh for whatever the next step brought. "It's not quite a full day on foot to where we're going. We can find a good spot to settle down for the night. Tomorrow is soon enough to find the next clue and dash off on another wild goose chase."

Sonar stepped up to his left as they neared the water. He smiled, lifted his chin, and drew in the scents. "Back to nature."

Jag heard the excitement in his voice mixed with a thread of worry. Something bad loomed ahead. His intuition told him so.

You can't save the world in a day. Sandman will still be out there no matter what.

He set his backpack down on a large flat rock and glanced across the landscape. The small waterfall threw water droplets in the air, the sound both loud and soothing at the same time. A tranquil pool received the abundance of water, large enough to quench the thirst of all the forest animals and still allow for plenty of bathwater at the same time. Crisp and clean, the liquid called to him.

Jag opened up all his senses, checking the vicinity for threats. Finding none, he gave in to temptation and started stripping down.

Sonar grinned over at him. "In a hurry to cool down?"

The heat and humidity weren't anywhere near comfortable this time of year. Jag ignored it as best he could, wiping at the continually dripping sweat with the back of his sleeve. He'd been through much worse and would gladly trade the dampness for the dry heat of the deserts. At least here, water was in abundance and he didn't have far to go in order to wash all the grime from his body. Much better than going weeks without more than a spit bath with a constant irritation of sand finding its way to his skin in Afghanistan. Hell, he'd eaten enough of the grimy stuff and inhaled more than that during one of the many sandstorms while stationed there. Not the land of the weak or pampered.

This place, on the other hand, suited him much better.

As soon as his last garment hit his bag, he shifted forms. He smiled at the unique feeling of seeing the world through his cat's eyes. Scents carried to him on the light breeze, so many more than in human form. His senses were sharper, his eyes keener. Instincts ruled.

So when his stomach growled with hunger, he lifted his chin, scanned the area, then leaped into the brush.

SONAR WATCHED Jag go with a wry grin on his face. The black jaguar didn't waste any time or mince words. He embodied the role of predator and most likely would return with a fresh kill.

At a more sedate pace, he pulled off his boots and clothes, putting them all next to Jag's on a nearby rock, well away from the silt. He'd handwashed clothes more times than he could recall, but preferred to avoid doing so on this trip, however long it might be.

His mind wandered back to Jag and the almost insurmountable odds they were up against. A serial killer who had painted a target on Jag's back who knew how long ago. Revenge. Jealousy. No matter the motive, it was there and wouldn't go away until one of them was dead.

Sonar recalled the two dead men they'd found and shuddered. The poor guys hadn't deserved such ruthlessness. No one did.

Resolve settled on Sonar's shoulders. One way or another, he'd stick by Jag and help him make things right. Or as right as they could be.

Bone-tired, he stretched and rubbed his eyes. Jet-setting all over the world wasn't all it was cracked up to be. Now, if only he had time to sit back and enjoy, play tourist, or savor the man in his company.

Just like I did earlier.

Well, yes and no. The hot, fast fuck, though pretty damn explosive, only whetted his desire for more. So much more. He could spend days on end exploring Jag's body, bending over and letting him shove that big cock up his ass, even getting a taste of Jag's cum as he sucked him dry.

Sex had seemed to take the edge off Jag. Thankfully. If that's what it took to keep Jag centered on the rest of the mission, Sonar had no qualms being a boy toy.

He grinned at the thought. *Boy toy. Never considered myself one of those before.* Yet, for Jag, he'd step into all kinds of new roles.

The more he thought about it, the more he came around to the idea that Jag would make a pretty damn good boyfriend. Protective and possessive were a given. Sonar hadn't glimpsed tenderness or softness, but instinctively he knew both were hidden deep inside Jag, reserved for only the special people in his life.

I could get used to that.

Sonar's own dating history was pretty dismal. One-night stands were a given, especially during his military career. Yet even before signing up, he had never found anyone that he could bond with, wanted to hang out with, or even remotely consider marriage material. Humans and shifters alike left him bored and flat. Love was all too elusive and he'd begun to wonder if he was even capable of the emotion.

Then Jag appeared in his life, hurt and reeling, on a direct course with destiny.

The timing sucked.

Right now, all he could hope for was acceptance as a colleague or perhaps friendship. From what he saw and understood, Mark still claimed Jag's heart, even in death years earlier. Which left Sonar very little hope of holding a small part for himself.

He recalled Jag's demeanor, his responses and attitude. Hope flared as he considered one large piece of the puzzle. Jag hadn't pulled away from his kiss. Instead, he'd grabbed hold and held on tight.

A man still in love with another wouldn't have been so easy to take to bed, so eager to screw like there was no tomorrow. Sonar recalled the blazing hot kiss and slowly bobbed his head. Jag had had three years to work through his lover's death, including killing the one responsible. Sandman had just reappeared and used every available opportunity to remind Jag of his loss.

Banish the bad guy, get away from memory lane, and Jag will be set free.

The inner voice spoke truth. Sonar clung to the gem.

A scuffing noise caught his attention. He turned, found the one responsible, and shook his head. Sure enough, Jag panted as he rested on a large branch in a nearby tree, his fresh kill hanging in the crook of the same tree.

Not the least bit concerned with his nudity, Sonar peered up at his teammate, planting one hand on his hip.

Unable to resist, Sonar stared up at Jag and decided to yank on his chain. "Gonna share with me?"

Jag flashed a fang and growled low in his throat. *Big-cat speak for "get your own."*

Sonar arched an eyebrow. "Temperamental. I swear."

Jag's cat eyes narrowed just a hair.

Determined to have a bit of fun, Sonar quickly drew up a plan of action. He morphed into his ocelot form, raced for the tree, and climbed up like a seasoned pro with the assistance of long claws that dug into the wood. Once he drew near, he reached out, latched onto one of the deer's legs, and started back down the tree.

Never in the wild would one of his brethren dare attempt to steal a meal from a mighty jaguar. Here, and with their shifter nature, Sonar dared.

Jag snarled, stood, and jumped down to protect his kill. Too late.

Sonar twisted his head, sending the animal falling to the ground. He leaped down, grabbed a hind leg, and trotted away. For about three steps. The deer halted suddenly. Swinging around, Sonar spied Jag on the head end, pulling back toward the canopy of the trees.

Not about to let go, Sonar yanked hard, saw Jag only marginally move, then dug in his feet as Jag started backing up, using the power of his hindquarters to drag both the deer and Sonar along.

Sonar growled and snarled, maintaining his fierce hold in the impromptu game of tug-of-war.

Jag eyed him for a long moment before dropping the deer.

Just as Sonar triumphantly spun around with his meal in tow, Jag pounced on him. Sonar hissed and struggled, only to find Jag's much-heavier frame pinning him to the forest floor, his mouth encircling the back of Sonar's neck.

A bit uncertain, Sonar stilled. He didn't believe Jag capable of outright murder, but he had pushed way past the boundaries of civil protocol.

To his chagrin, Jag took a snug hold of Sonar with his powerful jaws, sharp teeth pressing into Sonar's neck, but gently, not near enough to break the skin. Jag picked him up and carried him, like a mother cat would a kitten, straight to the water's edge, and dropped him in.

Sonar plopped into the water, came back to the surface, and gave a token hiss. The effect was quickly ruined when he sneezed.

Jag yawned wide, swished his tail, and shot Sonar a haughty look filled with self-importance.

Resignation overcame the tad bit of indignation over being carted around like a cub. No adult male would tolerate such insolence. But Sonar couldn't get all pushed out of shape. Not when Jag snorted at him, went back to his kill, and inclined his head toward Sonar.

Stepping out of the pool, Sonar strode over, shook the water from his coat onto Jag, then settled down at the rear of the downed animal. One glance told him Jag intended to share without a single complaint.

With a grin to himself, Sonar dug in.

Chapter 9

"WHAT WAS Mark like?" Sonar asked as he sipped a cup of hot tea.

They'd spent the day in their beast forms, eating, napping, even a quick game of chase. The downtime had done him good, as his ocelot was now content. He could say the same for Jag, noting the lines of stress had eased from the man's forehead and around his mouth. He'd even smiled a couple of times in the past hour, despite the monumental mission and heart-wrenching circumstances.

Which is why Sonar hated to throw out the question now. But his gut told him a clue lay somewhere close by, just out of their reach. Something big and mighty important.

Jag glanced in his direction, crossed his legs, and scanned the forest around them. A hardness returned with a slight tensing of muscles.

Sonar sighed. "Let me tell you where I'm going so we can figure this out together. We've already decided that Sandman and Mark were close, really close. Something happened to rip them apart, allowing Mark to find you."

"Yeah."

"Granted, it could have been anything that caused the rift, but it doesn't make sense to me that Sandman could keep his evil ways secret for long with Mark. Maybe he found out?"

Jag cocked his head. "If he did so, I can't see him keeping his mouth shut. He always cheered the underdog and wouldn't sit idle if he knew Sandman was busy carving up humans as a new hobby."

Thankful that Jag seemed only a bit pensive with the line of conversation, Sonar continued. "So, logic leads us to believe Sandman was once normal." He did the quotations in the air. "And something caused him to snap."

"From what I understand about that sort of mental illness, it starts early and only escalates with time." Jag shook his head. "Mark was sweet, good, and loved to play around. He was the embodiment of everyone's brother and friend." Jag's lips thinned. "Don't get me wrong. He could kill when necessary, but always in protection of himself or others." He sighed. "I teased him often that he was too innocent for the Army. Death and destruction weren't him at all."

"What did he say?"

"That he belonged with me. At my side through thick and thin." Jag's words faded as he turned his head.

Sonar saw the still-raw grief and warned himself to tread carefully. "If they were dating, would his family know anything about Sandman? Perhaps he told them about the breakup?"

Jag swung back around to face Sonar. "Maybe, but what does it matter? I already know what he looks like. Mark is dead. Sandman is enacting revenge, presumably out of jealousy."

"Maybe it does or doesn't matter. I'm just having a hard time believing that he survived a direct shot to the chest. I've seen you in action. You don't miss. Even if you were off an inch, the chances of him surviving were slim to none."

"If he were a human, that would be true." Jag leaned forward to rest his elbows on his thighs and prop his chin up with his clasped hands. "He has to be more than that."

"I agree." Sonar nodded and took another sip of his drink. "But I still can't get past the idea of even a shifter surviving such a wound."

Jag sighed. "I've been through all this a thousand times. All it does is give me a headache without changing the facts. He has to be taken out, no matter what he really is. Human, shifter, or the devil himself."

"Are we sure a simple bullet wound will do the trick?"

"Unless he's a ghost or a god, I pretty much guarantee that a bullet will work. If not, I suppose we can cut a couple of wooden stakes to stab through his black heart."

Sonar snorted at the image Jag's words provoked. "I have a feeling I don't want to get close enough to him to find out if that's a viable way to do him in."

Jag's face pinched as he met Sonar's gaze. "If anything happens to me, get on the satellite phone and call Mac. His number is programmed in. He can pull all kinds of strings to get you to safety."

Sonar frowned. "I'm not going anywhere without you."

"If I'm dead, there's nothing anyone can do for me." Jag's flat tone struck a chord with Sonar.

Obviously Jag had come to terms with his own mortality. Most would be antsy or afraid. Jag just spit out the truth like he was reading from a boring instruction guide with directions on assembling a wooden shelf. While that bode well for the mission, Sonar's inner cat snarled in displeasure. It was as if Jag had already decided the outcome. And he lost.

A sudden thought clicked in Sonar's mind. "Wait a minute. You said Mark was human."

"He was."

"Then how did he get to be in an all-shifter unit?"

Jag's lips thinned. "I recruited him. We met. Fell in love at first sight. I didn't want to be away from him for weeks or months at a time. Mac agreed to let us work together." He grimaced before sighing wearily. "If not for my selfishness, he'd still be alive today."

"You don't know that." Sonar thought for a second. "You said it yourself that he didn't want to be parted from you. Seems to me Sandman is one particularly determined bastard. He went to great lengths to destroy Mark, just like he's doing now to you. If Mark was back home, alone, he'd have been vulnerable. An easy target. No telling what horrors he would have suffered at Sandman's hands. The way I see it, because of you, Mark lived longer and damned happier than if he'd stayed behind. You protected him from a much worse death."

A dawning of understanding crossed Jag's face, as if for the first time he saw the truth and could let go of that one parcel of guilt. "I never thought of it that way." His softly whispered words spoke of newfound insight.

Sonar dipped his chin in acknowledgment. "You being together granted him a gift—time to spend with the man he loved. Don't regret that."

Silence ensued for several minutes as Jag stared into the wall of trees surrounding them. Finally, he rustled around and turned his attention back to Sonar. "We'll bed down for the night. Tomorrow we'll hit the trail and see what we can find." Jag took a long drink from his canteen.

"What do you live for, Jag?" Sonar wished the words back as soon as he saw Jag's eyebrows furrow and his eyes snap with anger.

"If you don't know that already, then you're dumber than a rock." The words came out gritty and harsh.

"Revenge might drive you now, but what about in the future, when you're done with this FUBAR mission?" Sonar pressed his advantage, needing to make Jag look at more than this moment in time. Living in the present was all fine and good for some. Jag needed to recall the happier times and regain hope. Without that driving force, Sonar didn't have much conviction that Jag would stand tall under such an overbearing burden.

Jag sat silent.

Just when Sonar thought he wouldn't answer, Jag's quiet voice carried to him. "I've known love, happiness, and terrible loss. Given another chance, I'm not sure I would do the same again."

Sonar blinked. "You'd rather never have loved at all than spend whatever time you had with the man you loved above all others?" With that attitude, Jag most likely would never open his heart again, the pain too great.

"I don't know." He blew out a breath, appearing more tired than Sonar recalled ever seeing him before. Considering how much they'd traveled in a short time, with little sleep that said something.

"Here's what I know. Love is special. Very special. Thankfully, we're able to love more than once in our lives. To give up for whatever reason sentences us to a damn lonely path." Sonar reached over to pat Jag on the knee. "Personally, I'd rather enjoy what time I had, share some laughs and love as I go, because none of us knows when our time is up."

"Easily said when you've never lost a spouse from senseless violence and spite." Jag's jaw ticked.

Sonar removed his hand. "True enough. I've never walked in those shoes and hope I never do. I'll say this, though, you're a damn sight better man than I ever could be. You survived and you continue on. Call it revenge for now, but you keep plodding along. That takes guts. I'll give you that." He stretched his legs out on the pallet and lay down on his side facing Jag. "Maybe one day you'll be able to see what I see and realize there's much more in this world than relentless hunting, missions, and heartbreak."

Jag didn't budge for several minutes. Finally, he stretched out on his blanket, his back to Sonar. "The world needs optimists and romantics."

Unsure exactly what that meant, Sonar started to ask, but bit his tongue. He'd pushed hard enough for one night. No sense in pissing Jag off when they both needed sleep badly.

With Jag nearby, Sonar relaxed, knowing that between the two of them, they were safe for the night. He keyed in on Jag's pulse and let the soft lub-dub lull him to sleep.

Chapter 10

JAG WOKE the next morning to find a fur ball staring at him out of slanted cat eyes from a couple of inches away. The sleek, spotted coat shined with health and cleanliness while the expression on Sonar's face could only be called mischievous.

"Bat ears." Jag grinned as Sonar opened his mouth and a small squeak came out. "Yeah, that's real intimidating."

Sonar tried again, a bit more growl in this vocalization.

"I fed you yesterday. I'd say today is your turn to scrounge up breakfast." Jag snorted as Sonar pinned his ears in annoyance. "Uh-uh. I'm not buying it." He sat up, more than tempted to scratch the small feline under his chin or run his hands over the gorgeous coat. While he couldn't actually understand Sonar's words, he could guess. Big cats were fairly simple in some regards. They were hungry, angry, playful, or sleepy. Pretty much everything else fell into those categories. The tone of his feline voice and body language clued him in to what Sonar wanted: breakfast on the hoof. Barring that, cooked over a fire or even pulled from their ration stores in their packs.

He recalled the day before. Whatever had possessed him to pick Sonar up by the scruff in his kitty form, carry him to the pool, and dump him in still amazed Jag. It had felt right at the time was his only excuse. The grumbling and spitting by Sonar only made the act that much more amusing. While he'd certainly never carried cubs around in such a manner, he couldn't help himself. Payback for Sonar trying to steal his hard-won meal. If he had offended Sonar with his playful antics, Sonar hadn't let on. Instead, he'd pretty much settled down, appeased, when he dove into the best portions of their food.

He couldn't think of a single shifter brave enough to try to dash off with the deer after he'd blatantly warned them away. Sonar, instead of going about his own business, seemed to take the fang flashing as a challenge. A bit crazy, but humorous at the same time. He had no hope of winning, certainly. Did that stop him? Not at all.

He'd actually enjoyed carrying the unhappy ocelot around in his mouth. The put-upon expression and small outburst by Sonar had only made him want to laugh.

Which brought up another puzzling query. Never would he have imagined sharing a fresh kill with another shifter. He was too much an alpha for that. Adult males of any species would be turned away. Primitive instincts and all that. Still, he'd pretty much let Sonar not only halfway cart off the deer, but then he'd let him have the tastiest bits. So unlike him. Hell, if the others back at home base heard of such a thing, they'd sign him up immediately for a psychological evaluation, thinking he'd lost his mind.

Maybe he had finally flipped his lid. Maybe he'd just wanted to give in for once, tired of always being on the defensive and fighting for every inch. Maybe something about his partner brought out the playful side, at least for a few minutes. A quandary for sure.

Who knows? It's not like it really matters in the scheme of things.

Still, he couldn't help but grin slightly at the enigma and contradiction. He'd fought tooth and nail against having a spotter. Now, not only had he grown accustomed to Sonar at his side, he allowed him privileges he'd afforded no other.

Sonar batted at his nose.

Jag frowned down at the bothersome cat. "I don't know what you want, but if you keep pestering me, you'll get dunked again."

Sonar rolled his eyes and huffed.

Jag bit back a grin. Sonar weighed in at perhaps thirty pounds. Pretty small compared to Jag's animal form, topping out around three hundred pounds. Yet Sonar carried enough attitude to rival the biggest cats on the planet.

Small but fierce. A tiger in a compact body. He'd give Sonar kudos for having a pair of balls, definitely.

Sonar turned around and started to walk away, only to pause and look back. He added a short cry.

"Okay. I get it." Jag stood up and followed Sonar, making their way through dense brush before finding a clearing of sorts.

Sonar bounded up a tree, found a dangling orange, and knocked it down.

Jag caught it before it could hit the ground. "Breakfast, huh?" He smiled as Sonar repeated the action, sending half a dozen ripe fruits into Jag's hands.

Once done, he leaped down and trotted back to their campsite, his head held high, and tail straight up in the air.

With a shake of his head at Sonar's self-importance, Jag returned the way they'd come with bounty in hand.

Several minutes later, he'd cut three of the fresh oranges into sections, adding the juicy fruit to their morning meal of bread and peanut butter. Although both carried more MREs, neither wanted to delve into the pasty meal if they didn't have to, not when better alternatives were available.

Sonar stood nearby, having just changed from ocelot back to his human form. Nude, he caught Jag's eye.

Ripped and toned, he would be hard-pressed to find much fat on Sonar's body. Muscles snapped with each graceful movement as if his natural feline abilities transferred to his human side as well. A wide chest flowed into a narrower waist and on down to powerful thighs. Jag noted each before his gaze landed on Sonar's half-interested cock. Thick and proportioned. Fully erect, it would most likely hit the above-average category in all measurements. Just the way Jag remembered.

Sonar turned and bent over to retrieve something from his pack, giving Jag a nice view of his upturned rear. Sleek and well-shaped, Sonar's ass not only drew Jag's attention, but could easily win a few contests for the best rump around. Perfect in every way. He could speak from experience on that one.

Hungry and in desperate need of a distraction, he picked up a slice of orange and popped it into his mouth, savoring the incredible sweetness of tree-ripened fruit. Shutting his eyes, he chewed slowly, not about to rush the small pleasure.

"You look like you're in ecstasy."

Jag opened his eyes to find Sonar staring at him with a wide grin on his face. "I'll admit, they're good."

"Uh-huh. You wanted breakfast. I delivered." Sonar pulled his clothes back on before sitting down and partaking of the meal.

"Yeah, yeah. You did a good job. Are you satisfied now?"

Sonar glanced at him over a piece of fruit and offered up a lopsided grin. "Maybe."

"I can tell you're high maintenance."

Sonar waggled his eyebrows. "I might be cheap, but I'm not free."

Jag laughed and quickly finished his meal. He considered heading toward the exact location of the next clue, but couldn't quite dredge up the courage or the motivation. Tired, he preferred to have a few more hours of downtime. His inner beast readily agreed, shoving to be released again.

Standing, Jag took a moment to strip down, smirking when he saw Sonar sit up and take notice. The spark of sexual interest in Sonar's eyes added to Jag's ego and cranked up his own libido.

He wanted the guy, but not like before. Not out of anger or a demand for tension release. Jag craved more. A link. A bond. Less mindless screwing and more personal fucking. However, now wasn't the time.

Sonar stuffed the last piece of fruit into his mouth and chewed. He arched an eyebrow. "Going *au naturel*?"

Jag answered with a shift. One minute he stared down at Sonar through human eyes, the next on an equal level through a jungle cat's vision. Sounds and scents became sharper, as did the subtle aroma of Sonar's arousal. Jag chuffed, turned, and dashed off into the thick woods.

He stopped a while later, perked his ears, and stilled. The sound of a branch being pushed aside put him on high alert. Jag swiveled just in time for a very familiar small feline to pounce out of the brush toward him. Jumping back, Jag watched as Sonar's trajectory fell short. Yet as soon as his feet hit the ground, Sonar leaped once more, this time to smack Jag in the side with his full body weight.

Jag didn't budge. Instead, he stared at Sonar with a definite put-upon expression.

He could have sworn Sonar grinned in his ocelot form before turning tail and sprinting away.

Unable to resist, Jag leaped after him. They raced through the brambles and ducked around trees until Sonar skidded to a halt at the pool. Jag followed suit, after slamming into Sonar and sending him tumbling into the water.

He sat back on his haunches and watched with amusement as Sonar pulled himself out, hissed, and finally shook the water from his coat onto Jag.

If he could have, Jag knew Sonar would have flipped him off.

He waded into the water and began swimming, his legs churning with ease in the small ripples of current. After heading to the falls and ducking under, he started back.

Sonar sat on the bank, his tail flicking.

Kitty with ambush on his mind.

Jag surged out of the water, bypassed Sonar who swatted at him, and bounded several paces away. A nearby tree caught his attention. He sprang up, found a large horizontal limb, and stretched out on his stomach.

Sonar tilted his head and stared up at Jag. Mischievously, he made a big overture of walking over to Jag's clothes, circling around, and lying down right smack in the middle. Still damp.

Jag roared quietly, a warning for Sonar to move his ass or get it moved for him.

Sonar blinked up at him, rested his chin on his front legs, and shut his eyes.

Like that worked. He chuckled to himself. Sonar didn't seem fazed by anything, especially Jag's posturing and not-so-subtle threats. *Give the guy credit for having a pair of brass balls.*

Jag stretched and yawned. The exercise had helped. He'd take a nap, get a good meal into their stomachs, then begin where they left off. With more challenges ahead, Jag savored the small reprieve knowing it would be a good long time before he could get away from all the drama once again.

Two hours later, Jag broke out the MREs and a couple of the remaining oranges for a more substantial meal. He felt refreshed, yet pensive. Whatever surprises Sandman left never boded well.

Sonar had also returned to human form, dressed, and packed up their camp, the earlier playfulness forgotten as they focused on the difficult task ahead.

They ate in companionable silence for a few minutes before Sonar spoke again. "If you weren't in the military, what would you be doing instead?"

Jag spared him a glance, not too upset despite Sonar's nosey nature, which pried into his personal life seemingly on a daily basis. "Never thought about it."

Sonar paused in midchew. "You've never considered what you'd do after retiring from your unit?"

"Nope."

"Why not?"

Jag picked up another section of orange. "There's no sense in planning for a future that isn't likely to come about. Focus on the present instead."

Sonar's eyebrows furrowed. "If you can't think of the future, how do you make goals? Dreams?"

"I don't."

"That's damn depressing," Sonar spit out with a hint of frustration.

Jag's ire rose a notch. "Let me tell you something. I wasn't one of those pampered kids who were spoiled beyond measure. I was raised on the streets with no one but myself to look after. Dreams didn't happen back then, and they don't happen now."

Sonar's mouth fell open for a second before he started eating once more. "Your parents didn't want you?"

Blowing out a breath, Jag told himself that his past was none of Sonar's business. Yet he found himself opening up anyway. "I didn't know my real parents. Supposedly they died when I was very young. The foster care system took me in."

"Shifters aren't thick on the ground. Why didn't another family member step up?"

Jag shrugged. "As far as I know, there was no one."

Sonar tapped his chin. "Odd. Shifters normally look after their own. Even another species would likely adopt a shifter child rather than leave it with humans."

"Again, no clue."

Jag continued on with his short explanation. "By the time I hit my teens, I'd been through six homes. The last one pretty much washed their hands of me. Probably relieved when I packed up what little I had and hit the streets."

"Sounds like some piss-poor foster parents."

Jag shrugged. "Not entirely their fault. No one knew I was a shifter, including me. I had problems adjusting and acted out in the process. The humans didn't have a clue as to my behavior and labeled me as a social deviant." He recalled the years on the street, struggling each day to find food and shelter and avoid the nastiness that went hand in hand with homelessness. Predators were always on the lookout for new blood. He'd managed to stay a step ahead. Barely. "I grew up fast, developed some skills, and found myself with a drive to do more. To get off the street and somewhere I belonged." He drew in air. "Long story short, I met another of my kind who got me on the straight and narrow. Later, I was recruited by Mac and his team. They took me in immediately, trained me in all kinds of things, and became the surrogate family I never had."

"So, you're killing yourself on these nearly impossible missions because you're indebted to them?" Sonar's eyes reflected pain and sorrow.

Having no need of pity, Jag offered up the truth. "No. I do it because I'm good and it's all I've ever known."

A long pause followed. "You've never had anything easy, have you?"

Jag narrowed his eyes at Sonar. "Life isn't easy. It's about fighting and survival. Nothing else matters." He took a long drink of his water and started cleaning up the site. "Get a move on. We've got some acres to cover today to reach the GPS destination."

Sonar opened his mouth, started to speak, then stuffed the rest of his sandwich in his mouth instead.

Quiet at last.

Jag scrubbed his face, shoved aside his fatigue, and braced himself for what lay ahead.

DOUBLE-CHECKING THE coordinates, Jag searched the area for anything resembling a clue that Sandman would have left. In the dense jungle, that could be anywhere and any variety of things. Large limbs from trees shaded the area while nearly overgrown foliage covered the ground. A man could hide a VW Beetle among the lush growth and it would never be found.

"There."

Jag twisted to find Sonar pointing to a nearby tree.

"There's a metal box nailed to it."

Anticipation grew as Jag neared the case. At least there wasn't a body this time. Or if there was, the jungle predators and scavengers would have taken care of the evidence in quick fashion. Opening the lid, he found another note. He plucked it out and slowly unfolded it, only to find a ring carefully tucked inside.

His mouth fell open as he stared at the gold band. *No. It can't be.* With trembling hands, he turned the ring this way and that, reading the inscription, checking out the etching along the outside. Finally, he held it up to the light, saw the tiny dent on one side and felt like a .45 caliber round had just slammed into his chest. His heart stopped and the air was sucked out of his lungs.

He fell to his knees, his whole body shaking with shock and sheer outrage. Jag's heart stuttered once more as sorrow poured over his soul.

"Jag? Jag?" Sonar touched him on the shoulder. "What is it?"

Jag managed to force the words around the lump lodged in his throat. "Mark's... wedding ring." Memories flooded his mind, all of the day he had slipped the ring on Mark's finger. The happiness, the love. The good days before life had turned to hell.

"Oh, shit."

For a long time, he just held the band, tears pouring down his cheeks, his grief as raw as the day Mark died by his side.

Sonar slowly slipped the note out of his hands. "With this ring, I thee wed. And so our game has gone full circle. We'll end where it all began."

The cryptic words cut Jag that much deeper, adding more agony if that were even possible at this very moment.

"The Valley of Death."

Sonar blinked at him, his lips turning down in a scowl. "That's one screwed-up motherfucker."

Jag agreed, but was too devastated with pain to comment. He'd put the past behind him years ago. Now, Sandman had turned back the clock and reopened old wounds.

"Are you sure it's not a replica?"

Jag wiped his face and drew in deep gulps of air, collecting himself a breath at a time. "Yes." He hadn't cried when Mark died, when he carried his body to the rendezvous, or when the chopper flew away with Mark inside. That waited until later, when he had laid Mark to rest, and for some time later. He refused to do so now. Not when Sandman waited.

"Damn." Sonar raked the area before turning his attention back to Jag.

"Mark drew the design himself. The jeweler made molds. The molds were destroyed afterward." Jag grappled with overwhelming loss, determinedly shoving down his emotions back into a safe place. He was on a hunt and feelings were a major distraction. "The small dent is there too. He hit the ring hard on a rock during training. Left a tiny flattened area right above the year." Jag lifted his chin and met Sonar's concerned gaze. "It's there. All of it."

Remorse and sympathy covered Sonar's face. His thin lips and sad eyes spoke of supreme contriteness and barely leashed anger. "That dickwad planned it all along. He had to have stolen the ring before the burial, knowing it would be a closed casket and no one would look." Sonar's eyes narrowed. "He was there. At the funeral."

Jag's iron grasp quaked and weakened. The thought of Sandman violating Mark's final resting place had sent shards of outrage through him. Taking it from the funeral home was only marginally better than if he had gone in search of it later. All that time Jag had scoured the earth for Sandman after Mark's death was a ruse, a setup. He felt idiotic and played.

Never again.

Forcing himself to stand, Jag regained his composure, pulling on the abundant amount of rage to push past the pain and focus on the goal ahead: killing the bastard once and for all.

Dropping the ring in his ruck for safekeeping, he strode north, the quickest route out of the jungle. He had a meeting with destiny and wasn't about to be late.

Absently, he noted Sonar tagging along, his steps muted despite the overgrown brush they tore through. Stiff movements screamed outrage, the body language unmistakable with Sonar. He exhibited the same emotions Jag felt yet had carefully sealed somewhere deep inside.

In all fairness, he should ground his spotter, drop him off at the closest base, and go ahead alone. He'd do it in a heartbeat if he thought Sonar would actually obey. But these past several days spent with the guy had taught him a few things. Namely, that Sonar was in for the long haul and he was a damn good man to have at his back. He respected the ocelot shifter and had found a kinship with him. A solid friendship had formed. Maybe more.

Jag could only hope Sonar's loyalty wasn't Sonar's demise. He couldn't bear to lose another spotter, another lover, especially one who had stubbornly refused to throw in the towel and leave his side.

They'd developed a closeness over the days. Although he had tried his damnedest to keep Sonar at arm's length, the pesky ocelot broke through his outer walls. Now, as Jag's friend, he put himself on the target almost as much as Jag himself.

The thought ate at Jag's gut and slashed open old wounds.

One way or another, I'll ensure Sonar makes it out alive. Come hell or high water. That was the least he could do.

Chapter 11

"WHY THE Army?"

Sonar lowered his binoculars and glanced over at Jag. "Unlike you, I grew up knowing what I was. My family blended into human society fairly well too. By the time I finished school, I'd figured out a few things. Namely that I sucked at people skills, couldn't ride a desk for any length of time, and needed a job where I could have the freedom to shift now and again in order to keep my sanity."

Jag nodded. "Makes sense. You went with your innate abilities, although the time to shift philosophy was a bit off the mark."

"No shit. One of the biggest challenges and frustrations to date."

Sonar returned to looking over the valley. For the past five days, they'd been all over the place, searching for clues and coming up empty-handed. After a ten-day hike to even reach the place to begin with. Military choppers hated to fly anywhere near the valley due to the frequent attacks launched at them by the insurgents. If not for the innocent villages in the flatlands, the US forces could have bombed the shit out of the Taliban and cleared the area. Unfortunately, that wasn't possible with so many people living there. Thus, they were relegated to fighting the hard way. Taking out one by one. Slow. Too slow compared to the numbers that kept cropping up.

With no exact location specified this time, they had miles of mountains, caves, and flatlands to scour. All had potential, but they focused more on the elevated areas rather than the villages. Sandman wouldn't be able to capture and cut up a man in the middle of a group of people. He'd be alone. High up. And protected from prying eyes. The role a sniper always preferred to take.

Sonar rubbed his chin. The stubble was quickly turning into a half-decent beard. One that was hot and itchy. As much as he'd love to take the time to shave it off, he didn't have that luxury. He and Jag were firmly entrenched in the area of highest insurgent concentration, the most ally deaths, and the greatest terrain obstacles. Vanity would have to wait until they finished their mission and could return back to base.

Which couldn't come soon enough. Impatient, fatigued, and more than frustrated, Sonar needed this mission to come to an end. Immediately.

He glanced back to Jag, noting the lines marring his handsome face. Though they had started switching off shifts in order to let each other sleep, it wasn't enough. No one rested well curled up in a cave, always on edge for an insurgent party to come across them.

"You know Sandman better than anyone else. Where do you think that bastard is hiding?"

Jag stared out across the ridge. A muscle in his jaw tensed. "My gut tells me near the location where he killed Mark."

"Where is that?"

"About three clicks northeast."

Sonar's shoulders slumped. "Right through the heart of Taliban country."

"Yeah."

What he wouldn't give for an Apache to come in with guns firing, drop a bomb or three, and clear the way. Since that wasn't a possibility, they were relegated to a game of trying to sneak by the deadly groups on patrol every night. Though many of the insurgents slept during the afternoon, traveling at that time of day still proved dangerous.

We just can't catch a break.

"Got a boyfriend?" Jag asked.

The personal question surprised Sonar. Rarely did Jag ask him anything more than facts pertaining to their present situation. He'd long ago decided Jag intended to keep their relationship strictly professional despite their make-out session back in Paris. The less Jag knew about Sonar, the more he could stay away. Sonar hadn't settled for that and kept tossing out queries now and again out of curiosity, to know his partner better and to help pass the time while waiting for their next move.

Not to mention Jag's question came a bit late since they'd already fucked. "No."

"Why not? You seem like the kind of guy that would attract plenty of attention." Jag wiped down his rifle, adding oil and removing sand in the process. In the desert, equipment dried out fast.

Sonar went with his standard answer. "No time."

Jag snorted. "That doesn't stop most people."

Twisting, Sonar met Jag's gaze. "I've had my fair share of pumping and dumping. I've grown up and want more than a quick fuck. Hard to find that in the middle of BFE, surrounded by humans, while being shot at."

"Touché." Jag's lips hitched up slightly at the corners.

Sonar knew they both recalled their one time together. Hot. Blazing hot. One of the best times of his life. The joining lacked tenderness but fit the bill for that particular moment in time. Next time, and Sonar knew there would be one, he'd slow things down, partake of Jag like an expensive, rich candy.

The momentary ease of Jag's features stole Sonar's breath. The man was a looker, even with a scruffy chin, signs of weariness written all over his face, and eyes dulled from lack of sleep.

This assignment couldn't finish fast enough. The strain wore them both down while Sonar worried for Jag's health. He'd taken quite a few shocks and rebounded back. How long he could do so without having a breakdown became an important question.

Sonar cussed his rotten luck and the all too elusive Sandman. "Have a long list of potential dates lined up?"

"Yeah, right."

Sonar turned to glance at Jag. "What? Don't tell me you scare potential suitors off?" He purposely added humor to his tone.

Jag snorted.

"Yep, I can see it now. You snarl and all the guys go running." Sonar chuckled softly. "Must be damn hard when you're such a surly-assed alpha."

"Bite me, pussy."

Instead of taking offense, Sonar laughed. "Gladly."

The brief bantering faded. Sonar sobered as he returned to his task, searching constantly for signs of movement.

At least we received a supply drop yesterday. The additional water was most appreciated. Fresher and better than the water they found running in a couple of caves. Drinkable if they added the purifying tablets first. It worked, but nothing tasted as delicious as good old bottled water from home. The MREs were chewy but took care of their nutrition needs—mostly. Weight loss was a given on these long missions.

"I have one single goal in life—eradicating Sandman. When and if I accomplish that, I'll figure out which direction to go from there." Jag bit the words out as if trying to convince himself of their truth.

Sonar bobbed his head slowly. "Understandable. One thing at a time. All those men will still be waiting for you when you get back to base." He turned his head as Jag stretched out next to him, his rifle at the ready.

"What's up with you and this legion of men? You must be hallucinating or damn horny."

Sonar grinned at Jag's flat tone. "Oh, so the men are for me. That's damn nice of you."

"You've lost your fucking mind." Jag angled the rifle slightly to the left.

"Must be contagious, then. You're the one mentioning suitors."

"I don't want any suitors."

"Sure you do." Sonar stared across the valley for the hundredth time. "You're one hot tamale with a big stick. Such a waste to not use it."

Jag paused. "Horny it is. Got it. Just don't expect me to ante up. My hands are full at the moment."

"We'll finish Sandman. After that, go on a trek to find all these fabled men you're promising me."

"Easier said than done."

"True." Sonar shrugged. "Not saying anything is a piece of cake. Just that things worth having are worth fighting for."

Jag snorted. "Spoken like a bona fide optimist."

Sonar halfway grinned. "That's me. Too much death-and-destruction mumbo jumbo gets me all depressed."

"You got that right." He took a moment to stare through his scope and make some adjustments using the dials on top.

Long minutes passed when nothing moved below. Jag eased his rifle off his shoulder and stretched his arm. "I'll take the night watch. You can get some sleep."

Sonar eyed him for a couple of beats. The command wasn't anything new since they were taking turns catching some shut-eye while the other stood guard. Yet something in Jag's tone made his gut clench with warning. "I'm taking the night shift. You need more sleep than I do."

"Not happening. You're sleeping tonight." Jag's voice turned hard as he glared at Sonar. "And that's an order. I'm not going to argue with you over this. Without sleep you're useless to me. So, either do as I say or call for an exfil right now."

Irate, Sonar stared right back. The last thing he would do was pick up the satellite phone and call for a chopper to pick him up. Not without Jag. "Don't do something stupid like wander off by yourself. To twist your own words, you're no good to anyone dead."

Jag growled low in his throat. "I'm not a fucking idiot, no matter what you might think."

Sonar blew out a breath and aimed for calm. "That's not even close to what I think about you. If you must know, you're one hell of a man. I'm honored to work as your partner now, would be thrilled to do so again after this mission is completed. Hell, I'll even ask you out on a date when you're ready to get back into the social world again."

Jag's eyes widened slightly. "A date?"

"Yep. Dinner. I'm buying. Steak and potatoes with all the fixings." He offered up a small grin. "I'll even pitch in for dessert. My treat, so no arguing over the check."

A ghost of a smile settled over Jag's lips. "Don't tell me you have cravings for chocolate?"

Sonar shrugged. "I'll eat anything sweet and scrumptious."

"What about that legion of men?"

"Why would I want those? You're definitely man enough for me."

Jag leaned in and brushed his lips over Sonar's. Stunned, Sonar took a split second to return the affection. He opened his mouth, allowed Jag entry, then took advantage in order to get another taste of him. He bit back a moan, poured his emotions into the action, and stepped it up a notch.

Just as the kiss started to explode into something more, Jag pulled away. He brushed his fingers over Sonar's cheek and met his gaze steadily. Desire and something more flashed in Jag's eyes.

Sonar felt the connection just as strongly. For a long moment, they remained still. Finally, Jag brushed his thumb over Sonar's lips and blew out a breath. "Unless we get to Sandman, and soon, we're not going to have to worry about who picks up the tab."

The moment of lightness passed just as quickly as it happened. Sonar adjusted his position, checked his GPS, and went back to watching the dusty mountainside for the tiniest evidence of human activity.

Just get through this. His reward, in the form of Jag, waited.

TWO HOURS later, they were on the move again. Sonar took the lead while Jag pulled up the rear. The old goat path they followed took them around a hill, over some rocky terrain, and would eventually lead them to another series of caves, one of them where they would set up for another night.

As comfortable as Sonar felt in their last perch, he understood constant movement ensured survival. To become entrenched tempted death in this region of the world. Vast numbers of insurgents, native to this area, prowled each night, on the lookout for any unfortunate soldiers traveling through the Valley of Death without the eyes of a drone way ahead of them. The Taliban were fast and crafty. They took advantage of every angle, the hundreds of caves, the known transportation routes through the valley, in order to set ambushes.

Thus, Sonar and Jag had packed up an hour before and began yet another hiking trek in order to get closer to their goal while avoiding the nests of the enemy presently hiding in wait.

Sonar paused at a fork in the path. "The right seems to make more of a beeline. The left, probably the scenic tour, but ends up in the vicinity. Which do you think?"

Jag studied both, then lifted his chin and narrowed his eyes to slits in order to stare into the setting sun. Using a hand to shield the brightness, he tried to make out potential pitfalls, obstacles, and cover along each one. Sonar did the same, then faced the other direction, a habit of watching their backs.

Sunlight glinted off metal on a ledge a few hundred yards away.

Shit.

Sonar tackled Jag, sending him tumbling to the ground just as shots filled the air. He rolled back to his feet, aimed, then flew backward when a bullet slammed into his Kevlar-covered chest. Breathing became a challenge but adrenaline and training kicked in. He immediately righted himself, shoved Jag ahead of him to the right side of the path, and ran crouched over for several paces before dropping behind some large boulders for cover.

"Fuck." Jag settled beside him, already lining up his rifle with the location the attack came from.

Sonar kept his head on a swivel, feeling way too exposed on the side of a hill, with nothing behind them besides a couple of bare bushes. Nearby enemy would rush to the sound of battle. It would be Sonar and Jag's rotten luck if they were flanked in the process. "We've got to find better cover."

Jag fired, the boom of the big gun nearly deafening in Sonar's sensitive ears with the proximity. He didn't have the time or luxury of slipping his noise-barrier headphones on with danger potentially sneaking up all around.

No other shots sounded.

Jag paused only a second before leaping to his feet. "Not stopping until we reach the first opening on the cliff face."

With those words, he sprinted ahead.

Sonar followed right behind. Another bullet smacked into his vest, burning like a branding iron, but Sonar kept hauling ass. To stop was to commit hari-kari by giving the insurgents an easy target.

In what seemed like an hour but probably was closer to five minutes, they navigated over the crumbled stones and cautiously stepped into the first large crevice they found. Jag, with his rifle slung behind his back and pistol in hand, slipped deeper into the darkness. One step at a time, he traversed the dusty cavern, finally holstering his sidearm. "We're good here."

Sonar nodded, too relieved and winded to answer.

Jag hurried back, catching Sonar just as he plopped down on his butt. "Where are you hit?"

Sonar swallowed, drew in a breath, and grimaced. Stung like hell. Still, he was alive. That's what counted in the end. "Vest took...."

Without waiting for more of an explanation, Jag started yanking the Kevlar vest from Sonar. He tossed it aside, drew his knife, and slit through Sonar's shirt effortlessly, without causing a single scratch on Sonar's hide in the process. His eyebrows furrowed as he ran his hands first over Sonar's chest, then his back. "Damn. Two hits."

He wasn't telling Sonar anything he didn't already know. "Felt like they were coming right through the armor."

Jag nodded, lightly pressing on the quickly purpling area adjacent to Sonar's left pec. "Bruised for sure. Hematoma, maybe."

Tossing his ruck to the ground, Jag pulled out a quick-relief ice pack. He snapped the two edges apart, waited a second for the coolness to happen, then placed it against Sonar's chest.

Finally catching his breath, Sonar glanced up at Jag, their faces perhaps a foot apart. "You don't have to care for me like this. I can do it myself."

Jag arched an eyebrow. "Right now, I think you've got all you can do to just suck in air."

"It's better," Sonar admitted. He tried a deep breath and winced. That wouldn't be comfortable for a while to come, obviously. Whether he had a cracked rib or just the breath knocked out of him, he didn't know. Neither would change the course of things.

"You took a bullet with my name on it," Jag whispered.

Sonar blinked at him and waited. When no other words came forth, he shrugged, then hissed in regret. "Seemed like the thing... to do... at the time."

The corner of Jag's lips hitched upward. "Uh-huh. Took that bullet, rolled to your feet, then returned fire before I could get my head back over my ass."

"Well, you do have a big ass." Sonar offered up a tired smile.

Jag grinned openly for a second, then sobered. "Thanks."

"Welcome."

Sonar stared into Jag's eyes, read the respect and appreciation, along with a spark of softness and caring. Too bad it disappeared just as quickly as it appeared, only to be replaced with steely determination.

He'd meant what he said earlier about going on a date with Jag. They just had to make it out of this hellhole first. Not an impossible task but pretty damn close.

"Let's make camp. We've got a couple of hours until darkness. Take advantage of it. You're definitely sleeping tonight while I'm on watch."

Sonar didn't bother to argue. He knew stubbornness and command when he heard it.

Chapter 12

JAG SILENTLY strode away from the cave, glancing back one last time to the place where Sonar still slept, safe and sound, well out of view. A moment of regret flared before reason took hold. This was the only way he could eliminate Sandman and keep Sonar out of harm's way at the same time. Since Sonar stubbornly refused to stay behind or well back, Jag had no choice but to sneak off in the wee hours of predawn. Besides, he'd been hit twice yesterday while saving Jag's ass. He'd done enough. Now it was Jag's turn to step up to the plate once and for all.

He'd read the signs and figured out last evening where Sandman holed up. As much as he wanted to charge ahead, he knew better. First he had to come up with a foolproof plan and that involved ditching Sonar.

Successful at both, he made his way up a nearly invisible goat trail to the far side of the hill, senses fully open to pick up every single sound, no matter how tiny.

The chess game was about to come to an end and he didn't trust Sandman to play fair. However, unless he missed his guess, Sandman had one flaw he could capitalize on: arrogance. The whole trip around the world showed Sandman loved to be in control, to make puppets out of people, and had a big-time superiority complex. That he could exploit. Not much, but hopefully enough.

The sandy path veered upward into a more rocky terrain littered with pockets of brush nearly stripped bare by hungry goats. The present leafless state suited Jag well, allowing him to glimpse what might hide on the other side.

Scenting nothing, he moved steadily forward, knowing that Sandman would have spent the night in a cave just like he and Sonar did. The Taliban still roamed at night and would have just as happily taken out Sandman as any other soldier. Too bad it couldn't be nearly so easy.

A few more steps placed him on the east side of the hill where more bushes existed.

The hairs on the back of his neck stood at attention as his gut clenched in warning. Immediately, he hit the deck and started crawling, using the vegetation as cover.

His right foot caught for a second.

Fear surged through him as he glanced back just in time to see the nearly invisible wire tighten. With a vile curse, he threw himself to the side, but not fast enough.

The gunshot rang loud in his ears as a sharp pain burned down his lower leg. The scent of blood filled his nostrils.

Sitting up slightly, he drew his injured leg closer for inspection. The calf had taken a direct hit, and now resembled hamburger. Blood trickled down in a steady stream from the wound. From what he could see, the muscle was still there, just filled with numerous holes that leaked valuable fluid with each passing second.

Shit.

He needed to shift and fast. The gunshot could be heard for miles and Sandman could be anywhere. Still, he had no choice. Unless he took advantage of his innate healing ability, he chanced bleeding out.

He started peeling clothes and equipment from his body in preparation for a necessary transformation to his beast. No sooner had he stripped down to his camos than the slight crunching noise of boots drew his attention. He jerked his attention toward the top of the hill.

Sandman stood silhouetted against the predawn sky with an evil smile on his face. He pointed his rifle at Jag and walked closer. "I see you found my advanced warning system. Kind of you to let me know you'd arrived."

Jag cussed himself for stupidity. Tripwires were commonplace in jungle warfare, but not as often seen in the desert. His inattention and eagerness to get to Sandman had caused the slipup and put him in a precarious position. Shifting would have to wait. He had bigger concerns at the moment.

Immediately, he reached for his pistol.

The cocking of a gun stopped him. "Uh-uh. Touch it and the game is over. Since I wanted to gloat a little first, I suggest you sit still like a good boy and listen up."

Jag narrowed his eyes but pulled his hand back anyway. With just his basic clothing, his knife and utility belt were all that remained of his weapons. A disadvantage, yes, but not as much as one would think. Years of training had made him adept at hand-to-hand fighting with martial arts and knives. Of course, he still had the grenade tucked away in the small storage pouch on his belt. That would ensure a fiery end to Sandman and him both.

For a long moment, he stared death in the face and made a decision. If there was no other way, he'd blow them both up. Even if he sacrificed himself in the process, he'd ensure Sandman never killed another person again.

Stopping about ten feet away, Sandman kept his rifle aimed at Jag's chest. "I bet you were in shock when you learned I'd survived."

Jag decided to play along. At least he'd buy some time to figure a way out of this mess, perhaps even taunt Sandman into a fairer fight, and discover some answers to the questions that had nagged him for the past few weeks. "You could say that."

"I'll let you in on a little secret. A few years ago, I signed up for an experimental study with active-duty soldiers. We were given injections laced with animal DNA. The purpose was to make our senses so much stronger than an ordinary human's. That worked fine and good. So, they did a few more. Seems the medication had a nice little side effect. We healed fast. Extremely fast. Even typically mortal wounds were fixable."

They were trying to turn him and the others into a shifter. Talk about one FUBAR experiment.

Jag blinked and forced himself to maintain a bored expression. "So you were able to just heal naturally? Your body knew what to do without direction?"

Sandman nodded slightly. "I just had to think for a second what I needed to do and it filled right back in. Easy as pie." He drew out the last words in sick appreciation. "I'm the best soldier ever. No one is my equal."

"That's what you think. I killed you once. I can do it again," Jag bit out in restrained anger. He needed to lash Sandman's conceit and push him into changing his plans.

Sandman laughed. "That's a good one. This coming from someone with a gunshot to the leg, no weapons close, and staring down the business end of a rifle."

Jag arched an eyebrow. "A child could win in this situation. Prove that you're the best soldier ever."

Sandman's mouth pursed for a moment as he stared down at Jag. "How?"

"Let's settle this the old fashioned way—hand-to-hand."

"You think you can best me with martial arts?" He sneered. "Not only do I have the senses of animals, I have their power and strength. Added to my years of karate experience and my black-belt status, and you're way over your head."

"Prove it."

Sandman inclined his head slowly. "First you get up and away from those guns."

Jag took to his feet, ignoring the shooting pain in his leg as he tried to put weight on it. Intent to never show weakness, he stepped steadily over several paces, well out of reach of his weapons. "Let's go already."

Never taking his eyes off Jag, Sandman slowly lowered his rifle to the ground, pulled his pistol out of the holster, then tossed it to the earth. He drew his knife and edged closer, his motion cautious and jerky.

For a second, Jag considered pulling his own knife, then decided against it. He could move better without having to worry about hanging on to the weapon. Truthfully, the blade slowed him down and proved a nuisance to him. He could kill with his bare hands much faster and easier than stabbing someone to death.

They circled each other.

"Bet you're wondering about Mark."

Jag snarled. "I know you were an item before Mark broke it off."

Sandman jumped in, slashed, and missed. "Mark and I were in love. He couldn't get enough of me or my big dick shoved up his ass."

Jag ignored the words, focused on his control, and constantly searched for an opening. He threw a round kick at Sandman only to have it blocked. He retreated as Sandman countered with a variety of punches and kicks in rapid succession. "Guess he must have come to his senses because he left you and found me."

Sandman's lips drew back in an angry grimace. "He didn't understand. Once we were together, no one else would work. He'd never find another man like me, as good as me. I tried to convince him of that, but he was too stupid to listen."

"So you decided if you couldn't have him, then no one else could either? You killed him on purpose." Jag lunged again, landing a jab to Sandman's cheek.

"No." The word ripped out of Sandman's mouth. He drew in some breaths and attacked again.

Jag defended each blow but felt his strength waning. The blood loss and moving around on his wounded leg was taking its toll. If he couldn't put Sandman down in the next couple of minutes, he'd be too weak to lift his hand.

"That shot was meant for you. I promised Mark that I'd kill you and get him back. Forever. You see, he didn't like the new me. Was afraid of my power and abilities. Said that the serum had messed with my mind. He was jealous over what I could do, is all. I told him I hadn't changed; he had. He went into a rage and told me that he'd moved on, found another man to replace me. He told me you were indestructible. You were the best that's ever been and no one could beat you." He aimed a kick at Jag's right leg, scored, and smiled when Jag began to hobble. "Guess he was wrong about that too."

Jag lunged for Sandman's arm, receiving a slash from the knife in the process. He jumped back just as quickly. "Mark loved me for who I was. We shared something special that you couldn't even begin to imagine."

"Not as special as what I shared with him. He was my pet, attentive to my every need. I wasn't about to let him go. No matter what."

"In the end, you lost. You killed him." Jag worked his way back toward his weapons. If he could get close enough, he could dive for one of the guns and end this fast.

Sandman shook his head, his eyes turning feral. "*You* killed him. If he hadn't been with you, he'd still be alive. He was mine. Mine! No one takes from me and lives."

The puzzle pieces clicked into place. "You started killing. That's when Mark ran."

"I grew stronger, faster, smarter than the rest. With every shot, I could see and feel the difference. Then the bastards stopped. Said it was too dangerous. That others couldn't psychologically handle the changes. Those fuckers were weak, unlike me. I was the supreme soldier, a predator who succeeded with anything and everything. Yet they took it all away. I needed an outlet and found a new hobby. Mark didn't know what it all involved but he became skeptical. Questioned me. That was his first mistake. His place was to please me, to obey, never to question. I had to punish him for that."

Oh, God. Mark. Jag didn't have a clue what Mark had gone through and didn't want to know. He shoved those thoughts aside and focused on taking down Sandman once and for all. Sandman blocked his way, standing between him and the stash.

Jag grimaced and tried to rotate around, only to be cut off once more.

"Come to find out he's one of the reasons they shut down the experiment. He went to them and made up lies. Said I was unstable. Too aggressive. Then he walked away. I promised to find him no matter where he went. Next thing I knew, he'd attached himself to you, sang your high praises, and set the ball rolling on your own demise."

Jag's heart stuttered hearing those words, but his resolve strengthened all the more. He'd make Sandman pay for what he had done to Mark and all the others.

"Why wait all these years?"

"Revenge is a dish best served cold." Sandman sidestepped. "I thought about it often, planned, decided the best course of action in order to make you pay, bleed, and suffer as you deserve for taking what was rightfully mine. For that, you'll forfeit your life."

Breathing hard, battling fatigue, and noticing his vision beginning to blur, Jag stepped up the game, knowing he had to end this now. He landed a solid kick to Sandman's thigh, which caused him to stumble. As he approached, Sandman lashed out with his leg, sweeping Jag's right knee, sending him toppling to the ground. Jag struggled to get up but it was too late. Sandman had pounced on top of him, using his weight to hold Jag down.

Their eyes met.

Sandman grinned as he placed the point of his knife against the center of Jag's chest. "I've dreamed about this moment. Spent some time deciding what picture to carve in your chest. It had to be special and fitting for the bastard that dared to take Mark from me."

Jag grunted as the knife started to press into his skin. He slowly moved his right hand closer, found the leather latch on the pouch connected to his belt. Getting it open, he ran his finger over the pin on the grenade.

The chips were down and he had one way out.

As he wrapped his finger inside the pin, a blur crossed into his vision. Furry and small, the animal leaped onto Sandman's back, growling as it bit the back of the man's neck and scratched him repeatedly.

Sonar. Jag recognized the animal and scent immediately.

Sandman howled, jerked back, and tried to throw the cat off. When that didn't work, he yanked on the animal's legs, smacked at its head, and even turned the knife in order to make a slit down the feline's side. Sonar was flung to the side, but immediately hunkered down for his next attack.

Jag threw himself back toward his guns, knowing if he didn't hurry, Sonar would end up dead. He stretched out, found his pistol with his hand, grabbed it up, aimed, and fired.

Sandman's body lurched as the side of his head exploded.

Jag lowered his gun and stared at the gruesome scene. "Enjoy an eternity in hell." Completely exhausted with the world starting to fade to black, Jag fell back to the ground.

SONAR BLINKED at the fallen man, noted the bits of skull and brain matter littering the ground. No one could survive a .45 bullet to the brain. Whatever Sandman was—human, shifter, or otherwise—he wouldn't be getting up again.

Sonar turned his attention to Jag, found him crumpling back to the ground from his sitting position. The gun slid from slack fingers to land at his side.

Fear propelled him forward, hurrying to Jag. Once there, he quickly changed forms, not the least bit concerned about his lack of clothing. Trivial things no longer mattered. Only Jag did.

He scanned Jag's body, noted the abundance of blood, and bit back a cry of grief. His acute hearing picked up Jag's weak heartbeat. Latching onto that, he drew his knife and cut Jag's clothing, searching for the worst wounds. It didn't take him long to find a hole in Jag's lower leg, which still bled heavily. The mess of tissue told him that the bullet might not have broken any bones but it sure tore the hell out of everything. It missed the artery, but the large hole leaked blood fast enough to end a man's life. His ankle seemed a bit off, but Sonar didn't sweat that small stuff. Quickly he turned Jag over, found nothing on the back, but a long, deep scratch to his arm. Rolling Jag back over, he noted the puncture wound on Jag's chest and knew deep, burning rage. If Sandman wasn't laying in parts nearby, he'd tear the motherfucker limb from limb. He dug in his pack, found a field dressing and pressed it over Jag's lower leg tightly while using his free hand to punch in memorized numbers on the satellite phone he'd picked out of Jag's pack from the ground.

"Man down. Repeat, man down. Request medevac on the double." He rattled off the coordinates, relieved when the other voice informed him there was a medical chopper in the vicinity and it would be there in minutes.

Jag's eyes slowly opened, widened, and finally focused on Sonar. "Got him."

"Yeah, you did." Sonar choked on the lump in his throat, not even bothering to wipe at the tears running down his cheeks. "Beat him, Jag. You have to fight and live in order to beat him."

"Too...."

"Shift. Right now. Just do it," Sonar alternated between begging and ordering. "There's not enough time otherwise."

"Never told you... you did a good job back there. One hell of a soldier... and friend. Thanks for having... my back." Jag's voice began to fade. "I wish...."

Sonar clutched Jag's hand and got into his face. "Shift, damn it. Because if I have to come to hell to personally kick your ass, I'll fucking do it." He slapped his hand on Jag's chest, saw him flinch, then growled. "Shift." Gathering his strength, Sonar poured every ounce of power into Jag, trying to force the change.

Nothing happened.

Just as a he began to panic, Jag cried out, morphed into a jungle cat, and remained still.

Immediately, Sonar checked Jag's injured leg, finding the bleeding down to a consistent ooze and the ankle area a tad bit displaced, but a definite improvement over seconds before.

The whir of an approaching chopper drew his attention. He tapped Jag's face, waited for him to open his eyes, and smiled down at him. "Once more, big guy. Kind of hard to explain why I'm hauling an injured kitty cat on a military helo, you know."

Jag blew out a breath, a sure sign of being put upon, and managed to switch back, with a hearty assist from Sonar. His eyes closed as his body relaxed into unconsciousness. Sonar took the opportunity to yank on his clothes, not bothering with trying to redress Jag. Even if he were dressed, the medics would cut away the material in a heartbeat. He'd saved them a step.

He scrambled, trying to figure out what to do next. The chopper would get them off the mountain and back to base on the double. But Jag couldn't go to the hospital. No way. One blood test would cause more than a stir. It would start the avalanche as far as shifters were concerned, jeopardizing each and every one of them, something Sonar couldn't allow to happen.

Sonar racked his brain before an idea popped into his mind. He scrolled through the numbers on Jag's phone, clicked down to Mac's name, and punched the button. The call was answered on the third ring.

"Jag?"

"Sonar, sir. Jag's down. Medevac is on the way, taking us down to FOB Thunder. He can't be seen at the hospital, sir." The forward operating base called Thunder was the closest to their location.

"How bad?"

"Shot in the leg. He shifted, so he's not bleeding near so much. But he's out cold, exhausted, and lost more than his fair share of blood."

"You just stay with him. I'll make a phone call. Don't let them take him to the hospital. There'll be a plane to pick him up momentarily and bring him home."

Sonar blew out a breath of relief. "Will do, sir."

"Good job, soldier. Hang in there and we'll have you home in no time."

Clicking off the link, Sonar shoved his feet into his boots.

The helicopter flew by. Sonar waved at the chopper and waited for them to turn and land. He gathered up their equipment, took one more look at the man who had caused such pain and havoc over the past several months, then turned his attention back to Jag.

Two men dressed in camouflage jumped out with a backboard in hand. They ran to Jag, scooped him up, and trotted back, placing their patient on the floor of the chopper.

Sonar jumped on board, not about to be separated from Jag, especially at such a crucial time.

They got to work immediately by shoving an IV in Jag's arm and rolling him side to side, checking for injuries. The closest man found Jag's lower leg wound. He stared at it, leaned down, then gestured for his assistant to take a gander. Confusion covered both men's faces.

Sonar pulled on a helmet and connected the communication link to the roof of the small area.

"What the hell, sir?"

"I'd say the wound is a week old and one hell of a mess."

Both medics glanced over at Sonar. He stared back at them unflinchingly. Shifting had saved Jag's life and was worth the risk. Even if the human medical teams ended up with more questions than answers.

Which meant it was time for a bit of explanation. "Hit days ago. He's been pushing himself nonstop. We field treated as best as we could." He leveled a firm look at the two men.

The older man scowled at him, censure in every line of his face.

Sonar bristled. "We're black ops. This is the first medevac available since his injury." With poor weather and bloody battles, medical choppers weren't always able to fly, let alone land. Let the people on board assume it was for one of those reasons.

The younger man nodded while the older one continued to frown in serious disapproval. He shook his head and went back to checking Jag's body a second time.

Sonar took the opportunity to rest, all the while keeping a close eye on Jag. As soon as they hit base, he had a battle to wage and another special transport to make with Jag.

The survival of their species depended on it.

Chapter 13

JAG AWAKENED groggily, slowly opening his eyes, before shutting them again as the bright sunlight nearly blinded him. The sound of curtains closing preceded the blessing of dimness in the room. He tried again, this time making out faces. It took a moment for the names to click. He was back home. With his shifter team family. "Mac?"

"Right here." The older man stepped up to his side.

Jag tried to sit up, but found a strong hand pressed against his chest. He turned his head and saw Sonar sitting in a chair next to his bed, presently preventing him from doing more than lying flat.

Memories flooded him. The fight with Sandman. The moment he prepared to pull the pin. Seeing Sonar in ocelot form tearing the shit out of the man in order to get him off. Jag recalled the second he latched onto his handgun, aimed, and fired. The satisfaction of seeing the resulting head wound and knowing once and for all the bastard now resided in hell. "He's dead."

"Thanks to you," Mac said.

Another man approached the end of the bed. Ronnie had a worried expression painted on his young face. "I'll tell you right now, any grenade I find in your house or pack *will* be turned over to Mac. Those are permanently off the order list as well."

Jag smiled sheepishly. "It was the only thing I could think of at the time." He hated that Ronnie had heard that part of the story and would have spared him the nightmare if he could have.

"Uh-huh."

"Good thing Sonar had your back. Not only did he get Sandman off you, he stuck by your side, and called me to help orchestrate a flight home. You both hightailed it off base almost as soon as your chopper landed. From what I was told, Sonar made one hell of a guard dog, refusing to let the medics take you to the hospital. He waited for your ride and got you back to us fast. I couldn't have done it better myself."

Jag peered over at Sonar, touched and awed by the other man's actions on his behalf.

"I couldn't let them test your blood, and they would have since you needed a transfusion. But we had to have transportation from BFE. I don't think you would have made it if I had to lug you around for a week before reaching civilization. It was a risk I had to take."

Jag's heart buoyed and pride hit him square on. Sonar had pulled the rabbit out of the hat despite the danger to them both. All for him. His feelings for Sonar came to the fore along with a healthy dose of respect. Still, he couldn't help grumbling over Sonar's intervention.

"You disregarded my order," he accused Sonar without malice or heat.

Sonar grinned unrepentantly. "Yeah, I did. As soon as I heard that gunshot, I knew you were in trouble. No one could take on that bastard alone, especially wounded. You were willing to sacrifice your life in order to take out Sandman. I couldn't let it come to that."

"Why?"

Sonar edged closer and pushed the hair away from Jag's face. "Because you're too good of a guy to let some stupid, psychotic prick take your life." Emotion and determination filled his voice.

"Okay, gentlemen, I think that's our cue to leave," Mac said. He paused at the doorway. "Take my advice. Hang on to this one."

Jag nodded once.

The room emptied quickly, leaving Sonar and Jag alone.

"Thanks." The simple word came straight from his very soul.

"Welcome," Sonar answered. His focus dropped to the floor before he scrubbed his face with one hand. That done, he met Jag's gaze steadily. "I'll have nightmares of that bastard nearly plunging that knife into your chest for the rest of my days," Sonar admitted.

Jag's heart tugged. They'd share that particular nightmare, no doubt about it. Still, guilt weighed heavily on him knowing he had added to Sonar's already hefty burden. He reached out and squeezed Sonar's arm, needing to reassure him and ease his concerns. "We make a pretty good team."

"That we do. Seems a shame to break up such a dynamic duo." Sonar worried his lower lip.

"That's why we're not going to," Mac's voice interrupted them.

Jag glanced toward the door to find his commander standing with arms relaxed at his sides and a shit-eating grin on his face.

"I've pulled rank on Sonar's brass. He's been formally transferred to our unit."

Jag smiled and met Sonar's eyes. "Think you can put up with a handful of cocky shifters?"

"I might be small but I'm mighty." Sonar laughed at his own joke. "Besides, I've gotten some practice dealing with one hardass already."

Jag rolled his eyes before turning his focus back to Mac. "I owe you."

Mac shrugged. "No sweat. Although the healer is back to put you through your paces."

Jag groaned dramatically.

Sonar chuckled. "That bad, huh?"

"You have no idea." Jag threw his head back on the pillow. "She's a canine and downright mean."

"Jaguar Mallow, you better not be slandering my good name." Misty stepped into the room, a small doctor's bag in hand. Speaking of small but mighty…. The wolf shifter might lack in physical size compared to the men, but she made up for it in sheer attitude, guts, and smart-mouth comments. None of them dared to mess with her.

She smiled at him mischievously, then held her hand out to Sonar. "Misty Trent. Tormentor… errr… doctor to Jag and the rest of this mangy group."

Sonar beamed up at her. "I think I like you already."

Jag groaned dramatically. "Not you too."

"What?"

Misty sat down on the side of Jag's bed. "Oh, ignore Mr. Cranky Pants. He's just lamenting the fact that I won the popularity contest and he didn't."

"Yeah, that's it," Jag quipped out. In all fairness, he adored the team healer. Like a pesky litter sister who yanked his chain any chance she got.

"Everyone scoot." She waved her hand.

Sonar stood. Jag grabbed his hand. "You're not leaving me alone with *her*, are you?"

Sonar eyed him in bewilderment. "Afraid you'll get all hot and bothered from her exam?"

Jag snorted. "First of all, you know I don't swing that way. Secondly, if I dared look at her as anything more than a healer, her mate would make a jaguar-skin rug out of me."

Sonar smiled wickedly. "That bad, huh?"

"Worse." Jag normally didn't yip or whine, especially when hurt. But he couldn't pass up the chance to banter with Sonar, not when he was so thrilled to just be alive, safe, and together.

The last word felt right so he didn't bother analyzing it too much. They'd bonded over the past several days, particularly in the mountains of Kunar. He'd learned quite a bit from Sonar and had his eyes opened to a few things. Namely, that he'd developed a taste for one small ocelot shifter with an odd sense of humor, no sense of self-preservation when standing up to a bigger, badder predator, and a unique ability to coat Jag with comfort even during the worst times. Add in Sonar's good looks and his droolworthy body, and Jag was sold.

The fact that Sonar was sticking around gave him the confidence and motivation to look beyond the next assignment, the next assassin job. He needed relaxation downtime. Maybe, just maybe, one damn hot sidekick to help pass the time as well.

Not to mention, that promised date loomed.

Sonar smiled softly back at him before stepping from the room.

His heart skipped a beat. He'd found something worth fighting for in Sonar.

"You and Sonar make a nice couple." Misty unrolled the dressing from his lower leg.

"Misty...." He added a warning in his tone. He and Sonar had barely started on the road to being a couple. Hell, one fuck session and a kiss didn't a relationship make. Until they had a chance to discuss what the future might bring, he preferred to keep everything on the down-low.

She rolled her eyes. "I know, I know. None of my business. However, as a healer, I'm charged with taking care of all of you, not just the physical aspect. Which means matters of the psyche and heart fall into my jurisdiction as well."

Jag groaned. Like a dog with a bone, Misty would latch onto a topic and refuse to let go until he offered up the answers she sought. Since he wasn't near ready to open his mouth on the subject of Sonar and had the tenacity to out-stubborn a mule, he simply shot her a glare. "We're friends. Comrades. Period."

"Uh-huh." She turned his ankle this way and that. "Your *friend* took care of you. Got you onto a plane. Just so happened one of our medics was on board. She didn't need lab work to determine you needed a transfusion. Sonar stepped right up for a direct donation, which probably saved your life."

Jag blinked at the information but didn't speak. He'd have done the same for a comrade in need in a heartbeat. Thankfully, shifters carried very similar blood, allowing them to donate to one another readily.

She returned his foot to the bed before having him pump his ankle in order to check his mobility. "Looks good. I set the broken fibula as soon as you arrived. The muscles are healing as expected. One more shift under your belt and you should be well on your way. I gave you a couple more pints of blood once you arrived, more as a safety precaution than anything. Sonar's blood had already stabilized you enough for recovery. Knowing how much he gave you on the trip over told me you were low. Too damn low. Coming in with less than half a tank was cutting it way too close," Misty scolded him as she gathered up another roll of gauze, tape, and scissors. She began rewrapping the area with practiced ease. "You might be sore and carry a limp for a few days, but you'll be back up to par before you know it, once you catch up on some sleep and allow your body to recuperate from pushing it way too hard."

"Good."

She finished her task quickly and efficiently. "Let me give you a word of advice."

"Do you have to?"

"Yes." She patted his arm. "That's one damn fine man you brought home."

He frowned at her. "Meaning?"

"Meaning, you might be blind to what's right in front of your face. So open your eyes, get your head on straight, and start living."

He opened his mouth, then thought better of arguing with her. Misty wasn't one to mince words or tiptoe around topics. She gave it to everyone straight whether they wanted to hear it or not.

She stared at him for a long moment, nodded slowly, then headed toward the exit. "I'll check on you later. Rest. Eat. Tomorrow is soon enough for you to be up and about."

Jag let his head drop onto the soft pillow and sighed.

He'd finished what he started and managed to live through the ordeal. Another mission wouldn't be coming down the pipe for a while, at least until he was 100 percent back on his feet. Probably a while after that. Which left him with time on his hands. Bushels of it.

Now what the hell am I going to do?

Sonar walked through the door with a large tray laden with food. He offered up a cockeyed smile. "I thought you might be hungry."

Oh, I am. Just for something that's not on the menu.

He ignored the husky voice in his head, sat up in bed, and prepared to take care of one of his needs. The other would have to wait.

THE DIPPING of the mattress awoke Jag from his doze. He glanced down at the end of the bed, found a large ocelot with sleek spotted fur walking toward him. They stared at one another for a couple of seconds before the cat stretched out beside Jag's hip, his head facing the door.

Jag studied Sonar in his cat form, realizing that he'd grown accustomed to having Sonar at his side every day and night, and having him here now provided a sense of contentment and well-being. While he might have Sonar's rear pointed his direction and his tail lightly flicking across his chest, the position didn't go unnoticed. Sonar was protecting him, just like he'd done back in the desert. Guarding him from what may come.

Jag's heart buoyed at the thought.

They might have started off pretty rough, and he certainly didn't make anything easy for the spotter he hadn't wanted from day one. Yet Sonar had stuck by him. They'd managed to find common ground, bonding along the way.

He owed Sonar his life. Twice.

How he would repay him, he didn't have a clue. At least Sonar had been reassigned to the shifter unit, so he'd be more at home and comfortable than surrounded by humans 24-7. That also meant they'd be teammates.

Jag had always been a loner. Until Mark. Before, he'd thought returning to that status was the answer. Then Sonar came along and showed him differently.

Once more, he appraised Sonar, who had curled into a ball, using Jag's hip as a pillow at his back.

The guy had guts; he'd give him that. And smarts too. Not everyone could have gone through what Sonar did—the endless days, the jet lag from trips all over the world. Being stuck with Jag, who had a sizable bounty on his head, making him just as much a target as Jag. Sonar had done just that and proven to be one hell of a partner along the way. Even his compassion and prickly words of advice had made a dent in Jag's usually repellent shield. He hadn't wanted to hear them then, and was not sure he wanted them now, but he knew Sonar spoke the basic truth.

Not that he'd ever tell Sonar that. The guy's head was plenty big enough already. Still, he couldn't resist teasing Sonar. "If you so much as think about farting…."

Sonar turned to look at Jag and chuffed, a snort in kitty language.

Jag ran his hand over Sonar's lower back, enjoying the sleek, soft coat under his fingers. "Thanks."

Sonar's whiskers twitched in acknowledgment.

With a weary sigh, Jag contemplated his current situation. Bedrest sucked. Tomorrow he'd get up and about, no matter what the healer ordered. He needed to shift another time or two, heal completely, and be back to training for the next mission that was sure to come down the pipe. He needed to sleep in his own room, move back to his house, and find what resembled a normal life before the next mission called.

Turning his head, he remembered that Sonar had arrived with just the clothes on his back and his ruck. The rest of his belongings were back at the FOB in Kunar Province. He made a mental note to tell Mac first thing in the morning. Sonar needed clothes, supplies, and a place to stay.

He considered the sole bedroom at headquarters that he presently occupied. Members of the team came and went at all hours of the night. Rest would be difficult enough if one knew each and every person who came and went. Sonar would be on edge, unable to relax, not sure about the happenings going on around him.

Which meant he needed another place to stay.

Jag blew out a breath. He'd take Sonar in. It was the most reasonable solution and the least he could do. Peace followed that decision, as well as a healthy dose of excitement. Maybe they could finally take some steps forward, seeing where teamwork might lead.

For the first time in quite a while, Jag threw caution to the wind and opened the blinds of his heart. Sonar would just have to be an exception to Jag's solitary rule. The thought made him smile.

Exhausted but content, Jag snuggled into his pillow and closed his eyes. The sound of soft purring lulled him to sleep.

Chapter 14

"I THINK you need to spend another day in bed." Misty lifted Jag's lower leg and gave it a thorough once-over. "It's still pretty rough looking."

Jag fisted the sheets in an attempt to control his building frustration. "Another shift will take care of it. You said so yourself."

She met his gaze. "That was yesterday. Today is a different day."

Annoyed beyond belief, Jag threw his legs over the side of the bed and stood. He shifted his weight from side to side, finding his injured calf sore and a bit stiff but nothing he couldn't deal with. "See? I'm fine." He repeated the action for Misty.

She blew out a breath. "You're not fine. You're recovering. Slowly." Her mouth drew into a line. "Truth is, I don't trust you to take it easy. You don't know the meaning of the word."

"Bullshit, lady." The harsh words came out as a near roar. He chafed at being down, couldn't take it any longer. His feline agreed readily. The need to shift forms and run free climbed to the top of the totem pole in priorities.

Mac appeared in the room a couple of seconds later. "What's the problem here?" Mac looked at Jag.

"I'm going out. Shifting and taking off. She said I could."

"Yesterday!" Misty crossed her arms over her chest. "Today that wound is looking a bit ragged. You need another day of lying around just to be sure."

"Not happening," he snapped.

They didn't understand. If he didn't get out of there and away from that damned bed, he'd tear the whole place apart. His big cat crawled under his skin, demanding to be let out. He'd woken up with the caged feeling, and it had only worsened through the day. By the time he finished lunch, he was about to lose his everloving mind. He was a man of action. Lying around wasn't in his genetic makeup.

Mac eyed him carefully as Jag approached. "Something tells me you'll be out there on the obstacle course just to show you can."

"Absolutely not." Misty backed up to block the doorway leading outside. "Walking around is enough stress for right now."

He leashed his rising temper. Barely. His inner beast yowled in frustration. *Soon. Very soon. Just a bit longer.* "I'll go over that fucking obstacle course if I want to." Jag snarled at Mac and Misty, who stood between him and the doorway.

"Just because you're pretty much healed doesn't mean you're ready to step right back into high-level training. You've been injured, lost a lot of blood. Hell, you haven't had a break in months. It's time you take one." Misty crossed her arms over her chest and glared at Jag like he was a poorly behaved kindergartener.

Which angered him all the more. He'd been responsible for himself since childhood. He knew his limits and, despite their rigid orders, knew he needed to get back out there today. "I don't need a break. I *need* to *run*." As shifters they should understand his great need. All of them, no matter the species, had to let their beast free now and again. To keep him or her caged was to ratchet up the tension, antsy feeling, and restlessness. If forced to go too long, the human side could eventually be overtaken by the animal.

Mac shook his head. "Running is fine. Training is a no. You're grounded for mandatory downtime, training included."

Jag opened his mouth, then closed it before he did something stupid like challenge his supervisor and get himself suspended, or worse, dismissed from the unit.

In truth, he understood Mac's position. He did need time to heal. To take that small vacation he'd been promised. However, right now none of that mattered as long as he could get outside, let the fresh air surround him, and just be free for a while.

And to get away from every single person on this earth for a while. Before he lost complete control of his demanding cat.

Sonar appeared wearing a pair of camos that Jag easily recognized as the set he wore the day they met, freshly cleaned. Jag hadn't seen him since Sonar snuck away when Misty brought Jag's breakfast. "I was going to go for a run this morning. Since I don't know my way around, Jag could go with me. I'll keep him off the obstacle course too. Free of charge." Sonar grinned.

Jag wanted to punch the smirk off his face. His skin rippled as his beast grumbled some more, oddly mostly placated with Sonar's arrival.

Still, he found himself snarling. "I don't need a fucking babysitter," he gritted out between clenched teeth.

Sonar held up both hands. "Whoa. Who said anything about babysitting? I'm going for a run. You're going for a run. Makes sense to run together."

Mac's gaze flicked to Sonar, then back to Jag. "Works for me. Misty?"

She nodded. "Running is fine. Just don't overdo it."

"As if." Jag took a step forward, then paused, remembering his promise from last night. "Sonar came in with just what he could carry. Think you can get him some camos and whatever else he might need?"

"Already done," Mac assured him. "His stuff is catching a flight and should be here in a couple of days. In the meantime, he's welcome to anything we have. As for a place to sleep, he can crash here if he wants."

Jag bit his lip, then went with his gut. "Here is too noisy and busy. He won't be able to rest."

Mac arched an eyebrow. "Then what do you suggest?"

Jag met Sonar's eyes. "He can stay with me. If... he doesn't snore and can pick up after himself." They'd just have to work out the details later. If Sonar grew to be a pain in the ass, Jag would simply duct tape him to a tree outside.

Sonar snorted. "I'm not the one that snores."

Jag rolled his eyes and strode through the door. He stepped out into the bright sunshine. Sucking in a deep breath, he felt the edgy sensation fade while excitement escalated.

None of the shifter unit would bother his clothes, even if they lay stretched out in the dirt. They respected one another's personal belongings and privacy too much to steal away with such items. Besides, unless a shifter wanted to walk around the compound naked, he had to return for his garments sometime. Hopefully, finding them in the same place he left them, dust, grime, and all. "Come on, Bat Ears. Looks like I'm to give you a grand tour."

"Yeah, yeah." Sonar stopped next to Jag, his arms relaxed as they hung at his sides. "You sure you're ready for this?"

"Just try to keep up." Jag immediately shifted into his animal form, shook his clothing off, then leaped into a run. He dashed this way and that at a full sprint until he reached the wooded area. The uneven terrain forced him to slow his pace, although not by much. His leg, albeit a bit stiff, held up as good as new.

Sonar kept up for the most part, despite taking three strides for every one of Jag's, a testimony to Sonar's conditioning and stubborn determination.

Finally coming across a stately tree with large limbs, Jag scaled it to the first fork, settled down, and panted to catch his breath. The high post allowed him see across much of the forest and surrounding land. Good enough for the moment.

Except for Sonar, who stuck to him like a burr.

The ocelot didn't blink an eye, just climbed up the tree, found a nearby branch, and stretched out like he owned the entire world.

Jag mentally rolled his eyes. Leave it to Sonar.

Amusement followed, as did another realization. He'd initially wanted to be alone today, having had more than enough of being penned up with people nearly constantly visiting his room. They all meant well, certainly. However, they only added to his overwhelming feeling of being smothered.

Now, hanging out in his big cat form, he found Sonar's presence tolerable. Calming. Wanted.

They should have been sick of each other after that marathon mission of endless togetherness. Not even close, at least from Jag's vantage point. Which added a bit of perplexity to his thoughts.

Sex with Sonar had been excellent. Awesome. Addictive. It just happened at a moment of severe stress when his control had slipped. Sonar didn't back down an inch, simply gave back in spades. Their hunger knew no bounds, but therein lay the issue. He wanted more of what Sonar had to offer. In order for that to happen, they needed to get some basics figured out.

Fuck buddy or something more? Friends with benefits or true lovers? Where do we stand?

The all-important questions for which answers remained elusive.

He studied Sonar, saw the expansion of the smaller cat's sides as he breathed, the wiggle of his whiskers, the slight twitch of his tail.

What do you want, Bat Ears? Can you handle being mine?

A soft sigh from a dozing Sonar was his only answer.

SONAR CRACKED open one eye, noted that Jag was still asleep, and yawned. He stood up on his branch, lowered his upper body before extending in order to stretch his hind legs. Energy hummed as he enjoyed the comfortable temperatures under the canopy of their tree. A slight breeze added a bit more coolness, making for a perfect summer afternoon.

How long they had napped, he didn't know. It couldn't have been long, considering the location of the sun. Long enough for him to feel refreshed, energetic, and a bit mischievous.

His gaze once more landed on Jag. The bigger feline took up most of the large branch, all four legs hanging over the sides as if to balance himself while sleeping. Jag's chin rested against the bark, his tail draped to one side.

In essence, he looked like one lazy house cat stretched out on his perch.

Sonar chuckled to himself. House cat would never describe Jag. Wild, primal, and downright dominating fit much better.

He'd never met anyone quite like the jaguar shifter. Would normally have been put off by the abundance of attitude and penchant for tossing out orders complete with a growl. Yet Jag rarely rubbed him the wrong way. Sonar instead saw the opportunities for pestering the typically temperamental guy, yanking his chain, and adding in a bit of play. Even when Jag snapped and turned downright surly, Sonar took it all in stride. His normally fairly laid-back personality reflected back on his inner ocelot. The beast inside didn't even get riled when Jag started flashing fangs. Not anymore. Instead, his cat stood up, took notice, and began to chuff in excitement.

Which was downright awkward.

Ever since that furious fuck session back in Paris, both Sonar and his beast had eagerly awaited a repeat performance. Sure, he knew tension relief had driven the sex that day, and personal emotions had little to do with the moment. He didn't mind. Long ago he said he'd gladly bend over and offer up his ass if it would help Jag decompress.

Truth in advertising.

Little did he know how absolutely terrific that experience would be. The best he'd ever had. They matched so well, pushed one another to great heights, then came nearly together in a fiery rapture. The sex would only get better once softer emotions played a part. He knew that for a fact. The problem was, how did Jag feel about taking things up a notch?

In crisis situations people gravitated toward one another. Relationships formed. Traditionally, they fell apart down the road as the base for their feelings crumbled. Did their coupling fit that description? Definitely. Could they transform from bedroom buddies and partners to lovers in the traditional sense? Possibly. He wanted that, yes. Jag had the tiebreaking vote. Unfortunately, he wasn't spilling any beans or dropping hard-to-miss hints about where he expected them to go from here.

I sound like a lovesick teen trying to figure out if another boy likes me and is going to ask me to the prom.

He snorted to himself and shook his head. *When did I get so mushy?*

Jag's ears flickered as if listening to Sonar's thoughts.

Sonar grinned. No sense beating himself up when more enjoyable pastimes could be tried. He stealthily walked down his branch toward the trunk of the tree. Once there, he found a relatively secure spot just above Jag. He found his balance, lay down, then dropped a paw to bat at Jag's ears.

Jag's eyes slowly opened in a decided glare.

Sonar kept his claws leashed but smacked the ends once more, laughing to himself as Jag pinned them against his head in obvious irritation. Rarely did he have the opportunity to harass another shifter, especially one as rigid as Jag. Somewhere between endless missions, killers, and his own personal losses, the poor guy had probably forgotten how to have fun. So, when Sonar enticed Jag into playfulness, it was so much sweeter.

Gracefully, Jag regained his feet. His shoulder height allowed him to stare just a smidgen above eye level at Sonar.

Not to be deterred, Sonar popped Jag lightly on the nose.

The flash in Jag's eyes gave Sonar a second of warning. *Oh, shit.* He leaped to the ground and took off at full throttle, Jag hot on his tail.

He hauled ass back to headquarters, barely able to stay ahead of Jag. The bigger cat had the advantage of size and stride length. Sonar, in his more compact cat form, won the hand in agility. He made some hairpin turns, acrobatic leaps, and managed to avoid Jag's attempts to knock him down. Jag wouldn't hurt him. Send him tumbling? Yes. Pounce on top and hold him down? Most definitely. Cause physical damage? No way.

Sonar smiled happily the entire time. Tag had always been a favorite game of his. The fact that he had bested Jag so far made it all the more entertaining.

"What the fuck?"

Sonar heard the man's voice, glanced to his right, and found a small group of soldiers with weapons in hand, walking toward the shooting range. Some more of Jag's team. *Correction. Our team.*

"Looks like the new kid bit off more than he could chew," another one replied before laughing.

Shows what they know.

He skidded, dug in with his nails, and flew toward the gathering. He felt Jag nip his hindquarters and turned on the afterburners. Like a flash, he darted past the men and hung a left turn around the corner of the headquarters building. He slammed on the brakes and barely managed to stop before bowling over Mac, Misty, and another man who had been pointed out to be her mate, Howler.

Jag slid to a halt right beside him.

Mac arched an eyebrow. Misty eyed Jag and frowned severely, no doubt concerned about his still-healing leg. Howler scowled down at them like a couple of errant boys caught in the act.

No one spoke a word for a long moment.

Finally, Mac blew out a long-suffering breath. "Retirement is looking more appealing every day." He shook his head, but Sonar caught the spark of amusement in the old bear's eyes and the hint of a smile.

Mac led the other two away, leaving Jag and Sonar alone.

Sonar trotted over to his clothes, changed back to human form, and started pulling them on. "I think I woke the slumbering dragon."

Jag followed suit before snorting. "You need your eyes checked. Last time I looked, I'm a jaguar." He started dressing as well.

"Yeah, yeah."

"Wake me up like that again and I *will* duct tape you to a tree and leave you there for the wolves to eat."

The threat would have sounded more ominous if Jag's tone hadn't carried plenty of amusement.

Sonar waved his hand. He glimpsed Jag's nudity, appreciated the dips, curves, and bulges for a long moment. Before he could get too worked up, he focused on the present: dinner and moving in with his new roommate.

The one who just threatened to tape him to a tree.

Sonar smiled saucily. *A tree? No way. The bed? Possibly.*

Jag rolled his eyes. "Don't tell me. The idea of being strapped down and being eaten by wolves turns you on."

"Well…." Sonar finished slipping on his shoes. "When you put it like that and change mangy wolves to a damn sexy feline, I'm all in."

"Horndog."

"Cat, thank you very much."

Jag sucked in air. "Yeah, well. Keep it in your pants, Bat Ears. It's dinner time and I'm starved." He shot Sonar one more glimpse and started walking back the way they'd come.

Sonar fell in behind, still wearing a smile.

Jag might talk tough and growl often, but his scent gave him away. He wasn't nearly as immune to Sonar as he would let anyone believe.

And that fact put a bounce in Sonar's step.

Chapter 15

"COME ON in. It's not much, but it beats living in a tent during the rainy season." Jag unlocked the front door, walked in, and dropped his ruck a few paces inside.

He heard Sonar shut the door behind him while a soft thud told him Sonar had deposited his heavy backpack next to Jag's.

"Nice place."

Jag swung around to find Sonar raking the area, checking out his new home for the next few days. *Or longer.*

Whatever came over Sonar to bat at him while he slept? Didn't the ocelot shifter know he played with fire? Obviously not. Jag mentally shook his head, still not quite believing he had joined in the game and nearly ended up with his nose plastered in Mac's groin before he could completely stop. That would have been more than awkward. Fun along the way, yet mortifying at the end. Thankfully, he managed to save face. Literally.

"I've got some food in the freezer. Won't take a minute to fix. If you'll unpack your dirty clothes, I'll toss them in the washer with my own."

"Sounds good to me." Sonar opened zippers and started mounding clothing.

Jag strode into the kitchen, taking a minute to wash his hands before starting the meal. Sniffing, he caught the unmistakable stench of decay coming from the corner. "Whoa. Smells like another science experiment might be growing in the fridge." He grabbed a trash bag and opened the fridge door. "Guess Ronnie forgot that part of looking after the house included eating or throwing away the food *before* it grew fuzzy."

Sonar peeked over his shoulder. "Give it another day or two and you might have a good stand of penicillin." He rubbed his nose and squinted. "On second thought, maybe not. That's pretty damn rotten."

Jag snorted. Hurriedly, he cleared out the moldy and decaying food, tossed it in the bag, before tying the top. A few steps later, he dumped the stinky mess into the trash can outside the house. After returning, he pulled a couple boxes of buffalo wings out of the freezer, poured them onto a cookie sheet, set the oven, and popped them in. That done, he dug through the fridge and frowned. Granted, he normally didn't have much fresh due to his being absent, but after clearing out the rotten stuff, almost nothing remained. He shut the door in a hurry. Changing gears, he opted for some canned mixed vegetables and a couple of large potatoes.

"What can I do to help?" Sonar dried his hands on a nearby towel.

"Get the canned stuff on the stove. I'll wrap the potatoes and stick them in the microwave. They'll be done faster that way."

"On it."

Sonar dug through a cabinet, found a pan, poured the contents in, and placed the pan on the burner after clicking it on. He opened doors, pulled out plates, and set them on the table. "Utensils?"

"First drawer past the microwave."

Jag watched the other man move fluidly, appearing more than at home in the kitchen. Not a typical hangout for men, especially shifters. "You don't seem the least bit intimidated by food preparation."

"Maybe it's because I'm not." Sonar lifted his chin and shot Jag a quick grin. "My mother had a firm belief that if you were to eat, you had to help out. That included cooking and cleaning. Not just in the kitchen, but the entire house."

The small fact fit well with how he envisioned Sonar. Not afraid to get his hands dirty, no matter the chore. "Good to know. Next time I'll let you cook."

"Whoa." Sonar held up his hands. "I do just fine with frozen foods, opening cans, and boiling water. Don't be thinking that makes me a gourmet chef."

"Well, hell. I had great visions of baked Alaska," Jag teased.

"So not happening. At least not from me. I wouldn't know where on earth to begin."

By the time the wings were done, Sonar had placed the rest of the meal on the table and filled their drinking glasses with ice. Jag set a bottle of soda on the table, poured, and went to fetch the main part of the meal, putting it in the center of the small wooden table bracketed by a wooden chair at each end.

They each filled their plates and started to eat hungrily.

"Not bad for a quickie."

Jag shrugged. "I'm like you. I won't starve. Just don't expect anything fancy either."

"Noted." Sonar took a bite of hot wing. "Ronnie is your cousin, right?"

"Yeah."

"You said you were raised on the streets. In foster care. Didn't know what you were. So, when did you finally learn you were a shifter and find family?" Sonar chewed slowly before taking the rest of the meat off the bone. He dropped the remains onto his plate and picked up another wing.

Jag glanced over at him and forked a bite of his potato. "I was living on the streets, barely making it on my own, when an older woman stumbled across me one day. I'd been sitting outside a grocery store, counting the change out of my pocket to see if I had enough to buy a sandwich." He swallowed and took a sip of his drink. "She stopped and looked at me. Most people ignored me and moved on. This woman, Constance, actually saw me. She bent over and whispered that she knew what I was, a jaguar shifter, and would be glad to open her home to me."

"Wow."

Jag nodded slightly. He remembered the day well. His angel had arrived not with white wings and a beautiful voice, but as a gray-haired woman with plenty of sass to spare. "I was stunned and immediately skeptical. But she persisted. When she touched my shoulder, I felt it. She was a shifter too."

"She took you in?"

"Yeah."

"How old were you?"

"Sixteen."

Sonar winced. "A lot of time on your own."

"I scraped by." Jag shrugged. He'd survived. That's more than he could say for others in the same situation.

Sonar prodded him to finish his story. "Constance is related to Ronnie?"

"She's his aunt. Never mated, never had children. So, she adopted me."

"What was life like with her?" Sonar took a large drink of his soda.

"Heaven compared to the streets. She wasn't filthy rich and she worked hard for what she had. It was so much better than I could remember. We had food, a warm house. Took me a while to thaw toward her." He broke into a grin. "She insisted that hugs were a great thing. I didn't agree."

"But you did it anyway?"

"Yeah. I came to love her, wanted to make her proud of me. She enrolled me in school and I spent a whole summer catching up. I guess, as a teacher, she couldn't stand to see anyone just give up on education."

Sonar smiled. "I bet you excelled. Street kids are smart. Have to be to survive."

Jag bit the meat off another small bone. "I did okay."

"And learned to give hugs?" Sonar's lips twitched.

Jag grinned slightly. "That too."

"She taught you how to shift?"

"Not really. I was an early bloomer in that department. By sixteen, I'd managed a shift or two. Pretty rough and took forever but I managed it. Constance helped me concentrate and zero in on the ability. She pointed out a few other things."

"Such as?"

"How to detect other shifters. Picking out the scent of their species. How to detect lies in humans. How to be strong and gentle at the same time." All important lessons that benefited him to this day.

"Do you still keep in touch with her?"

"Yeah. When I can. She's the mother I never had." He made a mental note to call her and let her know he'd returned safe and sound. Like any mother, she worried when he was away.

"Gonna kick me to the curb if I sneak in and play with your ears again?" Sonar's lips turned up at the corners. The teasing brought out an amused spark in his blue eyes.

Jag couldn't resist joining in the fun. "You do and I just might ship you to Siberia."

Sonar arched an eyebrow. "Siberia, huh?"

"Yeah."

"Damn cold there."

"Yeah."

"I'd freeze my tail off."

"Then we'd call you Bobtail instead of Bat Ears."

Sonar snorted, bit back a smile, and lost. "Gee, thanks. I like that one *so* much better."

Jag grinned widely. Belatedly, he realized he'd laughed more than he had in a good long time. Sonar's sense of humor proved contagious. For that, he'd almost tolerate having his sleep disturbed by a spotted pest. Almost.

Sonar cleaned the vegetables off his plate and went back to eating wings like they were going out of style. "When did you join this motley crew?"

"A few years back. I went to college and got a degree, to please Constance, knowing that I'd never be one to sit in an office surrounded by humans, day in and day out."

"How did you find them? It's not like the shifter unit is advertised or anything." Sonar tilted his head as he cut up his baked potato. "Hell, if I'd have known about them, I'd have made a beeline for this place."

"Shifter Central is pretty off the grid. Understandably so. For the most part, you don't find them. They find you."

"Is that how you enlisted? They approached you?"

"Yeah. One of those career days in college. I had nothing better to do that day and figured I could at least walk past all the tables in the auditorium and see if they had anything to my liking. One of the recruiters picked me out, pulled me aside, and told me that as a shifter, I had a natural inclination to be a soldier. After a couple of visits, I agreed." Jag took a drink to wash down his food.

"Nice."

"It works. For now."

"I've met a few so far. Everyone seems tight-knit."

Jag finished the last wing and wiped his hands on a napkin. "We are. This is family. Much like Special Forces teams who become brothers in training, we do the same. Some didn't have much support before coming here. Others did. We're ragtag, for sure, but once a Predator, always a Predator."

"Ah ha. I was beginning to wonder if you guys had a nickname for yourselves." Sonar smiled at the label. "Better than 'Furballs R Us,'"

Jag snorted. "Say that to the wrong guy and he'll commence whup ass."

"Something to look forward to." Sonar gulped down the rest of his drink. Finished, he collected the dishes and took them to the sink.

"Did you call your family and tell them you've been transferred?"

"Yeah, I did that earlier. Told them I switched to a more specialized unit, presently stateside for as long as that lasts. Mom was pretty happy to hear that."

Jag placed his plate and utensils in the sink. "It must have been nice growing up in a loving family and knowing what you were the entire time."

Sonar stuck the plug in the bottom of the sink, turned on the hot water, and added dish soap. "Oh, I don't know. Nothing is perfect. Growing up with a sister was a bit challenging at times." He leaned in close. "Don't tell anyone, but Mom has some damning photos of me dressed up like a baby doll for my sister's tea party."

Jag's eyes twinkled as his mouth lifted into a wide smile. "Now that I have to see."

"So not happening." Sonar started washing, enjoying the familiar chore. It always reminded him of home when all his family worked together after a big meal.

Jag pulled a couple of dish towels from a drawer. He spread one out on the cabinet. The other he kept in hand, taking the first of the utensils from Sonar right after they were rinsed.

Never one to see housework as more than a necessary evil, Jag was a bit surprised at how much he enjoyed himself. He and Sonar worked seamlessly, their chatting filling in the silence, so the task passed much more quickly.

If anyone would have told Jag a while back that he'd be happily washing dishes with another man while shooting the breeze, he'd have called them ten kinds of crazy. Yet here he stood, pretty damn content.

Except every time Sonar leaned close, he caught a whiff of his unique scent. Musky. Woodsy. Manly. Enough to get his attention and get his engine ready to rev at a moment's notice.

And if I don't get my mind off him, I'll be sporting a boner even camos can't hide. He opted to pick up the conversation where it fell off. "You didn't mention you spoke with your father."

"He was killed when I was fourteen."

Jag paused and met Sonar's eyes. "I'm sorry. Tough age to be without a father." He automatically accepted the clean plate, dried it, and placed it on the small, growing stack of clean dishes on the counter.

Sonar nodded. "He was a bank manager. Some idiot tried to rob it. Dad stepped in the line of fire to protect his employees. He might have gotten away with it, but he tried to tackle the guy. The gun went off, killing Dad instantly." Sonar's voice faded.

"I can see where you get your bravery from." Jag reached over to squeeze Sonar's shoulder.

"Nothing compared to you." Sonar rinsed the last fork and passed it over.

Jag accepted it, wiped it with the towel, and started putting away the dishes. "Don't go there. I'm no saint or superhero."

Sonar let out the water and wiped his hand. "You've overcome some pretty fucking bad odds. That's to be commended."

Jag blew off the compliment. He hated praise. Never knew how to accept it. Instead, he preferred a quick pat on the back, a "good job," and being left to go about his own way. Opening the fridge again, he plucked a couple of beers from a shelf and tossed one to Sonar, who caught it easily.

After popping the top, Jag made his way into the living room and sat down in his favorite recliner, a comfortable recliner Constance had bought from Goodwill for his first apartment.

Sonar followed along, plopping down in the center of the couch. Sprawling was more like it.

Jag noticed how Sonar lounged on the couch, especially after placing his beer on the coffee table and spreading his arms over the back of the couch.

Wonder if he does the same in bed or maybe he's a secret cuddler.

And I'm so not going there.

"I'll take the couch."

Jag shook his head. "No reason to. There's a perfectly good bed in the room next to mine."

"Thanks."

"No problem." Jag took another drag from the bottle. "Bathroom is the first door on the left. Your bedroom is the last."

"Got it." Sonar stood up, collected his ruck, and made his way to the bathroom.

Jag watched him go, noting Sonar's powerful build and that fine ass Jag had fucked once before.

Sonar paused at the entrance to glance back at Jag. "Siberia, huh?"

"Yeah. Siberia."

"Well, shit." Sonar entered the room and closed the door behind him.

Jag smiled.

Whatever was to come in the foreseeable future, at least it would be pretty damn entertaining with Sonar around. Not to mention the eye candy he sported as well.

Shaking his head at his rampant libido lately, Jag turned back to the necessary chores at hand. He unloaded his backpack, tossed the clothes into a couple different piles and carried them to the laundry room. He returned, gathered up Sonar's clothes, tossed some in, and started the washer. Task done, Jag lugged his half-empty pack to his bedroom in order to unload the rest.

Absently he dug through the pockets, removing each item, checking it, before either setting it aside to change out or replace it. He methodically worked from side to side and front to back, going over every item. All were essential, and if he found himself in a pinch, he'd need them to survive. Thus, he checked them fairly often, trading out when necessary. His career didn't forgive laxness or ill preparation.

Jag's fingers dug deep, hitting something small and metal. He pulled back and stared at Mark's ring. Slowly he rotated the golden band in order to read the inscription. His heart stuttered, emotions welled up, and tears sprang to his eyes. Memories assailed him, everything from their first meeting to their marriage, and then some, played like a slideshow through his mind. Pain returned as he saw once again the moment Mark had been killed.

He closed his eyes and shoved away from the horrific memory in order to focus on the happier times. The goofy smile Mark had on his face when Jag slid the ring on his finger. The brightness in his eyes. The bubbly happiness as their dream finally became real.

Jag blew out a breath, opened his eyes, and eyed the ring more.

So many memories, nearly all of them good. He'd had five wonderful years with Mark. More than some people get. With that scrap of wisdom, he stood up, walked to his dresser, and pulled a velvety box out of a drawer. Jag opened the lid, saw his own ring inside, then gently placed Mark's matching one right next to it. The bands kissed in the confines of the small protective container.

Jag smiled sadly at the irony. He'd give just about anything to bring Mark back for one more embrace.

If wishes were horses....

He took another long look before closing the lid, the slight snap signifying the end of one life and beginning of another.

Jag replaced the case in the drawer and shut it. *The past is the past. Nothing can change that. We remember and move on.* He recited the words of wisdom he'd read at one time. Somehow they seemed fitting right now.

The sound of footfalls in the living area drew his attention.

Three years ago, he hadn't thought he could ever open his heart to another man. Today he knew better. And the man who fit the bill had just finished with his shower.

Jag quickly replaced the items he'd removed and zipped up the backpack once more before leaving his room and striding down the hall.

He caught sight of Sonar standing in a pair of loose gray sweats and a long-sleeved T-shirt. A pair of white athletic socks completed the package. His short hair had been combed, yet still held plenty of dampness, testament to a thorough cleaning and quick towel dry. Sonar turned and grinned. "Your turn."

Jag nodded, ignoring his body's great interest in his roommate. No matter the clothing, Sonar made for excellent eye candy. Jag flashed back to their one time together, felt his cock begin to harden, and cussed himself for lack of control. They'd just arrived home, were exhausted, and he wasn't about to chance ruining a potentially developing relationship because of his randiness.

He forced his mind back to the business at hand. "If you want to grab the laptop out of my bedroom, you can start writing up your report."

Sonar groaned dramatically. Jag empathized. He still had to do his as well.

"In your bedroom, huh?" Sonar's smile turned wicked. "Checking out porn sites in bed?"

Jag rolled his eyes, flipped him off, and headed to the bathroom.

He didn't need porn. He had his own perfectly built male model feet away. A definite temptation. One he hoped to sample again soon.

Chapter 16

"How are you doing?"

Jag leaned back in his chair and stared at Mac drolly. He'd been summoned by Ronnie this morning to report straight to Mac's office. Typically, such an order didn't bode well. For Jag, it normally meant another assignment had come down the pipe. However, he didn't expect that to be the case. Not this time. Not now. "Good as new." He rocked his foot from side to side. "Not even stiff."

"Good to know." Mac eyed him critically. "I've read all the reports. That was one hell of a mission."

His gut proved right once again at Mac's comment. "Yeah." Jag wasn't sure where Mac was taking this conversation but prepared for a grilling.

He and Sonar had both turned in their reports yesterday, leaving nothing out. Mac had the ability to read between the lines way too easily. Better to just put it out there and deal with the fallout rather than suffer the Spanish Inquisition, otherwise known as a conversation with his boss.

"Now, level with me. How are you really doing?"

Damn Mac and his ability to read people. More than once Jag had wished for a commander who stuck more to the books and was less involved with the members of his team. He preferred more hands-off, but Mac didn't seem to like that style of management. He watched over his group, treated them all like sons, and stuck his nose into their business seemingly on a daily basis. Most of the guys blew it off as parental caring. Since Jag had grown up without much of a father figure, the level of involvement Mac insisted upon didn't always make Jag comfortable.

Still, it was nice to know the old guy cared. Mac had his back. There was no doubt. Three years ago, Mac had been a godsend, a solid support after Mark's death. He had opened his door to Jag, checked up on him, and offered a shoulder and a listening ear when the emotions ran free. Jag took him up on it a time or two. He hadn't regretted it then or since.

He took a second to formulate an answer. "Off-balance but quickly finding my feet." Truthfully, the constant reminders cut him to the core and would have done more if not for his spotter.

"That bastard didn't pull any punches. Yet you were able to hold it together and complete your mission. That takes some balls."

Jag shrugged. "I didn't have any choice. Besides, Sonar did more than his fair share of load-handling all along the way. Without him, I'm not sure I could have come out ahead."

As much as he had resisted Sonar's presence at first, he had grown to understand a few things as the mission continued. Sonar was a damn good man to have at his back, smart and perceptive as well. Without him pushing and stepping up to the plate, Jag knew he most likely wouldn't have made it back home. "He kept me focused and saved my life a couple of times too. He got us back home."

Mac's chair squeaked as he leaned back, placed his elbows on the armrests, and steepled his fingers against his chin. "You're a survivor, so I have faith you could have made it alone if there was no option."

Jag shook his head. Always before he had wanted to remain alone and solitary when working, especially lately. Now he knew Mac had been right all along. Without backup in the form of Sonar, he'd have been horseshit crazy, if not waiting in line for the permanent check-in to hell. "No way, sir. I thought I could, but I was wrong."

Slowly Mac bobbed his head. "I believe you. As stone-cold brave as you are, I would have expected even you to break under such relentless pressure. No one could have handled that kind of torment. I'm not sure others could have even with a spotter along."

Jag twined his fingers and waited. His heart sped, but he didn't feel the overwhelming, wrenching pain that had once become a daily suffering. *Time heals all wounds.* At least well enough to soften the pain now and again. The trek through Sandman's game of heartbreak had reopened some wounds, sure. Years of acceptance and carrying on lessened the blow. Add in Sonar, and he had managed to scrape by, his hide and emotional health mostly intact.

When Mac remained quiet, Jag spoke up. "Credit Sonar. Without him I'd be one psychological nutcase right now." The soft admission carried truth.

Mac sat forward. "I've noticed the two of you formed a tight bond while out there."

Here we go. "Yes."

"He's tough. Fearless. More than capable of fitting in with the elite team."

Jag nodded. He wouldn't have mentioned the group to Sonar if he hadn't thought the ocelot shifter could hack it. "True."

"So?"

"So what?" Jag knew what Mac dug for. He just wasn't ready to open up that particular can of worms.

"I've seen the looks between you two. There's more than sniper and spotter there."

Why again do I have a commanding officer that is more like a Jewish mother than a hard-nosed drill sergeant? "We're friends."

Mac arched an eyebrow. "I'd wager you both might want more than that."

Worse than having the sex talk, I swear. Jag shot Mac his most bored expression. "Mac...."

Mac held up one hand. "None of my business, I know. This is coming from me as a friend, not your superior. I haven't seen you as relaxed or happy in years. Sonar seems to be responsible for that change. I can see it. The whole team can. They've all commented on it, so take my word of advice. Hang on to that. Happiness is rare and fleeting in our business. If Sonar gives you that, then you're damned lucky. Keep him."

Jag wasn't sure what to say. Knowing he'd been the topic of gossip around base didn't rile him too much. The guys were always yapping about someone or something. The fact that Mac picked up on the subtle nuances between Jag and Sonar didn't surprise him either. Mac missed nothing. Besides, Mac had told him what Jag already knew: he and Sonar clicked.

He just needed to find the right time to talk to Sonar and find out if his partner was on the same page.

A knock at the door interrupted them. Lily, Mac's secretary, stuck her head in the door. "Sonar's here to see you, sir."

"Send him in."

Jag glanced up and met Sonar's curious yet slightly worried gaze as he walked into the room.

Sonar took the seat next to Jag, tilted his head toward Jag, then turned his attention to Mac. "You wanted to see me? Er... us?"

"Yes. Yes, I did." Mac folded his hands on his desk. "I've read over the reports and am very pleased with how everything turned out. Both of you did an exceptional job under extenuating circumstances. Not everyone could have pulled off what you guys did."

"Thank you, sir." Sonar answered.

Jag smiled to himself at Sonar's stiff military protocol. He'd settle down with time. None of the shifters stuck to such formality for long.

"That being said, there's a couple of things we need to attend to." Mac pinned Jag with his gaze. "You need a psychological evaluation before you can go back on active duty. You're scheduled with Dr. Howard—" He checked his watch. "—in forty-five minutes. After that, you're on leave."

"But...."

"No buts. Go watch some whales, visit an art museum. Build a castle in the sand. I don't care what you do as long as it doesn't involve training. The last thing I need is Misty nipping on my ass about your recovery and missed downtime."

Jag didn't bother to argue. He knew an order when he heard one. "Yes, sir." Being ordered to see the shrink wasn't a shocker. After all he'd been through, Mac didn't have much choice but to ensure Jag could still handle his job. He'd be grounded until the guy gave him a thumbs-up.

"Good. Take a couple of days. I'll have Dr. Howard's recommendation on my desk by tomorrow. We'll go from there."

"Fine."

Mac turned his attention to Sonar. "You'll need a day of orientation. There's paperwork, rules, special unit protocols that you need to be made aware of. Your physical exam has to be done as well. All that starts now. Misty is expecting you in fifteen minutes in her office."

"Yes, sir." Sonar's shoulders lowered as if the tension slowly drained from his body.

Jag knew the feeling. It had taken him years to sit comfortably in front of Mac. Big, burly, and downright scary, Mac could make the strongest man wet his pants when on the warpath.

"Dismissed."

Standing, Jag led the way out of the room. He paused in the hallway and waited for Sonar to catch up. "Orientation. Let me tell you how much fun *that* is."

Sonar snorted. "Speaking of, which is it going to be? Whale watching or building castles in the sand?" Sonar quirked a grin at Jag.

Jag flipped him off. "Smartass. Enjoy your exam. Misty doesn't know the word gentle."

Sonar slowed his steps. "I thought she was just going to listen to my heart and lungs, then tap a rubber hammer against my knee."

Jag grinned ruefully. "Wishful thinking, Bat Ears. That woman will know you inside and out before you're done."

"Well, hell."

"Just remember to turn your head and cough while she's checking out your junk." Jag laughed and sauntered out the door.

"Asshole." Sonar's retort carried to Jag's ears.

He just chuckled all the more.

Chapter 17

COMPLETELY WORN out, Jag entered the front door of his home, lifted his nose, and drew in a mix of delightful scents. Sonar and pizza. After the endless session with the counselor, he needed downtime, food, and quiet to decompress. The particular combination that awaited him promised all that and more.

He'd spent about two hours in his psychological exam, which seemed more like an eternity. Probing questions drew out his whole story from before and his latest mission. He ran the gamut of emotions, from anger to deep grief, forced to relive the worst days of his life. After the session finally ended, restlessness drove him to get away for a while, to be alone, and regain his composure. He had spent most of the afternoon in his jaguar form, running through the dense woods, physically working out the adrenaline that surged through his veins at the harsh memories. When his energy ran out, he changed forms, found an old downed log, and cried.

"Hey, just in time. Pizza should be done in a few minutes."

Jag walked farther into the house until he found Sonar sitting on the sofa, his long legs stretched out in front of him. He held a beer bottle in one hand, the television remote in the other.

Eyeing Sonar, Jag found him no worse for wear. Not that he expected anything different after a day of sitting around on his ass. "Passed the physical exam with flying colors?"

Sonar rolled his eyes. "Yeah. And you were right. That woman doesn't know the meaning of gentle."

Jag attempted a grin and failed. Amusement proved beyond his capabilities right now. "Told ya." He made his way to the kitchen, opened the fridge, took out a beer, and returned to sit down in his recliner. He'd been sitting all day long, but it still felt good to just kick back and take a load off.

"That bad?"

Jag sipped his drink before meeting Sonar's curious gaze. For a second, he debated blowing everything off. Common sense told him

Sonar would pry it out of him anyway. Besides, trust earned didn't waver because of one shrink visit. "Yeah."

"Want to talk about it?"

Jag shrugged. "The doc knows how to needle every fine detail out of a guy. Felt like he was literally probing my mind."

"Ouch." Sonar leaned forward, resting his elbows on his knees.

"Rehashed everything. Mark's death. The hunt for Sandman. The last assignment." Jag picked at the label on the bottle. "I'm drained."

"What do you need?"

Jag peered up to see the concern written clearly on Sonar's face. "Just food and a hot shower."

"Coming right up." Sonar smiled slightly and started to stand.

"I told Mac you anchored me, reeled me in, and kept me sane. Told the wizard that too." The wizard was Marine slang for a psychiatrist.

Sonar sat back down. "Okay."

"I meant it." Jag swallowed another sip. "You kept me from going off. I owe you."

"We're a team, Jag. That's what we do for each other." Sonar strode over and squeezed Jag on the shoulder.

The touch sent a wave of comfort through Jag's body. His tension immediately eased as if Sonar had drawn out the remaining ill effects with a single hand. He craved the salvation Sonar offered and something more. Something lasting. Looking up, he caught Sonar's eyes, saw the tenderness reflected on Sonar's face, and decided to throw out the question that sat on the end of his tongue. Just as he opened his mouth, the timer dinged loudly.

"Dinner's ready."

Jag shut his mouth and nodded, the moment interrupted and gone. For now. He'd find another time to coax out Sonar's feelings and expectations.

Beer in hand, he followed Sonar to the kitchen, collected a couple of plates and napkins, and took a seat. Sonar set the meal in the center of the table and they both dug in.

"What are you going to do with the rest of your leave?"

"Once I talk to Mac, I'll know for sure." He couldn't enjoy himself away from base until he knew the results of his evaluation and how it would affect his future with the Predators.

"When should he know?" Sonar bit into his pizza with gusto.

"Tomorrow morning. I'll go to headquarters with you and talk to him." Jag finished his first piece and grabbed another.

Sonar eyebrows furrowed. "Are you worried?"

Jag shrugged. "The way I see it, I'm as sane as I ever was." Which was true. He'd been grounded three years ago for over a month while he processed all that had happened with Mark's death and his hunt for Sandman. That had given him plenty of time to think, to heal, to work through the worst part. He'd chafed to return to duty the whole time, but Mac stood firm. Rightfully so. Because of that, Jag had been able to shoulder this latest round of torture. Sandman had reopened past wounds; that was a given. Yet Jag had had time on his side, which made them less traumatic than if they had been fresh. Not to mention Sonar right there supporting him every step of the way.

"Good to know. Here I thought your smartass attitude might fade."

Jag grinned. Sonar knew how to add a grumbling note of humor into just about any situation, a talent Jag appreciated. "No such luck."

"Well, shit."

A MUTED scream woke Sonar instantly. He glanced around the darkened room, heard the distressed sound once more, threw the covers off, and darted to Jag's bedroom. His heart sped as a number of scenarios, none of them good, raced through his mind. He skidded to a halt beside the bed, searching Jag's face in the process, his advanced eyesight allowing him to see with ease despite the lack of artificial light.

His gut knotted as Jag let out another cry, his hands fisted in the sheets, his mouth open, eyes closed, and a face frozen in a grimace of absolute agony. Great tremors wracked Jag's body as he twisted and fought against invisible bonds.

"Jag. Jag. Wake up. It's a dream. Just a dream." Sonar called to him, knowing better than to try to shake him awake. Muscle memory sometimes lasted forever, as did survival instincts. Anyone dumb enough to touch a highly trained military person as he thrashed in a nightmare was risking his life. Jag wouldn't aim to hurt him, but he couldn't control his reflexes either. Much better for both of them for Sonar to hang back and coax him from his nightmare. "Jag, I'm here. Just follow my voice. Come back to me."

Sonar empathized with Jag. He'd woken up more times than he could count in the very same way, although always alone. He didn't have any doubts what the nightmare entailed or stemmed from, not with their recent world tour filled with painful memories, death, and frustration.

Jag drew in a tortured breath and jerked. His eyes flipped open. Awake, but not quite.

Sonar tried again. "Come on, Jag. I'm right here. Just follow my voice. You're safe. I promise."

Gradually, Jag's body lost the intense tightness and began to relax into the mattress. His facial features eased as well. Ragged breathing leveled out as Jag's eyes began to focus once more.

"Hey there, big guy. You're okay. Just a bad dream." Sonar sat down on the edge of the bed, knowing the worst had passed. "Back with me?"

Jag wiped at the sweat on his forehead, his gaze scanning the room before latching onto Sonar. "Shit."

"Bad?" Sonar reached out to lightly grasp Jag's hand. He needed to ground Jag and physical contact did just that. As much as he wanted to draw Jag into his arms and hold him, he dared not. Jag had way too much pride and prickly tendencies to know how he would react.

More than that, Sonar just wanted Jag to heal. To be whole again. To not suffer any more at the hands of Sandman in the form of flashbacks and dreams.

Jag sat up in a rush and slouched. He looked straight ahead at the wall. "Aren't they all?"

Sonar scooted back to give Jag a bit more room but remained close enough for their legs to touch. "Yeah, but I have a feeling this is beyond bad."

For a long time, Jag remained mute. His breathing returned to normal before he lifted his head once more. "Sandman."

Sonar nodded. Not surprising after Jag had spent an extensive amount of time in a counselor's office today, purging his emotions by reliving the worst days of his life. "Mark too?"

Jag shook his head and met Sonar's gaze. "No. It was you."

Sonar blinked at the intensity in Jag's amber eyes. Possession, need, and white-hot desire all rolled into one. He cupped Jag's cheek and rubbed his thumb over the light amount of facial stubble. His stomach flip-flopped as his heart picked up speed. Sexual tension crackled through the air as Sonar absorbed what it meant for Jag to dream of him. Before he could say anything, Jag bracketed his head, pulled him close, and sealed their lips with a fiery hunger.

Sonar opened and gave back, needing Jag's touch more than his next breath. He sucked on Jag's upper lip, then pushed his tongue inside, enjoying a quick game of tag before seizing another taste.

With a moan, Jag broke contact and stared into Sonar's eyes. "Are you sure?"

"Hell, yeah. I want you. Can't you tell?" He gestured down at the tent in his sweatpants.

A small grin grew on Jag's face. "Nice." He reached over and rubbed Sonar's dick through the loose clothing. "Very nice."

Biting back a groan, Sonar absorbed the splashes of sultry sensation flowing through his blood. Hotter than he ever recalled, he couldn't wait to feel Jag's bare skin under his hands, sample his big cock, and send Jag right over the edge in the process. "I need you. Damn."

Sonar placed his palm on Jag's crotch and caressed, easily feeling the erection underneath.

"Shit." Jag stood up, dropped his pants to the floor, then undressed Sonar in a slow tease. First the shirt, soon followed by his pants.

Standing, Sonar kicked free of the shackle of pants. He licked his lips as he stared at Jag's exquisite nude form. His broad shoulders, tapered waist, six-pack abs begging to be kissed. The thick, jutting arousal that bobbed with each movement. His own libido skyrocketed. "So fucking sexy." Sonar wrapped his fingers around Jag's dick and caressed.

Jag pressed their lips together once more. Sonar lost himself in the hot, deep kiss as Jag ran his hands over Sonar's chest, trailing down to discover his rampant cock. White-hot need washed over Sonar at Jag's exploration. "Need you. Now."

Sonar whimpered as Jag nipped his chin almost playfully. He caressed Jag's body, giving in to the almighty urge to nip and lick, especially over Jag's nipples. A nibble brought them to pebble hardness and earned a low grunt of pleasure.

Strong hands cupped Sonar's ass and squeezed. He sighed at the intimacy while running his tongue up the column of Jag's throat. Another passionate meshing of lips followed.

Jag broke off on a gasp. "You're driving me crazy."

"Damn, I hope so." Sonar grinned.

"Smartass." Jag smiled. "Stretch out on your back." He walked over to the bedside table, plucked a tube of gel out of a drawer, and climbed on the bed at Sonar's feet.

After grabbing a pillow, Sonar got comfortable, spread his legs, and watched Jag's face with keen eyes. He read lust and longing, heady want, and a spark of something more. Something softer.

Before he could analyze his findings more closely, Jag leaned over and drew Sonar's aching cock into his mouth.

Sonar's hips arched as he threw his head back into the pillow, the delightful pleasure rocketing him toward the pinnacle.

Jag flicked his tongue over the sensitive head before swirling all around. He sucked, laved, bobbed, and finally moaned. The vibrations radiated through Sonar's entire body.

He writhed, glanced down to watch, and panted.

Jag kept him on the brink for a moment longer before pinning Sonar with his gaze.

Sonar's breath caught. The intimacy of staring at one another hit close to home. He trailed his fingers over Jag's cheek, needing to give back.

Last time they'd had sex was a desperate need to escape reality and to reaffirm life in the midst of heart-wrenching pain and chaos. Maybe the nightmare precipitated it, but Jag wasn't acting like using Sonar was a simple physical outlet. This time meant so much more. Sonar could feel the difference in Jag's touch, his kiss, his slow, gentle motions. This wasn't about the nightmare; this was about two men coming together with affection. Making love to one another.

Jag sat up, opened the lube, and squirted a generous amount on his hand. He coated his cock in a couple of smooth strokes before adding more. He maintained eye contact as he found Sonar's hole, dipped two fingers inside, and spread the slippery gel around.

Sonar bent his knees, allowing easy access to the place he needed Jag the most. The in-and-out motions foretold of a grand loving to come. He couldn't wait. "More. I'm ready for more."

"Patience." Jag added a third finger into the mix.

Sonar bit back a small cry at the stretching burn. He blew out air and focused on the pleasure. Quickly, the discomfort faded completely. The same would happen when Jag covered him. Taking Jag's big cock had been a challenge the first time, yet full of rewards. He had no doubt this round would prove even better.

Just as Sonar hit the point of begging, Jag removed his hand, scooted forward, lined up their bodies, then pushed in languidly. He lowered his upper body to rest on his forearms and brushed sweet kisses over Sonar's chest and face.

Pressure stole Sonar's breath. He forced himself to push back, to open up and invite Jag in deeper.

Jag took the hint, moving forward a centimeter at a time. The deliberate pace made Sonar's head spin. He lifted his legs until his knees rested against Jag's sides. The new position shoved Jag's cock deeper and rubbed Sonar's hot spot at the same time.

Sonar's hiss turned into another moan of heightened pleasure.

"Okay?"

Sonar met Jag's gaze steadily. "Yeah. Oh, fuck, yeah." He ran his hands through Jag's hair and pulled him down for another kiss, this one filled with passion and unspoken words. Sonar gave as he'd never given before.

Jag began a leisurely rhythm, short, deep jabs at first that transitioned into longer thrusts. Each one brushed Sonar's gland, sending a near-constant rain of erotic fire through his system.

The inherent closeness of the face-to-face position gave Sonar everything he needed and more. He ran his hands over Jag's back and sides, exploring to his heart's content. He lifted to meet Jag's penetrations, wrapped his legs around Jag's back, and hung on for a journey of the senses. The slapping of their bodies filled the air, as did the spicy scent of sex. Jag's grunting and pants spurred Sonar onward despite the sedate pace.

"So fucking tight. Hot." Jag kept the speed unchanged, but added more strength to each downward movement.

"Yes." Sonar nipped at Jag's earlobe. "Oh, shit. Right there." He latched onto the bright sensation, grabbed Jag's ass, and tried to pull him deeper. To join them so well that nothing could tear them apart.

However long they kept up the sweet interlude, Sonar didn't know. Time failed to register with Jag's loving attentions taking center stage. Sonar couldn't get enough. Always tiptoeing toward the pinnacle, but refusing to go over. Not yet. He was enjoying this moment way too much for it to be done in a few seconds. Besides, he needed Jag to be right there with him for the powerful climax sure to come.

Sonar met Jag's open mouth with his own. He licked Jag's upper palate, then his lips. Instinct drove him to pull back and expose his own neck, to show his submissive role, while receiving Jag's everlasting thrusts. His balls drew up and a tingling at the base of his spine warned of imminent orgasm.

"I'm going to," Sonar gritted out between clenched teeth. Valiantly, he tried to stem the tide—only to postpone it for a few brief seconds.

"Come already, babe. Let me feel your ass dance on my cock as you do." Jag grunted, shoved in deep. Once. Twice. A third time.

Sonar saw stars. He cried out as the first pulse of cum hit him in the chest. Hard waves of bliss surged through him, in time with each stream jetting from his cock.

"That's it. Come for me." Jag began to groan. He lowered his angle, plowed in hard and fast, before stopping with a harsh, muted roar.

"Fuck." Sonar felt the warmth of cum from Jag's fully lodged cock in his ass. The knowledge added more fuel to his slowly ebbing fire.

The last moment slipped away, leaving Sonar sated and satisfied. He opened his eyes to find Jag resting on Sonar's chest, his breathing still ragged.

Sonar cupped Jag's cheek. When Jag lifted his head, their eyes met. Sonar's heart flipped over. "We're good together."

"Yeah." Jag turned his head to press a kiss to Sonar's palm. "Damn good."

Seconds ticked by while they stared at one another. Sonar grappled with what to say. The tender admission sat on the tip of his tongue, but he couldn't force it out.

Jag also remained mute. He nuzzled Sonar's neck, lapped at his earlobe, and ground his pelvis against Sonar.

"Keep that up and we'll both be wearing my cum." Sonar grinned wickedly.

"And that's a problem why?" Jag arched an eyebrow.

"Well, when you put it that way…." Sonar pulled Jag down for another hot kiss. He wrapped his legs around Jag's back and whispered against his lips. "Fuck me again."

Jag didn't even hesitate, much to Sonar's delight.

Chapter 18

"I'LL CATCH you at lunch."

"Sounds like a plan." Jag watched Sonar amble down the hall, noting the powerful movement, the perfectly shaped ass, and the carriage full of self-confidence. Sonar put other men to shame with his physical looks, at least in Jag's opinion. Sonar slipped through the door and out of sight. Too bad. He'd provided some nice scenery.

This morning Sonar had a gamut of training assessment before being placed in one of the training rotations permanently. Until a mission came around, that is.

Jag sighed wearily. He'd finally gotten to sleep last night after sex with Sonar. Between the release and Sonar wrapped around him, he had drifted off peacefully with no further nightmares. Thankfully. Still tired, he felt more refreshed than expected. More than enough to waltz into Mac's office and hear his fate.

Images of last night popped through his mind. The heady lovemaking. No pump-and-dump sex like the first time they'd been together. That had been all about tension release. This time was a far cry from average in the form of lovemaking. He'd been around the block enough times to know the difference. Tender, sweet, and intense described the way he and Sonar had come together. He couldn't mistake the currents flowing between them. They'd been friends with benefits before. Now, the scales had decidedly tipped in favor of something stronger, deeper, and more lasting.

Sonar soothed him, amused him, and made a damn good partner. He also brightened up the days and supported Jag in so many ways. Jag knew the score. Prepared to open up about his feelings, he had to find the time to sit down and have a serious discussion with Sonar, get an indication of Sonar's wishes, and plan a trajectory from there. Entirely possible if life didn't keep getting in the way.

Maybe we'll just have to finally have that date Sonar promised back in Kunar. The idea put a smile on Jag's face. About time they actually did something more than go through the motions as roommates and occasional lovers. A bit of romance never hurt either.

First things first.

Jag made his way down the hall toward Mac's office. Finding the office door open, Jag tapped anyway, drawing Mac's attention.

"Jag. Come in." Mac scribbled on a couple of pages before shutting a manila folder and staring at Jag.

Quietly, Jag took one of the chairs in front of Mac's desk and waited. Patiently. As only a sniper could do.

As usual, Mac's expression gave no indication of his thoughts.

"I thought you were on leave." Mac's gruff tone came across without bite. He crossed his arms on his desk and watched Jag like a predator skimming an area for prey.

"Thought I'd stop by and see what those psych results showed before I head off to the beach to build sand castles as ordered."

Mac snorted. "The day you take a shovel and bucket to the beach, I'll resign and help you bury the body."

Jag halfway grinned. Mac would do it too. He had known his commander long enough to say that for a fact. He leaned back in his seat and folded his hands on his lap. "What's the verdict?"

"Getting right to it, huh?"

"No sense wasting time."

Mac nodded slightly. "Dr. Howard put you through the ringer, in his own words. He decided you were either one damn tough man or were completely pathological." Mac smirked. "I'd wager on the former."

The small vote of confidence steadied Jag's nervous concerns. "So I passed?"

"With flying colors. Howard recommended a day or two of leave before getting back into training. He also said to keep you on home base for a couple of weeks, just to let you rest up from about three too many missions in a row without mandatory downtime. I concur."

Relief spread through Jag. He'd been reinstated, almost making that torture session with the shrink worth it. Almost.

"After you check in with Misty." Mac stared at him sternly. "If she clears you for training on that leg, I'll give you free rein."

"Yes, sir." Jag didn't expect anything different. This part didn't faze him in the least. He knew his leg had healed perfectly and he'd regained his previous level of strength, agility, and abilities. Misty might turn him inside out, but he'd easily pass all her tests. "Anything else?"

Mac pursed his lips. "You look more relaxed. I don't suppose that has anything to do with Sonar or the fact that you're carrying his scent?"

Jag shrugged. He refused to enter into that topic, at least right now.

"Take it from someone who's been there. Sonar and you are a team package. On and off duty. Hang on to that."

"Matchmaking again?" Jag recalled the similar spiel from Mac before. He didn't question Mac's perceptive nose or his good intentions.

"Everyone needs a hobby." Mac smiled unrepentantly.

"And you picked *that* one?" Jag rolled his eyes.

"Yeah, yeah. Don't you have a physical exam to take?"

Standing, Jag noticed the flash of amusement in Mac's eyes. Nothing got past his commander. Just another reason he liked the old man so much. "On my way." He started toward the door.

"Jag?"

He turned back. "Yeah?"

"Be nice to Misty. She's a bit temperamental today."

"Wonderful," Jag answered drolly. He showed himself out and strode straight to the healer's office.

Misty sat in her seat, staring blankly at the computer screen.

Jag sighed and knocked. "You're expecting me?"

She startled, then smiled. "Yes. Come in, drop trou, and have a seat on the exam table."

"Geez, Misty. Don't I get dinner first?"

She snorted and broke into a reluctant smile. "If you're good, I'll give you a lollipop afterward. How's that?"

He saw her concerns wash away for the moment and patted himself on the back. Misty might be a bit rough, and goodness knew mated to one of the biggest canine jerks around, but she was part of the team. That made her a sister. One that he happened to care quite a bit about. "What flavor?"

"Oh good grief. I'll bring in the whole box and let you have your pick."

He grinned. "Can I have two?"

She shook her head and sighed with exasperation. "Fine. You can have two. *After* we're done. So get stripping."

"Damn, woman. You've got a hankering to see me naked awfully bad." He ducked as she swiped at him and hurried into the adjoining room, the tinkle of her laughter following her.

SONAR WALKED into the modest cafeteria, wearing his new special camo, provided by the unit first thing this morning. He marveled at the chameleon-like qualities to the fabric, the same stuff he'd seen Jag sport in Afghanistan. A nice upgrade from regular fatigues, especially in the field.

Spotting Jag, he walked over, trying to judge his partner's mood by his expression. As usual, sternness ruled the moment.

Sonar dropped his ruck next to an empty seat at Jag's table. "Hey."

Jag lifted his gaze and raked Sonar from head to toe. "Nice duds."

"I thought so." Sonar grinned as he noted the relaxation in Jag. The lack of jaw tension, the carriage of his shoulders. Presumably all went well with Mac. He'd get the details as soon as he grabbed some grub. "Be right back."

After filling his tray, Sonar returned, plopping down in the seat next to Jag. He drank thirstily before picking up his fork and digging in. "How did your meeting go?"

Jag popped a grape in his mouth. "Good. I've got leave for another day then back on the training schedule."

"That's great." Sonar knew Jag would pass with flying colors if only given a chance. The jaguar shifter had to be one of the toughest men he knew, mentally and physically. No one else could have stayed the course and held it together. At least no one Sonar knew. "Missions?"

"Grounded for a couple weeks because I missed my last mandatory downtime about three months back. Supposedly I'll get a decent vacation down the road, but for now I stay at home base."

"Sounds like a good deal." Sonar didn't know all the facts, certainly, but so far Mac and the rest of the unit impressed him. Thorough, yet caring. Attention to details and to the whole solider made them stand out above some of the other regular military units that didn't always even know the names of those serving under them.

"How about you?"

"Not too bad. Got fitted for uniforms. A new weapon. Seems today is Christmas come early."

Jag grinned.

Sonar's heart tugged at the sight. Before, he'd worried that Jag would snap and lose himself along the way. Now, he realized that Jag had battled his inner demons and won. The fact that he could enjoy life proved inspirational and compelling.

"Felines." A tall, dark-haired man set his tray on the table.

Jag glanced up and flashed his fangs.

Sonar eyed the newcomer. He recognized the wolf shifter as the healer's mate, though they hadn't formally met.

"Mangy wolf." Jag took a drink of his water. "Sonar. Howler, Misty's mate. Poor unfortunate woman."

Howler snapped his teeth. "Keep it up, cat. I'm in the mood to kick someone's ass today and it might as well be yours."

Sonar blinked. With all the apex predators running around, surprisingly he hadn't noticed any fighting. Until now.

Jag remained calm, even aloof. Howler's grip on his utensils tightened until his knuckles turned white. His jaw ticked.

Wolf about to blow a gasket.

"Nice to finally meet you, Howler. Heard good things about you." Sonar worked to break the tension.

Howler spared him a glance. "Sonar. What a moniker."

"Yep." Sonar grinned. "Gonna tell me how you came by Howler?"

"He's a wolf. They howl at the moon," Jag replied.

Howler frowned. "Not even close."

"Uh-huh."

Sonar got the impression these two men had never seen eye to eye. Not the best of friends, they were still devoted teammates. Thus, they could tease one another. All part of the game to get the other guy's goat.

"He's called that because he howls when he comes." Another man with reddish-tinted hair took the chair next to Howler. "He's so damn loud the whole compound can hear him."

Howler glared at the newcomer.

"Sonar. Grizzly. The name says it all."

Glancing up, Sonar appraised the massive man. No misidentifying that one. He was built like his animal half and possessed an unmistakable bear scent. The big guy dwarfed the tray. Hell, he made the table and chairs appear to be designed for kindergarteners rather than adults. Tall, wide, and clearly extremely powerful, Grizzly put off an attitude of "don't mess with me" combined with "go ahead, I haven't killed anything yet today." Sonar's inner beast hissed and would have retreated if it had been in charge. "Grizzly." Sonar tilted his head marginally in greeting, not exactly comfortable with the latest addition to the table.

Grizzly dug into his food, peering up at Sonar now and again. "New guy, huh? Ocelot?"

"Yeah."

"Bet you run fast."

Sonar bristled. "Faster than a big old bear, that's for sure." He braced himself as a scowl covered Grizzly's face. Just as he prepared to use his tray as a weapon to bash over Grizzly's head and get the pulp beaten out of him for doing so, Grizzly smiled.

"I like you."

Settling back down, Sonar resumed eating, still keeping one eye on the huge man across the table. "Good to know. I like living, after all."

The bear shifter laughed. "Spot on."

"Okay. Got to ask. Is there a big bear shifter community around? Or are you a loner?"

Griz grinned. "Oh, there's a community. Bears are social, don't you know?"

"Really? Since when?" Howler quipped.

Grizzly ignored him. "A few prefer to be solitary, but we have a few groups hiding among the humans. Just look up championship high school football teams and you'll find a few of the cubs playing."

"Makes sense. Anyone the size of you would be hard to miss. Football coaches would be drooling."

"Yep. Hide in plain sight, so to speak." Grizzly took a forkful of meat and put it in his mouth.

"My family was isolated growing up. By choice. Shifters seem to stick together as a rule, but my family seemed to be the exception." Sonar eyed Howler. "So, tell me. Big-time shifter pack?"

"Wolf here. Packs are a given."

Sonar grinned. "Let me guess. You're the alpha?"

Jag and Grizzly snorted. Howler scowled. "That would be my father, the dominant prick."

"Which is why he's here with us. Can you imagine that kind of attitude taken with an alpha?" Jag smirked. "I see balls of fur flying."

"That's pussy fighting, you dickwad," Howler snarled.

Sonar bristled. "Goes to show what you know, dog breath."

"Hey now. No need to get personal," Grizzly replied, his intense gaze locked on Howler.

Howler shook his head. "Great. Grizzly made a friend. Things must be looking up."

Grizzly's amusement fled as he snarled at Howler. "You're asking for a pummeling."

"You think you can?"

"Has anyone gotten a good whiff of Misty lately?" Jag tossed in as he forked a bite of meat into his mouth.

Sonar and the others stared at him.

Howler lowered his fork as he leaned forward. "What in the hell are you talking about?"

Jag swallowed. "She examined my leg this morning. Just thought she smelled different."

Howler arched an eyebrow. "Different how?"

"Still carrying your scent, buddy. That's for damn sure." Jag glared at him. "No need to go ripping heads off."

"Then what?" Howler demanded.

"Something softer. I don't know. Just different, but not in a bad way." Jag took a long drink. "Go sniff her yourself and find out."

Howler left his tray in place and strode out of the room, no doubt making a beeline for Misty's office.

"Okay. Curious minds want to know. What does she smell like?" Sonar asked.

Jag ate another spoonful. "New hair product."

"Holy shit." Grizzly's mouth gaped open. "Howler's going to go nuts thinking it's something big."

Jag grinned. "Yep."

Sonar chuckled. Nothing around this place had appeared dull since his arrival. He doubted it would ever be.

He studied Jag for a long moment, saw the residual smile, and felt a sense of rightness. After all the turmoil, he was finally home. *With the man I've fallen for. Head over heels.*

"Let's go out to eat tonight. My treat. As promised." Sonar found himself tossing out the offer before he could recall they had company.

Grizzly blinked at them. "As in a date?"

Jag kept shoveling in food. "Okay."

"You two a couple?" Grizzly popped a french fry in his mouth.

Sonar and Jag shared a look, rife with promise. Sonar's stomach flipped as his blood began to pound once again.

"We're still figuring some things out," Sonar answered.

"Damn. Romance in the air and I'm always the last to know."

Jag chuckled and spared Grizzly a glance. "Someone has to be at the end of the line."

Griz snorted and went back to eating.

Blowing out a breath, Sonar smiled wide. Jag's silence spoke volumes, all in a good way.

Chapter 19

THEIR FIRST date. The one Sonar had promised him back in Kunar. He hadn't thought much more about it until Sonar blurted out the offer. No way would he refuse. More than free food motivated him. Time with the man who snared his interest proved irresistible.

Jag tucked his beige short-sleeved Oxford shirt into his jeans and checked himself in the mirror one last time. Casual yet comfortable. He snapped his dark-faced watch on his left wrist, turned, and left his bedroom.

Sonar stood in the living room, dressed in a similar state, albeit in a light blue that complemented his eyes. Every motion pulled the shirt snug in one location or another, outlining Sonar's physique.

Jag enjoyed the view and knew more than he would be appraising the ocelot shifter this evening out on the town. "Ready."

"Come on, then. We've got a reservation. If we're late, they'll give it away to some poorly dressed idiot waving Ben Franklins around." Sonar gestured toward Jag's SUV.

They climbed in. Jag took the driver's seat, started the engine, and headed for a laid-back steak house that traditionally served delicious meals. Even better, the place was owned by a shifter, wolf to be exact, and catered to others specifically. Humans weren't able to pick up on the nuances, not like shifters could. The scents alone spoke of who and what had been in the vicinity recently. Lots of felines, a few canines, even an ursine or two. The city didn't sport a large shifter population, but those who lived nearby made this particular restaurant a common hangout. With two dining areas, shifters were afforded relative peace and distance from their human counterparts, a plus in Jag's mind.

"I think Griz just about fell out of his seat today."

Jag grinned. "Yeah. Not much knocks that guy off balance. Nice to see he's human. Well, mostly." He hadn't wanted to blab about him and Sonar. Not yet, anyway. Griz wasn't a huge gossip, but Jag wasn't dumb either. News of their date had probably circulated around the entire team before afternoon training sessions began.

No matter. In order to spend time with Sonar, he'd endure tons of ribbing from the guys.

A few minutes later, they sat down at their allotted table, in a corner, well away from human customers and their penchant for eavesdropping. Only one other couple occupied the farthest dining room, both felines if Jag's nose proved correct. Jag and Sonar ordered their drinks and food after a quick scan of the menu. The waitress assured them the meal would be ready soon and hurried off to attend to another table.

"I've been looking forward to this," Sonar admitted.

"Yeah. Me too."

Their eyes locked and held for a long moment. Jag saw Sonar take a deep breath, his nostrils flaring slightly. His lips quirked up at the corners, enough to give away his happiness at Jag's declaration.

Just as Sonar started to speak, the waitress arrived with their drinks.

Sonar watched Jag take a long sip and smirked.

Jag's internal radar pinged. "What's so funny?"

"Oh, just that I thought you were quite the alpha with a stick up your ass when I met you. Now, I can see it's a team requirement," he whispered. His voice traveled no further than Jag's ears.

Jag reached for his napkin and flipped Sonar off in the process. "Wimps need not apply."

"Ain't that the truth." Sonar took a drink and returned his glass to the table. "I'm surprised you all can get along. All that posturing and alphaness. It's a testosterone factory around that place."

Jag laughed. "Nice way to put it." He considered his words for a second. "Everyone has their own story, but we all share something in common. Most are outcasts from their family groups for one reason or another. I pretty much raised myself on the streets and in the wilds of the jungles. That much you already know. Howler, Griz, some of the others have tight family units that exist as a society among the humans without being noticed or bringing about attention. All fine and good except the guys don't really fit in and aren't comfortable conforming to the traditional family expectations. They've found their way to the team, have all excelled, and discovered a new, more accepting family in the process."

Sonar nodded. "Makes sense to me. I just never knew." He glanced around the room before turning his attention back to Jag. "I guess I had it easy, growing up with a good family. Granted, there was no pack and only human children to play with, but I didn't complain. Hell, I didn't know I was different until my early teens when Dad pulled me aside and explained a few facts."

"The birds and the bees?" Jag asked.

Sonar rolled his eyes. "I knew about that a bit earlier."

Their meals arrived. After thanking the waitress, Sonar continued where he'd left off. "To tell the truth, I was damn relieved to know I wasn't just hallucinating about that other voice in my head. For a while, I thought I was destined for the loony bin."

Jag cut his steak into smaller pieces. "Been there, done that. The first time my inner cat spoke, it about scared the shit out of me."

Sonar chuckled.

"Once I figured out what I was and where the voice came from, I set down some basic rules."

"Yeah, right. I can tell you two are still bickering at times."

Jag took another drink and met Sonar's curious gaze. "What? Don't you ever argue with yourself?"

Sonar grinned. "More than I care to admit." He sipped his water. "It's pretty cute the way your face scrunches up when you're debating with your cat."

Jag snarled. "Cute? Not even close."

Sonar just laughed. "Now that's the Jag I know. Not about to take any shit off anyone without a stern scowl."

"You're asking for it."

"Oh, yeah." Sonar waggled his eyebrows. "Depending upon what 'it' is, I'm all in."

"Horny, huh?" The slight whiff of arousal carried easily to Jag's nose. A common-enough finding with Sonar around. Hell, he could say the same about himself. Put Sonar in the vicinity and he couldn't help but notice a few things. Like the man's prime build, his natural confident carriage, his perfectly shaped ass....

Memories of last night flashed through Jag's mind. He doused them quickly before his body could respond with a hard-on from hell.

Sonar arched an eyebrow. "Maybe."

"Uh-huh. Something tells me you enjoyed last night."

"Big time." Sonar's eyes sparkled. "Like I said, we're good together."

"Damn good."

Jag met Sonar's gaze for a beat longer before delving back into his meal.

"I think we're worth a try."

Sonar's comment drew Jag's attention full force. He chewed and swallowed, reading Sonar easily from across the table. He thought about possible responses, then went with his gut. "Took the words right out of my mouth." The answer was right on the mark.

Relief and happiness radiated from Sonar as he beamed. The action tugged at Jag's heartstrings.

I'll give it a shot. Nothing to lose.

His inner beast chuffed in agreement.

Who am I to argue with such wisdom?

He laughed at himself, grinned, and took another bite, pretty well pleased with life at the moment.

SONAR DASHED ahead, his short fur coat shining under the slowly descending evening sun. Jag followed at a more leisurely pace as they explored the woods in their feline forms.

Dinner had been spectacular. Good food. Great company. Even the conversation remained light and teasing. All in all, a pleasant experience, one he would definitely repeat.

Too bad he couldn't sit back and digest his delicious meal. Sonar nagged him into taking a run through the cool evening air. Jag groused but tagged along anyway. Ocelots had the energy of a toddler hyped up on sugar, Jag decided. He made a mental note to wear Sonar out before their next meal so he could enjoy some peace after. Jaguars napped after a large meal; they didn't run around like a kitten chasing a butterfly.

Sonar zipped by again.

Jag studied Sonar's compact body as he gracefully traversed the uneven terrain, leaping over a downed tree trunk, and landing surefooted on the other side.

Sonar.

All through this mess, he'd been there, asking no more than to be treated like an equal and to watch each other's back. He'd led Jag back to his humanity, just like he was leading Jag through the outskirts of the training grounds now. Never once had he complained. Instead, he had stood in the trenches, chewed Jag's ass when necessary, and put a humorous twist on life that Jag had grown to appreciate.

Sonar climbed to the top of a decent-sized rock, swung around, and batted at Jag, smacking him on top of the head.

Jag frowned up at the little troublemaker and snorted.

So he wants to play king of the hill. I'll show him king of the hill.

Gathering his strength, he jumped on top of the rock, shouldered Sonar aside, and gave him a nudge right off the back.

True to his tenacious nature, Sonar returned in a flash, nipping at Jag's front legs, and shoving his lighter weight against Jag's much larger body. Jag simply sat down, flicked his tail, and stared at the small ocelot.

Sonar flashed his fangs and growled.

Jag rolled his eyes before lazily pulling his lips back to reveal his much larger canine teeth.

Obviously unimpressed, Sonar slapped him on the nose with his paw, claws sheathed.

Jag uttered a warning growl.

Sonar did it again.

You're asking for it, buddy.

The third hit prompted Jag into action. He stood up, grabbed Sonar by the back of his neck with his teeth, lifted him up in the air, then headed toward headquarters. Sonar squirmed, growled, and complained with each and every step. Yet he didn't fight the hold. Instead, he hung there like a disciplined ruffian child who dared not push his parent's temper any further.

Jag smiled to himself, laughing at Sonar's grumbling in kitty form. While Sonar probably didn't appreciate being treated like a cub, he also didn't seem too upset by it. If another shifter had tried the same thing with Jag, he would have been pissed. Sonar seemed to take the check in stride, being sure to offer up the proper amount of complaint along the way to maintain his ego.

Closing in on the headquarters building, Jag used one paw to open up the screen door and slip inside. Once there, he didn't stop until he found the breakroom, filled with a handful of team members just lounging in companionable bantering.

All eyes turned to him. A snicker broke the silence, followed by quiet chuckles, then rowdy laughter.

Jag sat down and dropped Sonar to the floor.

"Look what the cat brought in," Howler said, tongue in cheek.

"Awwww. Jag brought us a gift. Isn't he cute?" Misty smiled down at Sonar.

Sonar huffed, stood up, and stuck his nose in the air. Haughty came to mind, with a bit of a put-upon expression mixed in. He playfully swatted at Jag's face again, turned on his heel, and sashayed through the room with his tail straight up in the air. He looked back at Jag, sneezed, then strode out of the area as if he were walking down the red carpet.

Jag chuffed in amusement. Give Sonar credit for balls and a sense of goofiness.

"I don't think being carted around like a kitten fazed Sonar in the least," one of the other men noted.

"Nothing does. That little ocelot is like a rubber ball. He bounces back. Pretty laid-back too. Otherwise, I'd say Jag would have sprung a leak from having his face scratched up." Misty turned her attention back to Jag. "What do you think? Should we keep him?"

Jag met her stare for a long moment, grunted, then took a page from Sonar's book. He strode out of the room, his tail swishing, and humor in his heart.

All because of Sonar.

Yeah, I'm keeping him. Whether he knows it or not, Jag's inner cat made the statement a fact. Jag didn't bother to argue, not when he knew the words to be the truth.

Chapter 20

JAG STEPPED up to the door of Mac's office and paused. The message had come to him earlier in the day that the boss wanted to see him. Alone. In his office. His gut clenched at the ominous words relayed by Ronnie. The summons could mean anything. Considering he had spent his single day off running errands, grocery shopping, visiting his adoptive mother, and hanging out with Ronnie, he hadn't had much time to get into trouble. Besides, it wasn't like he'd take a nineteen-year-old kid anywhere dangerous.

Today he'd been training on the obstacle course and in the pool. The end of the day neared and he still needed to clean his weapons before going home for the evening.

He rapped lightly on the door.

"Come in."

Jag opened the door, stepped through, and closed it behind him. Mac sat in his large leather office chair. He glanced up, gestured to the remaining seat across the wide wooden desk, and clicked the mouse on his desk a couple more times. "Jag. Have a seat."

Plopping down, Jag stretched out his long legs and braced himself for whatever was to come.

"I've been working on something and needed some clarification about events in your report."

Curiosity piqued, yet he didn't show it. Snipers rarely showed anything at all. Just sat and waited for their opportunity to strike. Or, in this case, find out what bugged Mac enough to earn an order to appear. "Okay."

"You said Sandman spoke about being part of an experimental group. Regular military personnel willingly agreeing to be injected with serum designed to give them animal traits?"

"Yeah." Jag recalled the fight with Sandman. The admissions. The taunting. The battle that nearly cost him his life. Tension rolled over him. He clamped down on it, keeping it in check. "He said he started to become faster. Stronger. He could heal any wound." Jag glanced up and met Mac's gaze. "He also said Mark encouraged him to stop. Was concerned about his new hobby."

Mac's lips pinched. "Of killing."

"Presumably so."

"Which means there's others running around who were injected with the same concoction."

Jag knew where this train of thought led. He'd been down this road before. "And if they are still out there, the question becomes if they are struggling with their sanity and losing it just as Sandman did."

"Exactly." Mac clicked some keys and focused on the computer screen. "I've been digging, but can't find a single hint about such an experiment taking place."

Jag shrugged. "No surprise there. The government isn't really known for being transparent, especially when they are doing morally wrong things."

"True, but it makes my neck itch." Mac was a career military leader. He'd been through hell and back more than once, according to what Jag knew. Not much worried Mac, but this did.

"What do you want me to do about it?"

Mac met Jag's eyes. "Nothing. We don't have any leads to follow. No evidence to present it up the ladder. Just the boasting of one demented sap."

"That was right. No way was Sandman just another human. Nor was he a shifter." Jag recalled the scent, the break from sanity evident in Sandman's eyes. "I believe he spoke the truth. Whatever experimental drug they gave him, mixed with animal DNA, toppled him over the deep end."

"And that's what scares the shit out of me." Mac ran his hand through his hair. "I've put others in the know on alert. If there are more out there, they will pop up."

"With dead bodies left behind?" Jag grimaced at the logical conclusion.

Mac sighed wearily. "We pray not." He blew out a breath. "If you remember anything else, let me know."

"Sure."

Jag waited a beat longer. He hadn't been dismissed to go. Either Mac had something else to say or he'd encourage Jag to hit the road.

Normally, Jag could tell the difference. Today it was a toss-up. "Done with me?"

"Not quite."

Pulling on his patience, Jag waited.

"I'm putting you back on training duty, but keeping you grounded from missions for the time being."

Not a surprise, since he'd mentioned it before, but irritation flared anyway. He hated being told to stand down when a threat, one such as another Sandman, possibly ran loose. "I'm more than capable of taking out another bastard now or next week." He added determination and plenty of self-confidence to his tone.

Mac stared for a moment longer before shaking his head. "It's too soon. There's a reason we have mandatory downtime."

Anger unleashed inside Jag. *Now he's grounding me? He's got to be fucking joking. All of a sudden my downtime has priority?* "That didn't stop you from pulling me right off on another op the moment I finished a long tour. Months with no downtime." He gritted his teeth. "Seems to me that's a load of bullshit and useful only when it suits your or someone else's purpose. So come up with another reason because that doesn't cut ice with me."

For the first time, Mac's face reflected regret. "I would never have sent you if there had been any other choice."

The softening in Mac impacted Jag in a major way. His ire cooled immediately. He'd seen Mac in all sorts of moods, but never once did he recall seeing such self-loathing or repentance like he did now. Jag sat for a moment and offered up the truth. "There was no choice. You said it yourself: there was no one else to send that wouldn't have gotten their head blown off. You didn't make the rules. Neither did I. Sandman did, which forced our hand."

The chair squeaked as Mac leaned back slightly. "Just the same, our hands aren't being forced now. That means you're still assigned to base for the foreseeable future."

Jag scowled.

Mac sat forward once more. "I played with fire once with you. I refuse to do so again. Rest. Heal. Take some time to come to terms with what life dealt out. Enjoy some time to just hang out with the team. You've more than earned it."

Understanding Mac's point, Jag backed down. With no direct leads or any indication that another insane freak-turned-serial-killer was on the loose, Jag didn't need to go haring off across the world. Nor did he need to argue with his supervisor and chance getting demoted or worse either.

"Heard a rumor."

"Oh?" Jag already knew where this conversation was headed. Mac's rueful grin gave everything away.

"Seems you've taken my advice in the dating department."

"Uh-huh." Less than twenty-four hours. The gossip mongers were falling down on the job. Typically, the whispered secrets flew as fast as the speed of sound.

"Glad to hear it. Pretty damn cute, you carrying him around like a mother toting a cub."

Jag couldn't hold back the wolfish grin. "He's damn tolerant, I'll say that. Grumbled at the treatment, but so far hasn't come back to kick my butt for it."

"That's something." Mac steepled his fingers and tapped his lower lip. "You mentioned he made a superb team player. Knew what he was doing out there."

Unsure where Mac was going with this conversation, Jag answered truthfully. "He had my back. Held his own. Even saved my ass. You saw that for yourself. He's a Green Beret. Tough. Tenacious. He's all man and goes above and beyond." He couldn't have given Sonar a better compliment. Hell, if not for Sonar thinking on the fly, he wouldn't be sitting there now.

He owed Sonar and then some.

More than anyone else Sonar had been at his side, supportive and encouraging. His presence alone made Jag's day brighter and gave him cause to work that much harder to get his marbles back in line. He knew something existed between the two of them and intended to pursue it, was doing just that. At the pace of a fat caterpillar.

"That's quite a recommendation."

Jag nodded. "It's true and earned."

Mac read from his computer screen for a second before latching back onto Jag. "A mission has come up. I'm sending Sonar out with Griz."

"Where?"

"Kunar."

Jag's heart lodged in his throat. Protective instincts leaped to attention along with a hefty dose of possession. He didn't doubt that Sonar could handle himself and a seasoned veteran like Griz on the front lines. Yet that didn't quell the sudden apprehension in his gut. "Let me go."

Mac shook his head. "We've just been through this, Jag. You're grounded."

He's sending Sonar out and grounding me. Talk about a FUBAR mess.

Jag's inner cat growled in anger.

Right there with you, buddy.

Sucking in air, Jag reclaimed his calm demeanor with difficulty.

Conflicting emotions warred through Jag. He needed Sonar safe and needed to be there to make sure that happened. Sitting back home and wondering would drive him mad.

Suck it up, soldier. Every other loved one has to do the very same thing. Sit and wait for word, either good or bad. He knew the drill, just hadn't been on this side of the fence before.

"What did Sonar say when you told him?"

Mac rested an elbow on the armrest of his chair. "I haven't told him yet."

Perplexed, Jag cocked his head in question. Normally, a commanding officer didn't approach an individual team member and tell them about another guy's assignment. It fell under the "need to know" category and simply wasn't done as a rule. "Then why are you telling me?"

A long moment passed before Mac answered. "I need to know how being parted from Sonar will affect you. You two are close. Real close. I want to make sure I'm not derailing something big by sending him off for a bit."

Jag blew out a breath. "I hate being left behind."

"Noted."

"We've got a good thing going. Absence won't affect that."

"Good." Mac grinned. "Don't worry. It's a short one. Safe, as missions in Afghanistan go."

Which meant little to Jag. He'd been to the war zone too many times to mention. Safety didn't exist when three groups of insurgents all put a price on US soldiers' heads.

Mac sobered. "You've been through a lot, Cole. I care about you and Sonar too. Hell, all of you people are like my own kids. Hormonal, back-talking teenage kids...." He waved his hand. "I want you to find happiness. My gut tells me Sonar is the key. So, if pulling him on a mission right now interferes with the natural progression of things, speak up now, and I'll put someone else on the hop."

"We're stronger than you think." Jag's inner cat agreed with a soft roar.

Mac studied him for a few seconds. "I believe you're right. In that case, tell Sonar I need to see him if you catch him before I do."

"Yes, sir." Jag slipped out, closing the door behind him. He didn't stop walking until he had left the building entirely and entered the famed obstacle course at the far end of the grounds. Once there, he leaned against a large, weathered tree.

Sonar was being deployed. Back to the same hell on earth they'd just barely survived and returned from. Worse yet, Jag wouldn't be with him.

Worry knotted Jag's stomach.

Griz was a veteran and perfectly capable of navigating the ins and outs of a war zone without a single scratch. That didn't mean accidents and screwups didn't happen.

For the first time, Jag saw a future without Sonar and it bothered him. Immensely.

He'd gotten use to sharing a house with the ocelot shifter. Eating meals together. Sitting around and shooting the bull. Hell, he even enjoyed Sonar's playful and obnoxious ocelot form. The thought of that piece of his life absent pushed his shoulders down and tugged at his recently gained optimism.

I can't tell Mac to leave him behind. I just can't.

Pride and reason kept his mouth shut when asked if he'd be okay with Sonar away. He didn't need Sonar in order to make it through the long days, although Sonar made them better. He didn't have to have a babysitter, a cheerleader, or someone to pester him into a game of chase. While not a necessity, he wanted that very thing.

He wanted Sonar.

Friends. Lovers. Everything they could be together.

The confession felt right, though tempered by the upcoming revelation that Sonar would be whisked away to a place where nightmares became real.

What the hell am I going to do?

Jag sucked in air and stared at the ground. He couldn't change Sonar's orders and refused to crawl back to Mac asking for Sonar to stay. The reality of their career choice hit him square. Men were continuously coming and going from base. Missions seemed endless. That was part of being in the military. He just hated the fact that Mac was sending Sonar without Jag to watch his back. Yes, he trusted Griz, but it wasn't the same.

Jag sighed with resignation.

Time was fleeting and he couldn't afford to miss a golden opportunity. He needed to open his heart and step up to the plate.

There's only one way to do that: have a talk with my Bat Ears.

JUST AS Jag placed the pan of lasagna on the table, Sonar walked through the front door. He carried enough dirt to rival a dried-off mud wrestler. Grime streaked his face and hair. For all intents and purposes, he appeared to have been ridden hard and put up wet.

"Damn. What did they do to you today?"

"Live fire training."

Jag flinched. He hated that part. Live rounds were shot above everyone's heads as they crawled through mud and muck to reach their destination. Though little danger existed, tell that to the body's instinctive adrenaline surge. He'd gotten used to the drill over time but still dreaded it above just about any other training regimen. "That sucks."

"Tell me about it." Sonar dropped his ruck in the foyer.

As much as Jag hated to, he needed to pass along the message before it grew too late. "Mac wanted to see you."

"I know. Been there already."

Jag's mouth fell open before he shut it again. "When do you ship out?"

"0200." Sonar tilted his head. "How do you know about my orders?"

Truth time. "Mac called me in first. Told me his plans. He wanted to make sure I wouldn't fall apart without you here, and he wouldn't be stepping in the middle of our dating." The words came out clipped. Jag still stung from Mac's declaration. Yeah, his commander didn't really ask if he would crumble without Sonar here, but that's what he read between the lines.

Sonar blinked then shook his head. "Unbelievable."

Jag tensed. "What?" His mind took that single word a dozen different directions, most of them bad.

"I've never had a commander give jack shit about me or my personal life. It was always putting a body in a spot, no matter who it might hurt." Sonar rubbed his face. "It's just amazing to me that Mac would care enough to run it by you first, get your insight, and then ask me to go."

Jag released the breath he'd been holding. As irritated as he was with Mac right now, he couldn't deny the facts. "He's a good man." Turning, he collected the rest of the vegetables and placed them on the table with the entrée. "Dinner's ready when you are." He filled their glasses with soda and watched as Sonar stripped out of his work gear and carried it down the hall. "Let me throw these in first. I'll leave a dirt trail through the house if I don't."

Sonar returned several minutes later wearing only his boxer shorts.

Jag feasted on the vision and committed it to memory. They didn't have much longer before Sonar would have to be back at base in order to catch a ride straight to hell on earth. "Sexy."

Sonar's lips hitched up. "Glad you noticed."

"How could I not? Parading in here naked pretty much guarantees I'll look."

"Uh-huh." Sonar took his usual seat at the table and started filling up his plate. "Smells delicious. I'm loading up. After this, MREs are going to taste like cardboard."

"Yep. Better hurry back before you starve to death out there." Jag sat down and added some lasagna and vegetables to his plate. His appetite gone, he forced himself to chew and swallow the first few bites, barely tasting the pasta at all.

Never before had he been so antsy about a mission. Granted, he'd always been the one going. Since he typically worked alone, no one back here fretted over him. *Well, not quite true.* The team was his family. They thought of him and kept him in their prayers. He knew that as he did the same for each of them. Even with Mark, he hadn't worried too much. They were together. He could watch Mark's back and keep him safe.

Like that worked.

He shook aside the morbid reality and focused on Sonar.

"Don't take this the wrong way, but will you be okay with me gone?"

Jag saw the concern in Sonar's eyes and wanted to kiss it away. "I'll worry. That's a given. I hate that we can't go together, but Mac has me grounded for a while longer. Too many missions in too short a time. So he claims."

"Which is true and you know it."

"That doesn't mean much. I can do another mission or three if need be."

Sonar patted Jag's leg under the table. "That's just it. You don't need to right now. Griz and I have this one handled. Next time, though."

"Yeah. Next time, I promise. You won't be going without me."

"Deal." Sonar grinned. He commenced eating, swallowing before speaking again. "Don't worry. I'm more than capable of taking care of myself and one overgrown teddy bear at the same time."

Jag smiled reluctantly. The thought of Griz as a cuddly sleeping pet proved downright amusing. "You might refrain from calling him that. I'm pretty sure he'll beat you to a pulp for that particular nickname."

"I like to live dangerously."

"Yeah, well, yanking Griz's chain falls under the stupid category."

"So noted." Sonar smiled and cleaned his plate. Standing, he carried his dishes to the sink. "I'm going to hit the shower, then spend the rest of the evening with you before I have to get back to base."

"Okay." Jag watched Sonar head down the hall. When the bathroom door shut, he went to work clearing the rest of the table, putting the leftovers away, and filling the sink with soapy water. He'd wash the dishes later. Right now he had other plans. Namely, cornering Sonar and getting some things off his chest.

A few minutes later, Sonar returned, wearing only a towel and a mischievous grin on his face.

Jag arched an eyebrow as his body caught fire. The scent of arousal filled the air, causing Jag's cock to harden instantly. He ignored it for the moment, focusing on the reality of their short time left. "You should probably sleep while you can. Kunar isn't the place for peaceful naps."

Sonar approached, stopped right in front of Jag, cupped his chin, and sealed their lips together. "I'll sleep on the plane. Right now I want a proper send off."

Those words ratcheted up Jag's libido by leaps and bounds. He met Sonar's gaze and slowly smiled. "As you wish."

"Oh, I like that." Sonar chuckled.

Jag rolled his eyes. "You would."

Sonar wrapped his arms around Jag's neck, pulled him flush, and kissed him again.

Jag allowed Sonar to take the lead, content with being in the receiving role for the moment. He wrestled with Sonar's tongue, sipped, and finally mimicked Sonar's actions. The heated foray rewarded him with another taste of Sonar. His appetite whetted, Jag trailed his hands over Sonar's body, caressing all the hills and valleys, memorizing every inch along the way. "You're so fucking sexy."

"So are you. When you're naked."

Jag laughed as he took the hint. Stepping back, he started peeling off clothes in rapid succession. He kicked free, tugged on Sonar's towel, and peeked at the glorious treasure revealed. "Nice."

Sonar's cock bobbed as if sensing the admiration.

Reaching out, Jag encompassed Sonar's shaft in his hand, skimming his thumb across the tip. "Very nice."

A low groan escaped Sonar's throat. "Maybe we should take this to the bedroom. Unless you planned on bending me over the kitchen table?"

The idea had merit. Jag arched an eyebrow and studied the table before rejecting it. "We'll save the table for later. Bed now."

"You don't know what you're missing." Sonar waggled his eyebrows.

"I'm pretty damn sure I do. And if you don't get going, you're going to miss it all entirely." Jag smacked his rear to get him moving.

"Okay, okay." Sonar hurried back down the hallway and disappeared into Jag's bedroom.

Jag took a moment to watch the sight of Sonar's perfectly rounded ass. The muscles snapped and stretched with each step, adding to the beauty and grace. His heart picked up speed as his dick began to throb in demand. Slowly he followed in Sonar's footsteps, turned the corner, and spied Sonar spread out on the bed, idly stroking his cock.

Jag bit back a groan at the gorgeous picture right in front of his eyes. "Damn, Sonar. You know how to get my motors going."

Sonar grinned wickedly. "Turnabout is fair play." He kept jacking himself languidly, right in front of Jag.

Unable to wait a second longer, Jag strode over to the bed, plucked a tube of lube out of the nightstand, and tossed it on the covers. The necessary task done, he climbed on the mattress, crawled over to Sonar, and ran the tip of his tongue in a line from Sonar's low-hanging balls, across the sensitive skin in between, then right up the underside of Sonar's erection.

Sonar lifted his head and hissed. "Oh, shit." He arched his back, thrust his hips upward, and threw his head back onto the pillow.

Jag repeated the tongue bath, lingering much longer, before taking the mushroom head of Sonar's cock into his mouth. He caressed Sonar's balls, gently rolling them as he licked Sonar's dick like a favorite treat. Without pausing, he flipped open the cap on the lube with his free hand, squirted some on his fingers, then dipped his digits into Sonar's hole.

Tightness and heat met him. Jag eased two fingers inside, spread them, and pressed farther. Over and over, he worked the sphincter to loosen the snugness. He added suction while changing the angle of his wrist, bumping Sonar's gland lightly.

"Oh, fuck, yes." Sonar drew up his legs and spread them wider, giving Jag unencumbered access.

"Right there?"

Sonar arched into his hand. "Yeah. Oh, shit, yeah." He began to squirm to lift, to clamp down on Jag's fingers as if he could draw them deeper.

Jag smiled wolfishly. "So sexy spread out like this. I can't wait to fuck you."

Sonar's eyes narrowed. "Do it already," he gritted out the words, followed by a whimper of desperate need.

Satisfied that Sonar was prepared enough, Jag coated his aching cock with more gel. The entire time he watched Sonar's expressive face, noted the tightening, the smoky darkening of his eyes. Lust rode his partner hard.

And I have just what he needs.

Jag stretched over Sonar's supine form and snagged a pillow. "Lift up." As soon as Sonar did so, Jag placed it under Sonar's hips. He scooted close, sat back on his heels, and positioned Sonar's legs so they draped over his thighs. The sharp angle ensured he'd rub across Sonar's hot spot each and every time.

He placed the leaking tip of his cock against Sonar's opening, and pressed forward. Resistance met him for a couple of seconds before the tight ring eased. Jag took advantage and began a slow descent, watching Sonar's face the entire time for signs of pain.

Sonar grimaced and fisted his hands in the sheets. His leg muscles grew taut.

Jag paused, encircled Sonar's thick shaft with his fingers and began to strum. "Almost there."

By increments Sonar relaxed. He opened his eyes and pinned Jag with his gaze. "More. Now."

"Topping from the bottom." Jag chuckled. "Why isn't that a surprise?"

A growl escaped from Sonar's throat, whether in delight or warning, Jag didn't know.

He gave Sonar's cock a couple more rubs before releasing it. Gathering his strength, he started forward again, not stopping until he hit bottom with a grunt.

Sonar arched and jerked, his body alternating between clenching tight and pressing nearer.

The fine line between pleasure and pain.

Jag patiently waited before starting to ease back just a hair. Lazily, he repeated the motion.

"Oh, ohhhh." Sonar tilted his pelvis as his mouth fell open.

"That's more like it." In no rush, Jag kept up the snailish pace, using short jabs to make the most of his penetrations and elevate Sonar's arousal at the same time.

Sonar reached down, latched onto his cock, and began to stroke in time to Jag's thrusts. That lasted for a while before Sonar's motions grew more frenzied, more frantic.

Jag began to pant. His cock started to throb, his balls tightened to the point of discomfort. Still, he stuck to the course, not about to come until Sonar blasted off first.

He grasped hold of Sonar's asscheeks, using the resulting leverage to shove in deeper.

"Fuck." Jag gritted his teeth as tension radiated through his body and centered on his dick. With his orgasm imminent, he increased the angle all the more, picked up the pace, and deliberately brushed Sonar's gland with every back-and-forth motion.

Sonar's face screwed up and his breathing became erratic. His hand flew on his cock. A whimper escaped the trembling lips just before a growly shout.

Cum pulsed from Sonar's dick, hitting him in the chest.

Jag watched, the scene so stimulating, in combination with the moist tightness of Sonar's ass that together they sent him right over the edge.

"Oh, fuck." He plowed in deep, keeping his strong grasp on Sonar's body, holding him still while his buried shaft streamed again and again.

A couple minutes later, he pulled free of Sonar's body, walked to the bathroom and cleaned up, then began washing Sonar with a warm, damp cloth. Sonar hadn't budged an inch besides letting his legs straighten out when Jag moved. His hips were still elevated on the pillow. If he was uncomfortable, he sure didn't show it.

In fact, Sonar exuded sated bliss. His face appeared as lax as the rest of his body. Contentment and satisfaction flashed in his pretty blue eyes, along with something else. Something rarer.

Finished, Jag took the cloth back to the bathroom, tossed it into the hamper, then returned to the bed. He stretched out next to Sonar, moved the pillow up to their heads, and wrapped Sonar into his embrace. They spooned together for a while, each still coming down from his climax.

For Jag, it had been one of the strongest and best of his life.

All too soon reality invaded. Jag checked the clock on the wall and cringed. His enhanced vision allowed him to see well in the dark, especially with the moonlight streaming in the window as it did now. Three hours until Sonar had to be back at base. "I wish we had more time."

Sonar rolled over and gazed into Jag's eyes. "I know, but I'll be back home before you know it. You can dream up all kinds of fantasies to play out while I'm gone."

Jag smiled sadly. "Will you be doing the same?" He knew Sonar would have his hands full with survival in that hot zone. Dreams of home came often. Unfortunately, those were daydreams. Real sleep took a back seat to war.

"With Griz?" Sonar snorted. "Sorry. He doesn't do it for me. Not like you do." His voice softened at the end. "Guess that goes to show what love can do for a guy." He stilled.

The admission sent joy racing through Jag. A little surprised at hearing the words, Jag committed the moment to memory as he kissed Sonar's chin. "I love you too."

Sonar breathed once more, a grin forming and growing on his face. "I wasn't sure…."

"Shh." Jag silenced Sonar with a quick meeting of the lips. "No doubts on my part. I've loved you probably since you stood toe-to-toe with me in that tent, telling me off. I was just too blind to notice."

"A closet sub, huh?"

Jag growled. "I wouldn't go that far."

Sonar cupped his cheek. "Maybe we've both been a bit obtuse. It doesn't matter now. What does matter is that we love each other and are committed to making this relationship work."

"Exactly. So you better hurry back to me or I'll hop on a plane and come after your ass," Jag promised with a stern command.

"You would." Sonar chuckled. "And it makes me damn happy to know you'd do such a thing for me."

"Nothing will keep me away."

"Good. Because when I get back, I expect quite the welcome-home party."

Jag stared at him before smiling. "A party with just the two of us?"

"Bingo."

"Consider it done."

Jag scooted closer, wrapping Sonar tightly in his embrace. He kissed Sonar's temple and nuzzled his cheek. "I love you, Steel."

"I love you too, Jag."

"Cole."

Sonar blinked at him. "What?"

Jag froze but didn't regret what he'd said. The moment was right. Besides, it only seemed fitting that the man he'd started to fall for weeks ago knew his real name. "My real name is Cole." Jag grinned softly, a bit amused at Sonar's astonishment.

Sonar's eyes widened before a slow smile appeared on his face. "I was beginning to think you were never going to tell me."

"Yeah, well, what can I say? You grew on me."

"Uh-huh."

"But don't spread that around. Mac and Ronnie are the only other ones that know."

"My lips are sealed."

"I hope not. I have future plans for them."

Sonar kissed him softly, tenderly. "So do I, love. So do I."

Chapter 21

RONNIE PLOPPED down in the seat opposite Jag. "Hey, cuz."

"Hey, brat." Jag glanced at Ronnie's heaping plate of food and arched an eyebrow.

Ronnie simply grinned. "What can I say? The ladies love me."

"Uh-huh." Jag forked a piece of baked potato. "Or they're just trying to fatten you up."

"Maybe." Ronnie dug in with gusto. "Either way, they still adore me. Even the new girl, Rhonda." His eyes lit up as a wide smile followed.

Was I ever that young? Jag shook his head. "Let me guess. She's caught your eye."

"Yep." Ronnie talked around a mouthful of blueberry cobbler. As usual, he started with dessert first. "Speaking of, I need some advice."

"About women? From me?" Jag blinked at the youngster.

A pink flush covered Ronnie's face. "Well, it's pretty much the same, right? Whether it's a man or a woman that I want to date?"

Jag held up one hand. "I can tell you about men, but women are out of my realm of experiences. Hit up Mac or Howler or one of the other guys for advice on them. I suspect they're a whole different species than men."

Ronnie blew out a breath before taking a long drink of his soda. "Okay. But can I ask you something else?"

"Shoot." Jag fiddled with his meatloaf, not really interested. The food wasn't bad; he just didn't have much of an appetite today. After hitting the obstacle course hard this morning before dawn, a ten-kilometer run, and finally time in the weight room, he was tuckered out. Not to mention he hadn't slept all that well since Sonar had been gone. Eight days and counting with still no word.

No news is good news.

The reminder was beginning to sound outdated and lackluster.

"You were going to blow yourself up with Sandman."

Jag took a bite of his dinner roll. He didn't care to have this conversation, but he wouldn't turn Ronnie away. The kid needed answers. He'd offer them up. "Yeah."

Ronnie peered down at his tray for a long moment before glancing back up. "Why?"

"It falls under the category of the good of many outweighing the good of one. In order for the killing to stop, Sandman had to be eradicated. I knew going in that I might have to take him with me. It's just what Special Forces do. We put others first."

Ronnie tapped the table, his youthful exuberance flattening into a somber expression. "If you were in the same situation again, would you go through with it?"

Jag didn't have to think twice. "Yeah. In a heartbeat. If Sonar hadn't come along, I would've pulled the pin. No hesitation."

"You make it sound too easy. As if you have a secret wish to die." Ronnie frowned, his eyes filling with worry.

So that's what has been eating at Ronnie since I returned. Jag sighed. He was as close to Ronnie as he was anyone else. The kid looked up to him, that was a given. Still, he refused to sugarcoat the truth. Reality sucked some days. Adults had to deal with it. Kids too, although in a different manner. He'd learned earlier than most that dreams and fairy tales weren't aimed in his direction. Everything he had, he'd earned. The hard way. "Listen, Ronnie." Jag lowered his voice. "No one I know wants to die. But I don't fear it either. We all have to go sometime. Some earlier than others. I figure if I can take an evil bastard out in the process, then my death will be worthwhile."

Ronnie's eyes teared up for a split second before he lifted his chin and sniffed. "Is that why you want to go back on active duty so bad? To get back out there and play Russian roulette with the devil himself?"

Jag studied Ronnie, discovering a few facts in the brief glimpse. Fear and worry exuded from every movement of Ronnie's body, in his jerky motions, his severe frown, his lowered gaze.

Ronnie's upset hit Jag hard in the heart. He knew Ronnie cared deeply and he'd seen Jag as a mentor for most of his life. Never had he wanted to hurt Ronnie, but the kid deserved the truth. "I want back on active duty because I'm a sniper. It's my job. I'm a decent shot and I can do some good to save our boys who need watching over in a foreign land. I need to protect them."

For a long time, Ronnie returned to eating without saying another word. "So, you're not going back because of the glory of killing or the need to push yourself until your luck runs out?"

Slowly Jag shook his head. "Kid, let me tell you something. None of us like to kill. We do it in order to protect our brothers and sisters. It's as simple as that." He sipped his water. "Besides, why would I want to end it all when I've found something to live for?"

Ronnie's eyebrows flew up. "Oh, damn. I knew that rumor was true! You and Sonar are a couple." He grinned cheesily. "No wonder you didn't want me showing up unannounced. Afraid I'd interrupt you and him going at it like cats in heat."

"Who's going at it like cats in heat?" Howler stopped by the table, pulled out a chair, then sat down.

"Sonar and Jag," Ronnie answered.

Jag groaned and rubbed his forehead. "No. We're not."

"Why not?" Turk asked as he borrowed a chair from another table and placed it next to Jag. The coyote shifter was known as the base's gossipmonger. Smaller in size and stature, Turk made up for sheer bulk with speed, quickness, and a tendency to be downright sneaky.

Why me? Too tired to get all pushed out of shape, Jag flicked his gaze over the lot of them. He didn't want to spill the beans about him and Sonar. Their love was new and he didn't want to share the news with the rest of the team. Not yet, anyway.

"Why not? Sonar is sexy enough. For a dude." A new voice added.

Jag blinked up at Tracker, the resident dingo mix, as he joined them. "I didn't know your gate swung that way."

Tracker shrugged, picked up his utensils, and cut his meat. "It doesn't." His long hair, a mix of yellow and black, had been pulled back into a ponytail. Typical for workdays. Rarely did Jag see Tracker with his hair down.

They all wore green camos, matching peas in a pod, so to speak. The fact came across as a bit amusing.

"Then how do you know Sonar is sexy?" Turk asked.

All eyes locked on Tracker. He stuffed a bite of food into his mouth and chewed. "I might be straight, but I'm not blind."

Jag grinned slightly. Who knew the womanizer of the bunch had been checking out all the men's asses too? "New hobby?"

"Nah. Lack of beautiful women. You know how it is. When you're away from the fairer sex for long enough, even the guys start to look tasty." Tracker kept a straight face.

Jag threw his head back and laughed.

Turk joined in.

Ronnie eyed Tracker with a mix of amusement and discomfort. "Next time you return from a long mission, you go visit Mac first. I so don't need you to be ogling my ass and having some wet dreams."

Tracker raked Ronnie with his gaze, then offered up a lopsided smile. "Grow into that frame a little bit more and you just might catch my eye."

"That's it. I'm going on a celery diet," Ronnie grumbled.

"I take it Sonar is off the market, then?" Howler nudged Jag with his elbow.

"Ask him." Jag shoved the inquiry aside.

"He's not here, so I'm asking you," Howler persisted.

Jag finished his roll and took a drink of water to wash it down. "If you nosey parkers must know, Sonar and I are a couple. Nothing in cement, but exclusive. We're still figuring things out."

Howler smiled. "Good to hear. About time you found someone to love."

One thing Jag adored about his work family, they accepted his gayness in stride. They might annoy him endlessly or yank his chain enough to drive him crazy, but they had his back. In all things.

"I'm getting there." The admission popped out. Love. He knew the emotion described his feelings toward Sonar. He'd meant the phrase when he whispered it to Sonar. Still, he didn't really want to share such intimate details with the men sitting at his table.

"Last time I saw, there's no time limit on dating." Howler finished his mashed potatoes.

"Better not be or the kid here is doomed to be an old maid." Tracker inclined his head toward Ronnie and grinned wickedly.

"Hey! I'm not in my dotage yet." Ronnie huffed dramatically.

The guys shared a knowing look. "Yet."

"You're all assholes." Ronnie went back to eating, ignoring the rest of them.

Amusement washed over Jag.

"At least we weren't out there looking for grid squares." Tracker chuckled.

Color rose in Ronnie's cheeks again.

"Just remember that when I return the favor, dipshit." Ronnie flipped Tracker off.

Jag chuckled, recalling the day Ronnie had moved heaven and earth in order to find a box of grid squares. Poor kid didn't have a clue those didn't exist except on computer generated maps or drawn on by human hands. They sure as hell didn't come in presorted boxes.

Tracker shrugged, unconcerned. "Rookie mistake, ya know."

"Whatever, canine," Ronnie growled.

"Spoken like a true pussycat," Turk answered without heat.

"Stick with felines, Ronnie. Dogs are downright mean." Jag finished his drink and smiled over at his cousin.

"Well, some of us are exceptions to the rule," Turk answered with a devilish grin.

"Brownnoser." Howler rubbed his finger over his nose as if the others hadn't heard his comment.

"I'm surrounded by bastards." Ronnie waved his hand. "I swear."

Jag took pity on him. Almost. "Just remember those bastards are the brothers you never had. They'll carry you when you're down."

"Hooyah." The chorus rang through the room.

Jag's cell phone rang. With a surprised frown, he plucked it off his belt, checked the caller ID, and answered despite not recognizing the number. "Yeah?"

"Jag?"

Sonar's voice came through a bit thready.

"Sonar?" Jag perked up. He knew the pair would have a satellite phone with them, but didn't expect Sonar to call. Times were tough, danger surrounded them, and chances to call home were rare. "Everything okay?"

"Yeah. Just had a break. Thought to check in."

Jag ignored the wide grins on the other guy's faces. He probably had a goofy smile on his face too. They might rib him for it later, but hearing Sonar's voice made it all worth it. "Coming home soon?"

"Not soon enough. We're getting closer, though."

"Griz isn't giving you a hard time, is he?" Jag couldn't resist teasing his lover.

Sonar snorted. "He doesn't know any other—" The sound of gunshots close by carried through the line loudly. "Shit."

"Sonar?" Worry rushed through Jag's mind. "Sonar? Can you hear me?"

The boom of gunfire that continued, louder this time, was his only answer.

"Sonar!"

The line went dead.

Jag lowered the phone, his heart in his throat.

"What happened?" Ronnie asked.

"Shooting. Then nothing." Jag could hardly breathe as the worst ran through his mind. *No. Just no.* It couldn't be. After all he'd been through. He'd just found love again with Sonar. Surely, fate wasn't that cruel. His gut clenched and churned.

Howler squeezed Jag's shoulder. "They'll pull out of this okay. Griz is one hell of a soldier."

Jag nodded, appreciating the pep talk, but unable to buy into it right now. All kinds of things could have happened. Namely, if Sonar and Griz took fire, they would have dropped the phone or disconnected in order to fight back. Just because he was there then gone didn't mean the worst had occurred.

It didn't mean it hadn't either.

JAG FOCUSED on the target nearly a mile away. He centered the crosshairs, blew out a breath, and took the shot between heartbeats.

"Center field low," the man next to him called out.

"Shit." Since the high-powered scope allowed him to easily see the dust kick up where his bullet landed, the spotter's commentary proved unnecessary and a bit chafing. Why Mac deemed he needed a spotter on training grounds, he didn't have a clue. The dry terrain with few barriers made for easy detection of targets and even misses. Certainly, Mac had a reason, however vague and elusive.

Jag realigned his scope and adjusted for the wind and downhill location before slowly squeezing the trigger. The target fluttered and fell. *Finally.* Two shots was one too many.

"Bingo."

Not for the first time that morning, Jag wanted to send his spotter away. Well away. Back to the dorm room of headquarters. Perhaps even back to his hometown, wherever that was.

Which didn't make a lick of sense.

The guy hadn't done a thing wrong, only served his purpose, and didn't even pester Jag with questions. The problem boiled down to a simple fact: he wasn't Sonar.

Who just happened to still be over in BFE, fighting in a war zone. Hopefully still fighting. No one had received word from him or Griz since that cut off phone call a couple of days back. If Sonar suffered a wound or death, they would be notified. Unfortunately, the military wasn't known for prompt, up-to-date news from the front.

Which left Jag out in the cold, worried sick, and barely sleeping.

Never before had he given much thought to what families and loved ones went through when their man or woman was away on deployment. He walked in those very shoes now and could definitely attest that the situation sucked. Big time. He'd much rather be on active duty tromping through caves, mountains, and goat trails in Afghanistan than be back at base waiting for Sonar to return. The days crept by. Concern proved to be a constant companion.

He forced himself to look on the bright side and be optimistic. Sonar would return. That's the way it had to be.

If you'd get your shit together, you could team up with Sonar on the next mission.

His peak goal and one he took very seriously. Well, one of them. The other centered around his personal life and involved waking up every morning with Sonar snuggled against him in their bed. Next time he wouldn't be left behind. Come hell or high water, he'd tag along with Sonar, watch his partner's back, and make sure they both returned home alive.

Together we're a force to be reckoned with. Had been before, would be again.

Sonar's presence in the house comforted Jag more than he cared to admit. He slept much better knowing Sonar was close by. Not to mention the first night when in ocelot form, Sonar had slept by his side. The purring and contact soothed him. Comforted him. Gave him an anchor to hold on to for the rest of the night and each one since. Sonar had helped lay a foundation for Jag to work from. He'd seen Jag at his worst and still stood by his side, both then and now. If only Sonar were here to be his spotter. His friend. His lover.

Damn, I miss the guy. He'd better get back soon.

His training regimen kept him busy, but not enough to prevent him from thinking about Sonar several times per day. He closed his eyes, recalled the shit-eating smile Sonar flashed when mischievous. The ripped body. The twinkling blue eyes. The gentle touch and those blazing hot kisses. The way Sonar cried out when he came under Jag.

Just call me sappy.

As soon as he returned, Jag intended to feed him, care for him, and once Sonar rested, make love to him until the cows came home.

"Left-field bogey, approximately twelve hundred yards," the spotter droned on. Cal was the guy's name. New to the unit, young, and a hyena shifter to boot. So far, he did his job, but Jag couldn't find common ground or click with him.

Not a surprise. He'd always been picky about his spotters. Mark, as a human, was the exception to Jag's rule of sticking to other feline shifters when forced to drag a spotter along for his missions. No matter the variety of cat, they shared common traits and abilities. That made for a much better well-oiled machine. Placing him with a hyena shifter threw some small monkey wrenches in the spokes. They functioned together because they had to, but Jag wasn't truly in his comfort zone. Wouldn't be until Sonar returned.

Whenever that might be.

He refused to consider the alternative.

He fired three times before hitting the target. Cussing fluently, he shoved another clip into his rifle. "Can't hit the broad side of a fucking barn." A thread of fear flared to life. He'd lost his edge. Shots were going awry for some damn reason. He never missed like this. Not even when he first signed up with Shifters Central. If he couldn't get back up to par and soon, his career as a sniper would hang in limbo. His stomach clenched as he berated himself.

Cal gaped at him. "At this distance, even the best sniper would be hard-pressed to hit the bogey at all, let alone in three tries."

Jag wiped a hand over his face and snarled. "This is child's play for me. I used to hit each and every one of those damn things on the first try. *Every time.* Hell, this range is like shooting fish in a barrel compared to the places I've been."

Cal shook his head. "Then what has changed?"

The question took Jag aback. *Why could I ace the course before but struggled now?* What had changed? Sonar MIA had to be part of it. Still, he'd been through some intense times. He could focus in the middle of absolute chaos, even with a plateful of worries on his mind.

"Your spotter." Mac's voice carried to his ears.

Jag flipped over in order to face his supervisor. Mac, dressed in familiar camos, strode up to where Jag still lay halfway on his stomach, preparing for the next round of accuracy tests. His expression remained blank, no hints as to what his prophetic statement meant.

"What about him?" Jag voiced the question on the tip of his tongue.

"Not Cal. Any spotter." Mac paused next to Jag and squatted down. "What's changed between the last time you flew through this course and now? Your spotter."

Understanding dawned. "Mark."

Mac stared straight at Jag, refusing to allow him to glance away. "Not just Mark. You were still on top of your game with Sonar too. Even alone, you didn't miss out in the field when it counted."

Jag processed his words. He glimpsed over at Cal, who wore a frown. "Cal is doing his job. He's right on top of things."

"It's not about Cal's performance. It's about your comfort zone." Mac pursed his lips and grew thoughtful for a moment. "You're relaxed and confident by yourself and with a man you trust with your life at your side. Mix it up and you're tight, unable to settle in completely. That reflects in your accuracy."

He has a point. From the get-go, Jag hadn't clicked with Cal. Not the guy's fault. It just didn't happen. Unlike when he paired with Mark and Sonar, the only two spotters he'd really worked with in the past few years.

A semblance of relief extinguished his momentary worry.

Mac stood up and started to walk off.

"Does that mean you're putting me back on solitary status?"

Pausing, Mac turned back. "No."

The lack of clarification froze Jag's heart for a second. Surely, Mac wouldn't pull him off active duty permanently. He hated to ask, didn't want to hear the words, but needed to know the answer. "Are you grounding me permanently?"

Mac shook his head. "Why in the hell would I do such a fool thing as that?"

Jag blinked at him. "Because I can't hit a single fucking target?"

For the first time, Mac's mouth hitched up. "Wait until Sonar returns. Once you two are reunited, I bet you'll breeze through the course with flying colors." Mac spun around and strode off only to stop once more. "Jag?"

"Yeah?"

"Sonar and Griz are due back in three days."

Jag took an extra second to absorb the news. He cautiously allowed hope to flare. "You've heard from them?"

"Yep. They're fine. Got into a couple of hot spots, but nothing they couldn't handle."

Relief washed over Jag. *Thank God.* The happy news couldn't have come at a better time. To know that Sonar would be back at base soon both cheered Jag and set his heart pumping with excitement.

Mac smiled. "I expect you to be at the firing range in four days and nailing every shot."

No pressure there. Jag snorted. "Yes, sir." He replayed Mac's words through his mind once more before grinning. *Yeah, I can do that.*

The knowledge that he'd be back on active duty, in a job he loved, sooner rather than later, buoyed his spirits greatly. Add in the fact that he'd be attached at the hip with Sonar once more and his world brightened considerably. Three more days.

With renewed optimism, he flipped back over and took aim. The target exploded with the first pull of the trigger.

Chapter 22

"HEY, HOTSHOT."

Jag spun around to find Sonar walking through the door of the headquarters lounge, his ruck strapped to his back and rifle in hand. Covered in dust, with rumpled camos, Sonar appeared to be truth in advertising. He'd literally just returned from the front. A short op, two weeks. Long enough for Jag to miss Sonar greatly. Hell, he even missed Sonar's back talk and his playful ocelot form.

"Damn, you're a sight for sore eyes." Grinning, he ambled over, raking Sonar with his gaze, searching for any signs of wounds. When he discovered Sonar appeared safe and sound, along with a new growth of dark whiskers, he drank in the vision of a fit male in his prime. One that just so happened to strum his senses, crank up his libido, and make him drool with want. He looked good. *Sex-on-a-stick good.* "Look what the bear dragged in." He knew Griz must have returned at the same time, as he and Sonar were teamed up for this mission, but couldn't take his eyes off Sonar in order to find out.

Sonar snorted. "I thought bears were supposed to be fun and laid-back. No one bothered to tell that particular stick-up-his-ass grizzly."

Jag threw back his head and laughed. Leave it to Sonar to grumble about his partner for the past few days. Not that Jag disagreed with Sonar's perceptions. He'd just learned way back when how to navigate around some of the more temperamental members of the group. Since Griz happened to be one of the worst, he could sympathize. "Looks like you landed on your feet, though." He stopped right in front of Sonar.

Sonar offered up a lopsided grin. "Always do."

Unable to resist, Jag cupped the back of Sonar's head and pulled him close. He meshed their lips together, his heart speeding when Sonar licked at the seam, then slipped his tongue inside. Opening his mouth, Jag allowed the foray for a second before seizing control of the kiss. He plundered deep and thorough, tangled with Sonar's tongue, before easing back a hair in order to suckle Sonar's lower lip. It had been way too long and Sonar tasted heavenly. Even with the facial hair tickling.

"Get a room!"

Sonar lifted his head enough to flip Griz off.

"Ignore him. He so needs to get laid," Jag whispered against Sonar's lips.

Griz growled in response.

Sonar dipped down to meet Jag's lips briefly. "I told him that. *Repeatedly.*"

"Guess he didn't listen?"

Jag eyed the bulky Griz, dressed identically to Sonar. Griz snarled and waved his hand dismissively. "Since there was a decided lack of women around and I was stuck with this pipsqueak, getting laid wasn't happening." He pushed past them and continued on his way.

"Guess that means you missed me?"

"Yep." Jag kissed Sonar once more before stepping back. The lines under Sonar's eyes, the dullness, combined with days of built up grime told him Sonar needed food, rest, and a hot shower. Not necessarily in that order. "I bet a couple of weeks of only Griz for company made me look pretty damn good."

"You have no idea." Sonar rubbed at his forehead.

"Come on. Let's get back to the house. You can clean up there while I figure out how to cook." Jag had the afternoon off, thanks to Mac. They both had to report in first thing in the morning, but the rest of today was theirs.

"That's just great. Half-starved, living off MREs, finally get home, and you're going to feed me an experiment in cooking?" His face morphed into a put-upon pout.

Jag smiled saucily. "Would it help if I taste tested it first?"

"Not really," Sonar grumbled. He rolled his eyes and started toward the door.

Quickly catching up, Jag grabbed hold of Sonar's ruck, throwing the heavy item over his own shoulder.

"Thanks."

"No problem."

"Everything okay? Did you need Misty to give you a once-over?" Jag eyed Sonar's movements, finding them fluid, if somewhat lacking in energy. Still, he didn't want to hurry Sonar home if he required the skills of a healer first.

"Nah. I'm good. Just flat tired." Sonar managed a half grin. "Food. Shower. Then bed calls."

"You scared the shit out of me. Hearing those bullets flying then losing the call…" Jag couldn't finish with the lump that appeared in his throat at the memory of that horrid moment.

"It got heated for a minute. Dropped the phone. It ended up pretty banged up in the action so I couldn't call back. By the time things settled down and we returned to base in order to check in, a couple of days had passed." Sonar scratched at his chin. "I'm beat. In one piece, but damn worn out."

Jag slapped him on the back. "No problem." He'd been there, done that way too many times before, returning to civilization dragging his tail from days or weeks of relentless tracking and sniping.

They made the moderate hike in mostly silence. As Jag's home lay just outside the base's borders, driving seemed lazy and redundant.

He walked up the steps of the front porch and held the door open for Sonar. "Go ahead and hit the shower. I'll fix something worthwhile."

Sonar shot him an appreciative look. "Thanks." He stepped inside, paused, and sniffed. "Home away from home."

The statement tugged at Jag's heartstrings. A smile tugged at his lips. "Hit the shower before your clothes turn into a dust heap. I'll toss them in the washer and get started on lunch."

Without hesitation, Sonar began stripping down. Jag arched an eyebrow but said nothing, too busy enjoying the show. Despite being covered in dust, dirt, and a couple weeks' worth of grime, Sonar still took his breath away. "Gonna shave that furry chin?" Most men on duty in Afghanistan grew out their beards for a couple reasons. They blended in more since the culture tended toward beards rather than clean-shaven faces. Secondly, while outside the wire, they had little time to worry about things such as vanity or extra hair removal.

Sonar scratched at the area. "Definitely. Itches like hell." He shucked his shirt so it rested on top of his boots and started on his pants. Pushing them down, along with his underwear, he soon stood in the living room in nothing but his socks.

Jag bit back a groan.

Their eyes met.

"Like what you see, huh?"

Jag snorted. "That's never been in question."

"Uh-huh." Sonar turned, and started for the bathroom. He paused at the door to shake his rear, grinning wickedly.

"You're such a mess." Jag chuckled. "Go on. Get in the shower before you leave a dust trail all over the house that someone has to clean up."

Sonar stuck his tongue out at Jag before disappearing into the guest bathroom.

Jag shook his head, gathered up the discarded clothing, and made a beeline for the laundry room. He started the washer and made his way to the kitchen. Far from a fast order cook, he debated for a second what to fix. Thawed hamburger meat in the fridge caught his eye. He took out the full two pounds and started making them into patties. Since he didn't have any way to fry potato slices, he went with nuking a couple of potatoes instead.

As the food cooked, he set the table, noting the sense of contentment that had returned. No restlessness, no fretting. Just a typical meal served at home on a typical day. The only difference? Sonar was back.

Thirty minutes later, Sonar sat across the table from Jag, dressed in a pair of sweat bottoms and an old ragged T-shirt. Clean-shaven, Sonar appeared years younger and perhaps a bit sexier than the mountain-man look. His damp hair and fresh soap smell gave off an intoxicating aroma, especially mixed with Sonar's individual scent. The shower might have perked up Sonar a bit, but Jag still read the deep lines under his eyes. Fatigue. Near exhaustion. Sonar needed rest and lots of it.

"Why did I smell a hyena when I walked through headquarters?" Sonar asked as he bit into his second hamburger, having already inhaled the first one like a starved man.

"New guy. Cal is his name."

Sonar paused in his chewing. "You've been working with him?"

Jag forked a piece of potato. "Yeah. Mac teamed us up."

A frown covered Sonar's face. "As a spotter?" A hint of anger or perhaps jealousy filled his tone.

"Yeah." Jag smiled to himself. He didn't want to piss off Sonar, but seeing the green monster rear his head proved good for his ego.

"Replacing me already? That bastard." Sonar's eyes flashed.

Jag waved his hand. "Now, don't get your pants hot. It's not what you're thinking."

"Then what is it?"

"He teamed me with Cal one day. I couldn't hit shit. Not Cal's fault. He was doing everything right. I just couldn't settle down. Mac appeared at the range. Told me that I was lined up for active duty again."

"That's great. I know you've been going stir crazy grounded here."

Jag inclined his head, blew out a breath, and offered up the truth. "I was so afraid I'd lost my edge. If I couldn't hit an unmoving target on the range, how in the hell was I supposed to hit a moving one a mile plus away?"

Sonar opened his mouth, but Jag talked over him. "Mac nailed it on the head. He said it boiled down to trust and comfort for me. I couldn't work with someone successfully unless I believed in them. Cal wasn't the doing the trick for me."

"And?"

"And Mac said as soon as you returned, he'd attach us at the hip again."

A slow smile appeared on Sonar's face. "You're going to be tied to me?"

"Seems like." Jag managed to keep a straight face. Barely.

"Poor baby. Stuck with obnoxious me 24-7. It's a definite hardship."

Jag lost the battle with amusement, giving in and grinning. *Something was going to be hard all right.* He kept the thought to himself. For now. "Mac's probably punishing me again." He shrugged.

Sonar snorted. "Yeah, right. Talk about punishment, hang out with Griz for two fucking weeks."

"Been there, done that. Never want to repeat that damn awful experience. He makes a Komodo dragon seem like a cuddly puppy." Jag took a long drink. "Good man. Terrible temperament. He must have flunked 'plays well with others' in preschool."

"No kidding. It's like having Godzilla for a partner. He's big. He's scary. He's at the top of his game and a downright menace to the enemy, but conversation skills are definitely lacking."

Jag finished his burger. "Well, think of it this way. If you ever have to be paired up with him, I'm bound to be with you. We both can suffer together."

Sonar smiled. "That makes me feel *so* much better."

Rolling his eyes, Jag started cleaning up the table. "You would."

Sonar cleaned his plate and drank the last of his soda before carrying his dirty dishes to the sink. He reached out and caught Jag's arm. "I wanted to be out there with you."

Jag's heart skipped a beat at the softness in Sonar's eyes. "Me too. At least we know from now on we come as a package deal."

"There's that." Sonar stood still for a moment, appeared as if he wanted to say more, then released Jag. "I guess I should hit the sack."

"You look ready to drop."

"I am."

Jag stepped closer and brushed his lips over Sonar's. "Welcome home, love. I'm so glad you're finally here."

Sonar smiled. "Me too." They stared at each other for a few seconds before Sonar turned away and left the room.

Jag watched him go. As much as he wanted to welcome Sonar home with a robust round of sweet lovemaking, he held off. Sonar was on the brink of absolute exhaustion and falling over in a dead sleep. Rest took precedence. That didn't prevent Jag from sneaking in before long and cuddling up for the remainder of the night, though.

He smiled happily at the impromptu plan.

I've turned into a snuggler. He shook his head in amazement. Leave it to Sonar to pluck every tender cord Jag possessed.

Never again did he want to be parted from Sonar. Staying behind was simply too tough. Thankfully, Mac seemed to understand his position as he all but promised to pair up Sonar and Jag for all future missions. And there would be missions. He was going back on active status. Relieved and a bit excited, he couldn't wait to get back out in the field. Not that he enjoyed spending days hiding out, snaking along the ground, searching for his target. That was just what he excelled at. He needed to get back on track and soon, prove that he hadn't lost a step, make a difference in the world once again.

His protective instincts roared to life once more.

If another mission called Sonar away, he'd be right by Sonar's side, watching his back. As they were meant to be.

Chapter 23

"No rest for the weary," Sonar blew out a breath. Still fatigued from the last endless mission, he pulled on his reserves. At least he'd had food in his belly and a good night's sleep before being placed back on the training field this damp, chilly morning.

He'd woken up with Jag wrapped around him like a protective cocoon. He savored that moment and regretted that they didn't have the rest of the day to lazily spend in bed.

Later. Definitely later.

"I thought it was no rest for the wicked?" Jag offered up a teasing grin.

Sonar rolled his eyes. "I'll have you know, I'm nowhere near wicked. I'm an angel."

Jag snorted. "Yeah, in sheep's clothing," he muttered under his breath.

With his exceptional hearing, Sonar picked up the mumbled words. He shook his head and bumped into Jag, sending him sidestepping in order to maintain his balance. "Way to knock me to my knees." He didn't think twice about his comment until an expression rife with lust blanketed Jag's face.

Sonar grinned ruefully. Sure, he'd thought the same thing. More than once, actually. Hell, he'd fantasized about him and Jag in just about every position conceivable. Made for excellent wet dreams. Unfortunately, he hadn't had the chance to try any of them out yet.

How many times had he thought of Jag while away? Too many to count. He had wanted nothing more than to stay at home today and pursue the sexual heat bubbling between them, but no such luck. Duty called in the form of training.

Since they woke too late to do anything else except get dressed, brush their teeth, and head to headquarters, nothing more than verbal teasing would be happening this morning. They'd picked up their weapons for the day, including the ammo, and strode directly for the firing range. The obstacle course loomed ahead for the afternoon, along with meetings. Thus, anything else had to wait. Unfortunately.

"Full of yourself this morning, I see." Sonar switched his rifle to his other hand.

Jag lifted his chin in the air. "Full of myself? Never. I'm good and I know it."

Sonar chuckled. "The question is, what are you good at?"

"That's for me to know and you to find out."

"Bring it on." Sonar's heart leaped and his libido purred at their good-natured teasing. He didn't miss the spark in Jag's eyes or the definite interest there. *Picking up right where we left off.* He found joy in that fact.

They walked up to a small group of men waiting for their turn at the range. Mac twisted, eyed the two of them, then gave a brief nod. "About time you two showed up."

Jag lifted his hand to shadow his eyes from the sun. "Based on the angle of the big orange ball in the sky, I'd say it's 7:57, sir."

A couple of the other guys laughed.

Mac's lips twitched. "Once a smartass, always a smartass." He patted Jag on the shoulder. "Nice to see you're back to form."

"Ready and able, sir."

"Brownnoser," Turk quipped.

"Conceited is more like it," Tracker added.

Jag flipped them both off. "If you two could only keep up…."

Both of the men growled. Jag halfheartedly flashed a fang.

Sonar shook his head and stepped between them to face Jag. "I thought we were working on this. You draw more flies with honey than vinegar, remember?"

Jag glanced over Sonar's shoulder. His lips hitched up at the corners. "I don't want to draw flies in the first place."

Sonar rolled his eyes and threw in his ace. "If you behave, you might get a reward."

Jag's eyebrows shot up. "What kind of reward?"

"Uh-uh. Not telling." Catcalls carried from behind him. Sonar ignored them. "Practice playing nice today and you'll find out. Later."

"I'd take him up on that offer if I were you." Mac stepped over to Jag's side. "We're a team, one way or another. Either you work together now and in the future or work out some of your aggression on the obstacle course later on."

Jag sighed dramatically. "See what I get for yanking their chains?"

"Compromise." Sonar held up one hand. "Save the chain yanking for after training. Deal?"

"Yeah."

Sonar turned to the two other men. They both grinned wickedly. "Yeah, whatever. But it's so much fun to rile him up."

"Paybacks, boys. Paybacks."

When no one else said anything, Sonar smiled up at Mac. "See? I learned a few things this past couple of weeks."

Mac chuckled. "I noticed that." He flicked his gaze over all his men. "We'll start with urban warfare training, one on each side of the line at a time. After that, it's target practice and then conditioning."

A chorus of groans followed.

Mac just smiled all the more. "Get your asses moving. It's too damn hot out here to stand around getting a tan."

Sonar nudged Jag with his elbow. "Are you fast enough to keep up with me?"

Jag stared at him for a second before grinning. "Is that a challenge?"

"Pretty much."

"Then live and learn, Bat Ears." Jag strode over toward the preparation area to load up his weapons for the course.

Sonar watched him go, noted the strut in his step, and smiled. *Oh, yeah. Jag has his swagger on.* He shook his head and followed in Jag's footsteps, wondering if he'd bitten off more than he could chew.

Maybe. But, Jag was worth every bite.

"STILL BEAT you by a half second." Sonar smiled over at Jag as they ate hot, freshly delivered pizza after a long day of training. Somehow he'd managed to best Jag in a head-to-head battle on the urban battlefield course. Sure, he'd challenged Jag, but never once did he think he'd win.

Jag rolled his eyes. "Are you ever going to let me live that down?"

"Maybe." Sonar took a hefty bite.

"Besides, I think it's time we talk about this reward you mentioned. I didn't rip anyone's head off, call them a pussy to their face, or threaten to shoot them in the ass. That ranks right up there with my best behavior."

"I'd say so."

"So, what's my reward?"

Sonar smiled to himself, catching the impatience and eagerness in Jag's voice. All day he'd tossed around the idea of what to do for Jag. Many options would've worked, but he wanted something special, something fun to take the stress off. Something involving nudity, bed, and rip-roaring sex. "After dinner."

"Tell me now."

Sonar gave in. Marginally. "Dinner first. Then we'll retire to the bedroom."

Jag grinned saucily.

Sonar unrepentantly burst his bubble. For the moment. "For a back rub."

Astonishment quickly morphed into amusement mixed with a hint of wickedness. "You're going to give me a back rub?"

"Yep."

"Are you any good at it?"

Sonar laughed at Jag's skepticism. "As a matter of fact, yes. I took a couple of classes in massage therapy way back when. While I might be a bit rusty, I think I can recall the basics."

Jag took another bite of his pizza and chewed, his gaze locked with Sonar's. "Interesting. Very interesting."

Intrigued, Sonar tilted his head as he picked up another slice out of the box. "What is?"

"You as a massage therapist. I never would have guessed."

Sonar held up his free hand. "Hey, I might have big mitts, but I know how to use them." He took a drink and shrugged. "It started out as a free class. I thought it sounded like fun. Once I got started, I liked it."

"So why are you a soldier instead of a massage therapist at some tropical resort?"

"Simple. I'm better at one than the other." He grinned. "I guess you can find out for yourself shortly."

"Sounds damn ominous."

"Try it. You might like it." Sonar waggled his eyebrows and finished his drink.

"What the hell. Nothing ventured, nothing gained."

"Bingo. So when you're done, hit the shower and I'll clean up the mess. I'll take a quick shower myself and meet you in your bedroom."

Jag emptied his glass and wiped his hands on the napkin. "You'll get no argument from me."

Twenty minutes later, the kitchen cleaned and dishwasher humming, Sonar heard Jag exit the bathroom. He'd taken one of the fastest showers of his life and tugged on a pair of sweats for comfort. Briefly he'd considered leaving them behind, but running around in the buff pretty much said "fuck me" rather than "relax while I give you a massage."

The tiny click of the door opening sent a rebounding zing through his system.

"Still wanting to do this?" Jag called out from the bedroom.

Sonar walked that direction, pausing at the threshold to take in the sight of Jag standing next to the bed, absently towel-drying his hair. "Yep."

If there ever was a living Adonis, Jag would fit the bill. Powerful muscles rippled with every movement. Wide shoulders, a broad chest, and chiseled six-pack abs added to the package. Dipping lower, Sonar noted Jag's cock quickly swelling under his rapt attention.

Sure, he'd seen Jag naked before, but the sight never failed to inspire and entice him.

Picking up the telltale scent of arousal, he smiled and shook his head. When they got down to the nitty-gritty tonight, and they would, they'd probably burn the house down with their passion.

A lopsided grin kicked up on Jag's face. "Let's get to it."

Sonar's arousal jumped tenfold before he leashed it firmly. *Reward first. Play second.*

Jag stretched out prone in the center of his mattress, his head turned toward Sonar. "Do your worst."

Chuckling, Sonar approached steadily. "That sounded bad." He pulled a tube of massage oil out of his pocket that he'd collected when Jag had hit the shower. The masculine scent provided relaxing aromatherapy while his hands would ensure the rest. He climbed on the bed, settling on Jag's left side. After squirting some oil on his hands, he rubbed them together, then ran them up and down Jag's back in order to spread some of the oil around before properly beginning. That done, he started to massage and knead, starting at Jag's nape and shoulders, the places where most people carried tension.

The soft hitching of breath told him Jag was enjoying his touch so far. Still, he needed to be sure. "Okay?"

"Yeah. You missed your calling. This is good. Really good." He went up on his elbows and lowered his forehead to his clasped hands, offering up his entire neck for Sonar's attentions.

"I'm out of practice, but it's like riding a bike I'm told."

"Not something you've done for your other lovers?"

Sonar kept rubbing, not put off by the question at all. "Nope. Most of them have been a blip in life. In and out too fast to pay much attention. Like I said before, I've been too busy in the military to stop and smell the roses."

Jag sighed in what sounded like blissful enjoyment.

"You get to be my practice dummy." Sonar continued his way down Jag's back once more, thrilled to feel the muscles relaxing under his touch.

"I'll take it." Jag blew out a breath. "I'm one pretty damn lucky guy. I have a partner who loves me and is good with his hands too."

Sonar chuckled. "True." He bent over and kissed Jag's shoulder. "I do love you. It's so good to be home."

Jag flipped over and grabbed Sonar's wrist.

Pausing, Sonar glanced from the place where Jag touched, then back to his face.

"I want you."

Sonar swallowed, his heart skipping a beat before galloping. "You have me," he replied straight from his soul.

For a long moment, they stared at each other before Sonar leaned in for a kiss. Light, playful, exciting. Jag cupped the back of Sonar's head and held him in place. Sonar opened wide and sucked on Jag's tongue, a precursor to what he planned on doing to Jag's cock.

Breaking apart, Sonar peppered kisses along Jag's throat and chest, then continued southward. "I'm going to suck you off."

Jag drew in air.

Sonar heard the sound and grinned wickedly. Not about to waste another moment, he scooted back until he sat down by Jag's hip, within easy reach of his goal.

"Stretch out. I want to lick your dick at the same time," Jag commanded softly.

Powerful lust flashed through Sonar's veins. He adjusted his position, turned up on his side, and scooted in close. Automatically, he lifted his top leg and draped it over Jag's shoulder, giving his partner total access. Now comfortable, he grasped Jag's cock in his hand, rubbed his thumb across the sensitive tip, and watched a bead of moisture emerge from the slit. Unable to resist, he lapped up the delicious treat, before engulfing the entire head.

Jag groaned and his hips jerked in reaction. The motion fueled Sonar's resolve even as Jag returned the favor, sending additional bursts of fire streaming through his body.

After taking more of Jag's erection into his mouth, Sonar moaned low in his throat, the vibration a response to Jag's aggressive sucking as well as a stimulant for his lover.

Sonar bobbed. He laved. He swallowed the whole length of Jag's cock and swirled his tongue from base to head and back again. Reaching lower, he found Jag's sac and gently rolled the balls within.

Jag added more vacuum as if trying to pull every last drop of cum out of Sonar.

He didn't have long to wait as Sonar escalated to the pinnacle at incredible speed. He tried to concentrate on his task but failed as the climax hit him hard. He cried out, shoved his cock deeper into Jag's mouth, and fisted the sheets. Wave after wave of erotic heat cascaded over him in time with the pulses of cum.

"Nice." Jag murmured against Sonar's quickly deflating erection.

Sonar drew in a deep breath, focused on Jag's still-full cock, and latched back on. He threw in every trick that he knew, then smiled to himself as Jag began to rock and jerk. He kept him on the edge, then lapped across Jag's sensitive slit over and over again.

With a muted roar, Jag emptied his load.

Sonar took every drop and asked for more. Only when Jag flinched from sensitivity did Sonar release his prize.

"Damn, Bat Ears."

"You liked?"

"Hell, yes." Jag sat up, his breathing still a bit ragged.

Sonar followed suit. "You're not too bad yourself."

Jag grinned wickedly. "I have a feeling I'm going to need a back rub with a happy ending fairly often."

"Maybe I can get one in return?" Sonar followed suit, settling beside Jag and waggling his eyebrows.

"Absolutely. Love is a two-way street." Jag sealed the promise with a kiss.

Sonar tasted himself on Jag's lips and sipped for more. "Mmm."

"Delicious." Jag tugged on Sonar's collar-length hair. "Keep that up and we won't get any sleep tonight."

As much as he wanted to play all night, Sonar realized it simply wasn't possible. They had early morning drills and needed to be fresh. The downside of a military career. Weekends were just another workday. He sighed in resignation. "We need some sleep if we're going to be halfway awake tomorrow."

"Yeah. Unfortunately." Jag nudged Sonar to his back, stretched out beside him, then pulled him into a spoon position.

Sonar leaned back against Jag's ripped body as Jag pulled the covers over them.

There's no place I'd rather be. "I love you, Cole."

"Love you too, Steel." Jag pressed his lips against Sonar's nape before settling them down for the night.

Chapter 24

"WHAT WAS your reward?"

Glancing up, Jag found one Turk leaning against a table. "Not saying." Jag slowed his pace as he approached the training area for the morning. Immediately, Tracker and Griz stepped closer.

"What reward?" Griz asked.

"The one he got for not shooting any of us in the ass yesterday," Turk answered with a mischievous grin.

"Oh, it had to be good. He's got that grin of satisfaction on today." Tracker shifted his rifle to his other hand, keeping the muzzle pointed to the sky.

"Limber and relaxed too," Griz pointed out.

"He must have gotten some. Big time."

Jag snorted. Not about to spill the beans, he kept his mouth shut.

He smiled to himself. The memories of last night replayed with multiple highlights in his mind. As promised, Sonar had turned him into a lump of putty. The mutual blow job after the back rub sure did the trick. Refreshed and renewed, he felt relaxed and pretty damn happy today. Sonar was back at his side away from the hot zone. Relieved, Jag vowed to make up for lost time.

He loved Sonar, more than life itself. Sonar returned his love. Every glance, every action showed exactly how Sonar felt. Jag soaked it up and treasured each moment. Committed and together, Jag knew he'd struck gold with Sonar.

"Well, whatever you got must have been pretty damn good." Turk pursed his lips. "Come on. Fess up."

"Still not talking." Jag shook his head at the guys' antics this morning. They were like a bunch of energetic and curious puppies, all needing to be part of the action.

"Hey, Jag." He glanced up to find Howler approaching. The man had a shit-eating grin on his face, which never boded well.

"Howler."

The rest of the guys gathered around, all with cheesy smiles.

Howler pulled a card out of his pocket and handed it over.

"What's this?"

"Just a little something from all of us guys."

Jag peered down at the name on the card and the amount. "Whoa. This is to the fanciest place around and way too much."

"We wanted to give you something. You and Sonar. Seems you two could use a bit of romance to seal the deal. As always, we have your back." Howler grinned wolfishly.

Touched by their consideration, he couldn't gather the energy to be upset by the guys' obvious interest in his personal life. Normally he'd tell them to mind their own business. But with this gift, he couldn't utter a single protest. Nor did he have the heart to confess that he and Sonar had taken that big step already and just not shared it with the rest of the crew. Although, technically, they'd only been on one date.

"There's more. A limo will pick you two up, take you to eat, and bring you back home."

He blinked at Howler. "Holy shit. You pulled out the stops."

Howler grinned. "Misty said romance was the way to go. I didn't dare argue. She's much better at this stuff than I am. Besides, we all owe you. Time to start paying back." He slapped Jag on the shoulder. "I'll let you break the news to Sonar." He turned and started the way he came, paused, and looked over his shoulder. "Take my advice. Make it a night to remember."

"Will do." Jag held up one hand in a wave good-bye. He found three sets of eyes fixed on him. All the men wore goofy expressions that made Jag want to roll his eyes in return. "Thanks."

"Welcome."

"Gonna spill the details afterward?"

He snorted at Turk. "Not on your life."

"Well, hell."

Jag chuckled and squeezed each of their shoulders in turn. "You guys are keepers. Thanks."

"No problem."

"Now scat before I'm tempted to line up dates for each of you." Probably not the scariest threat he'd ever made, judging from the smirks on the men's faces. Jag turned to go in search of Sonar when Ronnie's voice stopped him.

"Jag. Wait up."

Pausing, Jag watched his cousin jog over, a paper in his hand. "What do you have there?"

"Compliments of the colonel. Day pass for you and Sonar for tomorrow. You're free this evening and all day tomorrow."

Jag took the offered golden ticket with disbelief. Mac handed out free passes rarely and only for good reason. The fact that he did so now spoke of his inner goodness and how much he thought of both Jag and Sonar. Enough to basically throw them together with nothing else to do for the next thirty-six hours or so.

Ronnie leaned closer. "Between you and me, I think the guys expect you and Sonar to do some major touchy-feely before you get back." He smiled ruefully. "Leave out the details, though. My ears! My mind! My sanity!" He held his hands up as if in surrender.

Jag threw back his head and laughed. "You're such a dramatic goof. The other day you were hitting me up for dating tips. Now you're covering your eyes and ears for fear you might overhear what Sonar and I do on our date?" He shook his head before slapping Ronnie on the back. "You're one of a kind, kid."

"Yep." Ronnie beamed as if he just received the Nobel Prize.

"Thank Mac for me while I go in search of Bat Ears."

Ronnie snorted. "Bat Ears? Does he know you call him that?"

"Yes."

"And he lets you live? That must be some strong bond between you two."

Jag thought about the statement for a split second. Truer words had never been said. Somewhere, somehow he and Sonar had forged a tight bond through the worst days of his life. Without Sonar at his side, Jag had no illusions that he'd be where he was today. Most likely, he'd have long since been sentenced to hell right alongside Sandman, compliments of that grenade. "You can say that."

Ronnie grinned softly. "Congrats, Jag. You deserve some happiness and I have a feeling Sonar is the guy who does that for you."

"I think you're right." Jag started to walk off before stopping again. "Just to be clear, you might stay away from the house while we're on leave."

"Yeah, yeah. I know. All that brain-bleach stuff and such. No worries. The last thing I need to see is my cousin's naked ass while he's rutting like a buck." Ronnie snorted, turned on his heel, and strode back toward the headquarters building.

What in the hell has come over everyone today? It's like they are all in cahoots playing matchmaker. The group was known for pranks, but never for giving two people a helping hand in the dating department. Odd, but pretty damn sweet too. With the gift card for a romantic date and a day pass to spend together, he and Sonar were pretty much being molded into a couple. Like Play-Doh. Jag grinned at the analogy. Fitting together wouldn't be a problem. It would be prying them apart in order to get back to work that would be.

JAG CLIMBED out of the limo, waited for Sonar to exit, then shut the door. The driver slowly pulled away, leaving the two of them alone back at Jag's home.

"I'm stuffed." Jag patted his stomach. "Great food. Just too much of it."

"Speaking of stuffed, did you notice our waiter's crotch?" Sonar trotted up the front steps.

Jag blinked at Sonar before following along. As a sniper Jag normally picked up on tiny details around him. Obviously not tonight. "I was too distracted by something else to pay much attention." Boy, was that the truth. He couldn't take his eyes off Sonar, having thoroughly enjoyed their evening together.

The night is still young.

The breeze brought an elusive aroma to him. Jag sniffed the air, picking up traces of familiar scents. All too familiar. "Do you smell what I smell?"

Sonar lifted his nose in the air. "Uh-oh. Think it's a badly planned prank?"

Jag shrugged. "Only one way to find out." He unlocked the front door, stepped through, and scoured the living room. His gaze landed on a trail of brightly colored condoms, still in their packages, leading from just inside the front door straight into his bedroom.

Sonar walked past him, pausing to stare at the floor and shake his head. "I take it this is their way of leaving a subtle hint?"

Jag's lips twitched. "Those animals wouldn't know subtle if it hit them on the head."

"Considering we don't carry disease and I'm pretty confident I'm not about to become the first man in the history of the world to become pregnant, what should we do with them?"

A sudden inspiration hit. "Leave them for now. We'll pick them up later. I can probably scrounge up a fishbowl around here somewhere."

Sonar blinked, confusion written all over his face. "A fishbowl?"

Jag grinned. "Ever been to college? The nurse's office at mine used to keep condoms in a fishbowl for free taking."

"Okay...." His lips thinned out in continued bewilderment.

"We have the fishbowl. Got the condoms. The only question remains is who gets to be the keeper of them?" Jag waggled his eyebrows.

Sonar caught on. He chuckled. "You're taking a chance on getting your butt kicked."

"What else is new?"

"This." Sonar met Jag's gaze for a second before moving close. Really close.

Jag pulled Sonar into his embrace, sealing their lips with unbridled passion. The first burst of need hit Jag hard. He'd waited seemingly forever for this moment, even though they'd been together less than twenty-four hours ago. Jag just couldn't get enough of Sonar, their newfound love, or the passion that crackled between them.

Sonar tilted his head and gave back with gusto.

Jag took control of the kiss. He dabbled, taking his time to lick at Sonar's lips before asking for entrance. Sonar's mouth opened on a quiet moan. Taking advantage, Jag slipped his tongue inside, plundering as he tasted Sonar deeply, leaving no crevice unexplored. For the longest time he simply meshed their mouths, enjoying the precursor and buildup as he reacquainted himself with the joy of kissing.

Passion erupted, lashing him to pick up the pace, to do something more than simply stand there. Jag pressed tiny kisses along Sonar's jawline as he worked on the buttons of Sonar's clothing, impatient to find bare, warm skin under his hands. Task complete, he shoved the unwanted material aside and rubbed over the hills and valleys of Sonar's bare chest and abdomen.

"Mmm." Sonar mirrored his earlier actions. "Off. Now."

Jag assisted by flipping the buttons himself before removing his shirt and tossing it aside. He took a moment to unzip his fly, push his pants down, and step out of the resulting puddle of clothing.

He peered over to find Sonar kicking free of his pants, leaving him in all his nude, splendid glory.

Muscles snapped and extended with every movement, a male body certainly in its prime. Jag licked his lips and dropped his gaze further. Sonar's erection stood boldly outward, thick and long. As he watched, a bead of moisture formed at the slit.

"Damn you're sexy."

Sonar grinned lopsidedly. "The same could be said about you." His eyes locked on Jag's cock.

Jag let him take everything in. Hell, he was doing the very same thing. They'd seen one another sans clothing before. Each time was better than the last. His cock hardened all the more with the teasing expression and rapt appreciation on Sonar's face. He felt like a man. A stud. Capable of damn near anything.

"Come here." Jag opened his arms, immediately cupping the back of Sonar's head when he stepped close and pulling him in for another searing kiss.

Sonar's hands acclimated themselves with Jag's torso before dropping to his aching shaft. With confidence, those same gifted hands rubbed and stroked him to a fevered pitch before smearing a bead of precum over the head.

Jag groaned as he reluctantly moved back a pace. "Keep that up and I'm going to blow right here and now."

"Is that a problem?" Sonar's eyes lit up.

"It is when I'd rather come inside your ass than on the living room floor."

"There's that." Sonar closed the distance once more. He reached out to pet Jag.

"Uh-uh." Jag latched onto Sonar's wrist and tugged, leading them into the bedroom. "My turn to torment you."

"Spoilsport."

"Complaints, complaints." Jag stopped next to the bed, swung around, and faced Sonar. He dipped in for a quick kiss while running his hands up and down Sonar's body. "I'll make this unforgettable. Promise."

They'd just started and already he was addicted. The taste, the scent of Sonar in full lust. The feel of his beautiful body. Jag couldn't wait to shove balls deep into Sonar's ass.

Sonar rubbed his nose against Jag's, then brushed his lips over Jag's. "I think we might even trigger the Richter scale this time."

Jag chuckled. "Don't tell Mac. He'll find a way to use that as a tactical advantage and farm us out."

Sonar snorted. "Like I'm going to talk dirty details to the old man? So not happening."

"Good." Jag nibbled on Sonar's lips. "Because you're mine. All mine."

"No other man will ever do for me," Sonar whispered.

"Since I don't share, that's probably a good thing." Jag worried Sonar's nipples into hard beads.

"Did I tell you that I love you today?"

"I don't think so."

Sonar brushed sweet kisses over Jag's eyelids. "I love you, Cole. You have my heart."

The words added a new dimension to Jag's arousal, spurring him higher and hungrier. "I'll guard it well. Will you do the same for mine?"

"Oh, yeah." Sonar smiled wickedly. "I'm small but mighty after all."

"That you are." Jag caressed Sonar's soft skin, enjoying the warmth and silkiness as Sonar mimicked his actions, leaving a trail of fire in his wake.

"I need you," Sonar admitted on a groan.

"And you'll have me."

So much sexual tension filled the air, he was surprised tiny sparks didn't brighten up the darkness of the room like glowing Northern Lights.

He'd never wanted another man more.

Jag seized control of the kiss, pouring all his emotions into the act. He moaned low in his throat, gripped Sonar's ass in his hands, and squeezed. "You've got me so hot."

Sonar chuckled, a harsh sound due to his rapid breathing. "It's only fair. I'm so fucking hard right now...."

Jag met Sonar's lips again with short, teasing caresses that allowed him a second to catch his breath and cool his jets before the next stage began. "Let's take this to the bed."

Sonar's smiled turned sinful as he reached down to stroke Jag's jutting erection. "In a hurry to fuck my ass?"

"More than you know." Jag lightly smacked Sonar's rear. "On the bed." He watched Sonar obey, crawling to the center on hands and knees. Once there, Sonar peered back at him.

Jag pulled a tube of lube from the bedside table, opened the cap, and squirted a generous dollop onto his hand. He stared at Sonar as he spread the gel over his shaft. Sonar's eyes locked on Jag's dick. He licked his lips as sensual lust covered his face.

Unable to wait a minute more, Jag took to the bed, stopping behind Sonar. He ran his hands over Sonar's back, along his flanks, and down his glorious rear. "Perfect." Collecting more lube on his fingers, he spread it around Sonar's entrance, before dipping one finger in.

Sonar gasped and rocked, his channel tightening around Jag's finger. "Yes. Oh, yes."

Jag grinned and added another digit. He twisted his wrist, spread his fingers, and started an in-and-out motion in order to loosen the snug sphincter in preparation for his penetration. "Like that, huh?"

"Shit, yeah."

"Then turn over."

Sonar twisted to look back at him. He blinked, but did as bidden. Once he lay spread out on the mattress, Jag edged between his open thighs. "Much better." He found Sonar's hole once more, adding a third finger this time.

A hiss escaped Sonar's lips as his face drew up in a combination of discomfort and high-flying pleasure.

Jag rested his hand against Sonar's opening, allowing his lover to adjust. He bent and flicked his tongue across Sonar's cock, which twitched and jumped at the contact.

"Mmm." Sonar arched his back, shoving his pelvis forward.

Taking the hint, Jag engulfed the head into his mouth and lapped away at the drops of salty precum leaking from the tip. He kept up the torment a bit longer, until Sonar eagerly rocked against his hand, his head thrashing on the pillow.

Jag considered getting Sonar off just like that but quickly discarded the idea. He wanted them both to rocket to the heavens while connected. He needed to come in Sonar's ass, to feel those muscles clamp around him, milk him.

Releasing Sonar's cock, Jag removed his fingers, scooted closer, and lined up his dick. He waited for Sonar to open his eyes. When he did, Jag began to inch inside, gradually, gently, watching for any signs of pain along the way.

Sonar's breath caught. He propped himself up on his elbows and rested his legs over Jag's thighs. His gaze bounced from the place of their joining to Jag's face and back again.

"Okay?" Jag slowed his ascent down to a crawl. They'd fucked before but each time was different and he wasn't about to take a chance on hurting Sonar.

"Yeah. You're damn big."

"And you want my big dick buried in your ass. All the way."

Sonar's eyes flashed. "Want it. Need it." He grunted as Jag surged forward once more. He lifted his pelvis and his mouth fell open. Dropping back to the bed, he whimpered, clutched the comforter, and blew out a deep breath. "Oh, fuck. More. More!"

Spurred on by Sonar's words, Jag hit bottom in one powerful thrust. He scanned Sonar's face and found only sexual excitement and building pleasure. "Still okay?"

"Yeah. Fuck me already." Sonar pinned Jag with his gaze. He lifted his hips and growled.

If he weren't so turned on, Jag would have laughed. Sonar wasn't a meek, submissive lover. He embraced topping from the bottom and made a damn nice piece of eye candy in the process.

Jag pulled away and slowly sank back in, testing the waters. When a sweet moan of need answered, he loosened the reins of his control, setting up a moderate pace of long strokes meant to hit Sonar's hot spot on each downswing.

Sonar grabbed his own erection and started tugging.

The sight just about sent Jag right over the edge. "That's it. Jack yourself off. I'm going to watch you come." He braced his hands on either side of Sonar's shoulders, took advantage of the leverage, and picked up both speed and power. Short, hard jabs that sank balls deep each and every time.

Sonar cried out, his hand flying over his thick dick. A second later, a pulse of cum fired through the air only to fall on Sonar's chest.

Jag growled as Sonar's body clamped down on his cock. Hard. He powered through, unable to stop with the pinnacle just out of reach.

Lowering his chest, he stretched out over Sonar, his bent arms taking his weight. Frantically, he pressed kisses to Sonar's face, his lips, his ear. "That was so fucking great. You're going to make me blow my load."

Sonar licked a line down Jag's throat. He reached around, grabbed Jag's ass, and pulled him closer, deeper, at the same time rolling his lower body to present his ass for Jag's pummeling. "Take me, Jag. Take what you need from me."

Jag didn't have to be told twice. He made each thrust count, grunting with the effort. Pleasure built and held, leaving him teetering on the edge.

Sonar nipped Jag's ear. "Come for me, baby."

Stars blinked in front of Jag's eyes as an overwhelming climax hit him square and with the power of a battering ram. He roared, buried his cock as deep as he could go, and shook from the violent orgasm. Pulse after pulse of hot cum left his body, each providing a crest of rapture, the intensity more than he'd ever known.

Awareness returned in the form of Sonar lightly caressing his back and nuzzling his cheek.

Jag blinked to clear his vision, then met Sonar's eyes. "Damn."

A bright smile appeared immediately on Sonar's face. "You can say that again."

"That was one hell of a ride."

"Uh-huh."

Renewed vigor enveloped Jag. Boundless energy and heady arousal quickly followed, along with an observation.

I'm fucking happy.

He grinned down at his partner and knew love. Bright, steadfast, deep love.

"Screw recovery time. I think you're up for another round." Sonar nibbled on Jag's chin.

Jag laughed. Indeed, his cock had returned to granite hardness and tingled with demand once more. "You good to go?" He'd wager Sonar hadn't taken the bottom role too often in life before lately. Combined with their exuberant sex life since pairing up, Jag was almost certain Sonar would be sore from their activities. Jag didn't want Sonar hurting. Ever.

"Try and stop me." Sonar grinned wickedly, clenched his muscles tight around Jag's still-buried dick, grabbed Jag's ass, and thrust his pelvis upward.

"Oh, fuck." White hot flames shot through Jag. Passion exploded.

Spurred on by Sonar's enthusiasm and insistence, Jag went back to work with a smile on his face and a light, joyous feeling in the vicinity of his heart.

Chapter 25

SONAR WOKE with the first hint of sunlight streaming through the window and right onto his face. He blinked into the glare and became aware of a couple of facts. First of all, Jag enveloped him like wrapping paper on a Christmas package. Second, Jag might still be asleep judging by his light snoring in Sonar's ear, but his cock was happily awake and ready to start the day.

Memories of the night before played through his mind. Sonar bit back a soft moan as a rush of arousal filled his own dick and flip-flopped his stomach. He and Jag had meshed well. Very well. The resulting climax still marveled him. Never had he been so turned on, so well loved, so happy. Well, not since before he met Jag. Since then the roller coaster had had some interesting twists and turns, with a few lows and many highs.

Snuggling with Jag, he felt protected, pampered, cared for. Loved.

Love. Yeah, the word described his feelings for Jag spot on. Had for a while. What started off as friendship for him soon turned into something more. They hadn't always been friends, but Sonar saw the potential for closeness, a bonding relationship. One of the best days of his life was when Jag had opened up and confessed his true feelings. Sonar understood how hard that must have been, how the leap of faith would have been particularly difficult for Jag. He appreciated Jag all the more for finding the courage to reveal his love.

I'll make sure he never regrets it. Sonar grinned to himself. They might bicker now and again, but nothing would sever their love. Neither took commitment lightly. If they worked at it, things would fall into place. Sonar didn't have a single doubt.

Sighing with contentment, Sonar soaked up the moment, wrapped in Jag's arms.

As warm and comfortable as he was, he couldn't stay there forever. His bladder tingled in warning, insisting he get up and about in a jiffy. Reluctantly, he extricated himself from Jag's embrace and slid off the bed.

When he returned from the bathroom, he paused to take in the delicious sight of Jag spread out on his back in all his naked glory. His morning wood stood proudly, as if begging for attention even while Jag snoozed.

With an excited grin, Sonar gently climbed back on the bed, settling between Jag's wide open legs. He wrapped his fingers around the base of Jag's dick and commenced licking it like a quickly melting ice-cream cone.

"Mmm." Jag lazily opened his eyes. "That's so fucking good."

"Uh-huh." Sonar swirled his tongue over the slit before opening wide and taking the mushroom tip into his mouth. He lapped and added a bit of a vacuum.

Jag's breath caught as his hips thrust upward in reaction. He placed one hand on Sonar's head, fisting his fingers in Sonar's short hair. His face screwed up in absolute bliss.

Sonar watched Jag's reactions, using every trick in the book to bring his partner the utmost pleasure possible. He took more of Jag's cock down his throat and growled, allowing the vibrations to add a new element to the blow job.

"Yeah. Shit, yeah." Jag sat up for a brief second before lying back down. His hand on Sonar's head tightened but didn't press down in the least, allowing Sonar to control the show.

Once again, Sonar purred.

Jag's body tightened, his hips rocketed upward. Head throwing back, Jag began to pant. "Fuck. You're going to make me come."

Spurred onward, Sonar found Jag's balls and rolled them between his fingers. He added more suction and flicked his tongue wildly all over every inch of Jag's dick. Time and again, he repeated the intimate caress, keeping his gaze locked on Jag's face. Each moan, each hitch of breath jacked up Sonar's arousal probably as much as Jag's.

An inarticulate cry carried to his ears a split second before the first stream of cum hit the back of his throat. Greedily he swallowed, never letting up on his motions until the liquid reward slowed and finally stopped. Only then did he trail the tip of his tongue up the length of Jag's cock, swirl over the top, and lap up the very last drop.

Jag shivered in response, his chest still heaving from the climax. "Damn."

Sonar sat up, grinning wickedly down at Jag. "Not too bad, huh?"

"Nowhere close. That was pure heaven." Jag blew out a long breath and returned the smile. "You might be a keeper after all."

Taking the comment in the spirit it had been made, Sonar flashed his fangs halfheartedly. "You might be a pain in the ass, but you're my pain in the ass."

Jag chuckled, reached up to grasp the back of Sonar's head, and drew him down for a kiss.

The act of affection carried passion despite Jag's recent release. Soft and sensual, Sonar opened himself to it. The aching of his cock combined with an undeniable need broke Sonar from the kiss. "How are you feeling?" Sonar asked as he searched Jag's face.

"Good. Very good," Jag answered with a wicked gleam in his eye. "And you? Sore?"

Relieved, Sonar shrugged nonchalantly. "A little. Enough to remind me you were balls deep in my ass last night, but nothing bad enough to prevent a little slap and tickle this morning."

"Is that an offer?"

Sonar smiled wickedly. "More like an order."

Jag groaned and smacked Sonar on the shoulder. "You're a handful."

Sonar glanced down at his erect cock and arched an eyebrow. "I'd say a bit more than that."

Laughter floated through the room. Jag shook his head in bemusement. "Incorrigible."

"Don't forget sexy." Sonar laid it on thick, thoroughly enjoying the teasing this morning. Sex wasn't always fun or humorous, but Jag made it so. He waggled his eyebrows.

"How could I? You've got one hell of a body. Not to mention a damn tight ass."

"Glad you noticed. Does that mean you're up for another round now?" Sonar slid off the bed, opened the top drawer of a nearby table, and pulled out a tube of lube.

"Always." The low growl in Jag's voice sent chills of excitement through Sonar.

He squirted some of the gel on his fingers as he returned to the bed. Settling next to Jag's side, he made a big production of smearing the lube all over Jag's hard cock. Up and down he moved his hand, grinning as Jag shoved his hips upward in an unvoiced plea for more.

"You're a tease," Jag gritted out between his clenched teeth. He moaned as Sonar rubbed his thumb over the broad head.

Sonar grinned wickedly. "Yep. Judging by the size of your dick, you don't mind a bit."

"True." Jag blew out a deep breath and growled. "Keep this up and I'll blow my load right here."

Sonar tsked. "Can't have that." Jag sat up and swiped the lube from Sonar's other hand. "Nope. Not when I can't wait to tap your ass again." He squirted some on his fingers, then motioned for Sonar to turn around, presenting his rear for preparation.

As soon as Sonar did so, Jag ran one gel-slickened finger along his crack, centered over his entrance, and pressed deep. Sonar moaned and pushed back, taking all of Jag's finger without difficulty.

"Oh, yeah."

Running his free hand over Sonar's back, Jag gently pressed a second finger inside, felt the snugness, and began a slow motion to test Sonar's soreness and to prepare him to take something much larger soon. He angled his wrist and bumped Sonar's gland.

"Shit." Sonar arched his back and shoved his hips back.

"Right there?"

"Fuck, yeah." Sonar threw his head back and gasped when Jag repeated the action.

Jag absorbed every moan, every hitch of Sonar's breath, savoring the knowledge that he brought pleasure to his partner. He'd missed this sort of closeness more than he ever imagined. To be so free with a man who meant more to him than his own life equaled nothing short of a miracle in his book. He was just the bastard lucky enough to have experienced it twice.

"Are you okay? Too sore to continue?" Jag continued gently.

"No. Don't stop. I need this. Need you." Sonar added a small growl to his order.

Jag chuckled. "Okay, then. You want me, you'll have me." He kept up with his task for a couple minutes longer, not stopping until his fingers moved easily back and forth. Only then did he remove his touch and sit back on his heels. For a second he considered Sonar's soreness and made a quick decision. Stretching out on the mattress, he kept one hand on Sonar's hip. "Ride me."

Sonar's eyes lit up.

Jag bit back a smile at Sonar's apparent enthusiasm. Obviously, he'd touched on a particularly favorite position. He filed that information away for later, took his throbbing cock in hand, and began to slowly caress himself while Sonar watched. "Climb on."

Sonar crawled over and straddled Jag's body, his erection bobbing with the movement and oozing a bead of precum along the way. He lined up their bodies, met Jag's gaze, and began to lower himself onto Jag's jutting shaft.

Languidly, he joined their bodies, stopping every inch or so to take a short break.

As much as Jag wanted to thrust upward and seal himself inside Sonar, he dared not. Instead, he clenched his teeth, forced himself to lightly play with Sonar's cock, and patiently waited for Sonar to accept the penetration.

Patience paid off as Sonar moved steadily downward, his face scrunching up in sensual delight mixed with a hint of pain.

Jag caressed Sonar's cock with confidence, hoping to help Sonar bypass the discomfort quickly and reach the point where only pleasure existed. "Almost there. You've about got it all."

Sonar sighed and sat down the rest of the way, hitting bottom with a grunt. He sucked in air, closed his eyes for a long moment, before opening them once again. As soon as they did, he bent over and sealed his lips over Jag's, engaging them both in a sultry game of tag within a fiery kiss. "Mmm." Sonar sat back up once more, rotated his hips, spicy lust flashing in his eyes. "Damn, Jag."

"Mine. All mine," Jag growled as he continued to stroke Sonar's cock. "Can't get enough of you. Of this."

"Then ease up a bit so I can ride you." Sonar nipped Jag's pec to punctuate the command.

"Bossy. Always topping from the bottom."

"Guilty as charged." Sonar's expression turned downright wicked. "Not enough. Not nearly enough."

Jag's arousal ratcheted up tenfold. He released Sonar's erection in order to cup his ass and squeeze. "Maybe I should point out you're doing the fucking. I'm just laying here."

Sonar laughed, a deep melodic sound that buoyed Jag's heart and sent another wave of pleasure zipping through his body.

Jag spanked Sonar lightly, bracketed his hips, and helped him lift a few inches before easing back down. "Yeah. Just. Like. That."

Bracing his hands on Jag's chest, Sonar picked up the rhythm, gyrating now and again to sweeten the experience. He absently played with Jag's nipples as he rode. "So big. So good." Sonar leaned in to mesh their lips once more, his lower body keeping pace at the same time.

Bright lights flashed through Jag's mind. He cupped the back of Sonar's head, held him tight, and plundered his mouth with all the passion rising in his blood. "You make me so fucking hard."

"Ditto." Sonar moaned and trailed his tongue along Jag's jawline. He ground against Jag before lifting, adding power to his strokes and pounding back onto Jag each and every time.

Jag grunted and lifted to meet each downward motion. He couldn't get deep enough, get there fast enough. His world centered down to Sonar dancing on his cock with precision and mind-blowing intensity. A low moan escaped from his throat as he watched the myriad of expressions flash across Sonar's face. "So fucking hot."

Sonar whimpered as Jag took his dick in hand, rubbing in perfect timing to each of Sonar's movements.

Unable to take his eyes off Sonar's face, Jag watched with building satisfaction. "You're getting close."

Sonar managed a nod before throwing his head back with a sharp cry. He rested his hands on Jag's chest and began to pump up and down in earnest.

Jag bit back another groan, focused on drawing out Sonar's pleasure, and sending him falling into a blinding climax. Only then would he let himself go.

Tingling along his spine warned him of impending orgasm. He snugged his grip on Sonar's cock, thrust his pelvis upward in counterpoint, and growled. "Come already."

Sonar plunged down on his cock, taking each and every inch within his body. He gasped, his face scrunched, and his mouth opened on a soundless cry. A split second later, rhythmic clenching milked Jag's buried shaft, squeezing and compressing, as if begging for his cum.

Instinct took over. He yanked Sonar down across his chest, licked his neck, and sank his fangs into the solid flesh at the junction of the shoulder. He cried out as powerful waves of ecstasy hit him hard, one right after the other, each accompanied by a pulse of release. All too soon, the crests of rapture slowed and finally faded away, leaving him breathless and wrung out.

He let go of Sonar with his teeth, allowing him to pull loose. Sonar didn't go far. After lying down on the mattress, he spooned up against Jag, still panting for breath.

Jag curled his body around Sonar, kissed the small wound he'd made, and sighed happily.

He'd marked Sonar as his.

Instead of concern or regret, he felt only contentment and happiness. The man he'd fallen for weeks ago now cuddled in his arms after one of the best rounds of sex ever.

I'm one lucky bastard.

As his breathing returned to normal, Jag held Sonar in his arms, sated for the moment. Protective and possessive. *Mine.* The word flashed through his mind. His inner cat agreed readily. Neither of them wanted to let Sonar go. For any reason.

They might have started out as friends, but now transitioned into lovers with more than enough passion to burn the sheets. *We're good together. Partners in every sense of the word.*

Sonar turned over to face Jag, using one hand to brush the locks of hair away from Jag's eyes. "Cole?"

"Hmm?" Too comfortable to move, Jag lazily readjusted his hold and settled back down into the soft pillow.

"I love you."

Jag smiled. Never would he tire of hearing that particular phrase. "I love you too, Steel. And, just for the record, I'm keeping you."

"Great. Now I'm a pet iguana." Sonar rolled his eyes.

With a snort, Jag smacked Sonar's ass lightly. "Better than an iguana."

"What's better than an iguana?" Sonar's lips twitched.

"I don't know. I'll come up with something, though."

"Yeah, yeah. I can't wait."

"Steel?"

"Yeah?"

"Thanks. For everything."

A true smile crossed Sonar's face. "No problem. Just remember you're stuck with me 24-7 from now on. We'll be attached at the hip."

Jag groaned dramatically.

Sonar laughed. "You'll have to pry me off with a shoehorn."

Jag snorted. "I'd rather get out the duct tape."

"Kinky." Sonar waggled his eyebrows. "Somehow I knew you'd be."

"I've never been until you came along. You must be a bad influence." Jag sighed with resignation. In truth, he didn't mind a bit of wildness in the sack. Especially if that involved Sonar.

"But you love me anyway."

"I love you anyway," Jag replied sincerely, sealing the deal with a sweet kiss.

Chapter 26

JAG AND Sonar dutifully knocked on Mac's office door. "You wanted to see us?"

Mac glanced away from his computer screen. "Yes, I did. Come in. Have a seat."

Sonar sat down first, a bit curious as to why they had been hauled in this morning. They'd returned from their day pass refreshed and frisky days ago, committed themselves to their training regimen, and hadn't even traded insults with the other guys lately. Maybe they had a mission, but Sonar wasn't sure.

Jag dragged his chair a bit closer before sitting. He stared drolly at Mac. "So, what is it?"

Mac's gaze flicked from Jag to Sonar and back again. "First of all, I take it things are going well for you both?"

"Yes, sir." Not that it really was Mac's business, but he bore some responsibility for getting them together.

Jag nodded in agreement. "Very well."

"Good." A tiny smile hovered on Mac's lips. "I can see the difference. Your training scores are way up as well. Together you two are excellent; apart you're average."

Jag turned to Sonar. "Nice to know that I'm pretty dull when you're not around."

Sonar bit back a chuckle. Ever since they started dating, Jag's sometimes sarcastic sense of humor had come out to play. Often. He shrugged. "What can I say? I have this effect on you."

"Uh-huh. All kinds of effects...."

"Gentlemen." Mac's firm tone pulled Sonar's attention back to him. "I brought you in here to tell you that you're both doing an outstanding job. I'll be holding you back from active duty for a couple more weeks before considering any assignment that might suit your talents after that."

"Great."

Excitement washed across Jag's face. Sonar could almost feel him bubbling with energy at the thought of getting back into the game. Jag needed to prove to himself that he hadn't lost his edge. The only way to do so was to just get back out there and do his job. Until that happened, there would always be a bit of doubt in his mind.

"It will probably be Afghanistan. Will that be an issue?" Mac's firm gaze bored into Jag.

Tension rippled through the air. Sonar held his breath, knowing what the thought of returning to that hellhole must do to Jag's mind and gut.

"I figured it would be and I'm up for the task."

Mac studied Jag for several more seconds. "If you're not, say so." His stern tone demanded honesty.

Jag glared back at the commander. "The past is behind me. Still hurts like a bitch now and again, but that's life. I can't let it rule over me anymore and I refuse to shirk my duty in fear. So, send me to goddamn BFE already."

Mac nodded slowly. "You've got your bad ass back, big time."

Jag snorted, but didn't say anything else.

"Is that all?" Sonar asked, more than ready to get moving again.

"Almost." Mac bent over. When he sat back up, he plunked a glass goldfish bowl on top of his desk. Bright, colorful condoms filled the container near to the brim. A piece of white paper with writing on it had been taped to the side of the jar now facing Sonar and Jag. "What I need to know is why anyone on this base in their right fucking mind might think I need condoms in the first place. Not to mention the nice instruction card attached." Sure enough the note stared at them with the words "straight and stalwart" written in black ink.

Sonar tried his damnedest to keep a straight face. He lost it in less than three seconds. He burst out laughing, noticing Jag sported a huge, amused grin on his face.

They'd batted around ideas on what to put on the label and finally went with a motto of one of the Army's regiments. Somehow it fit so much better.

"I have no idea, sir." Jag's lips twitched but he didn't break.

Mac eyed Jag skeptically. "Uh-huh." He shook his head and sighed. After grabbing a pen, he jotted a note on another piece of paper, securing it to the glass with a couple of pieces of tape. "Here. Pass this along."

Surprised, Sonar blinked at his commanding officer. "To whom?"

"To whoever in the hell you want. Just get it out of my office."

Jag picked up the fishbowl, tucked it under his arm, and stood up. "Is that all, sir?"

"Yes, now get your butts back to work."

Sonar regained his feet and led the way back out of the office. Only once they were in the hall, the door shut behind them, did he stop for Jag to catch up. "What did he put on the jar?"

Jag lifted it up to eye level and chuckled. He spun it around to face Sonar.

"We come in the dark." Sonar laughed once more. "Which regiment is that?"

"No clue, but damn, Mac hit the nail on the head with that one."

"Which leaves us with the question of where to drop this little surprise off." Sonar racked his brain. "Lunch room or Misty's office?"

A truly wicked grin spread across Jag's face. "Misty's office. Let Howler find this and go off the deep end."

"You're *really* asking for your ass to be kicked now," Sonar advised.

"Bring it on." Jag made a beeline for the healer's office just down the hall.

Finding the office empty, Jag placed the fishbowl in the center of Misty's desk, turned on his heel, and strode out before anyone could wander by and catch him in the act.

Sonar kept a lookout. "All clear."

"Good." Jag turned a corner and started toward the main entrance.

"You do know she's going to catch your scent on that bowl, right?" Sonar pointed out.

"Yep. Mac's too."

Sonar rolled his eyes. "Like she's going to blame Mac for this."

Jag grinned wolfishly. "Paybacks, buddy. Paybacks."

"Yeah, yeah. Just remember that when I have to scrape you off the cement with a putty knife."

"As if." Jag snorted and stepped out into the sunlight.

"How DID you put up with me through everything?" Jag asked as he shoveled a spoonful of chili into his mouth.

Not much in the mood to cook, they had pulled some frozen dinners out and heated them up. Added in some cheese and a few crackers and they'd called it supper.

Sonar shrugged. "You were an asshole from time to time." He recalled the day they met in his tent at the forward operating base. Fangs were flashing all around.

"Still am," Jag added honestly.

"Not really." Sonar sipped his soda and set the glass back down. "I knew of your reputation to start off with. Hard not to have heard about the best sniper around. Once I realized what you were, things clicked. If you'd have been any other way, I'd have questioned your alpha nature."

Jag arched an eyebrow. "Been around many of us?"

"Oh, a few." Sonar grinned. "They all run around with a stick up their butt." He considered the rest and sobered. "Once I knew what you were facing, I realized how strong you were. Dedicated. Relentless." He paused for a second. "I don't know of another person who could have gone through what you did and still function at an expert level, let alone return to being a smartass and fairly happy."

"A man does what he has to do." Jag's quiet words were filled with solemnness.

"Yes, but a lesser man would have crumbled under the weight you carried." Sonar shook his head. "You're an inspiration. To all of us."

"I'm just a soldier, nothing more."

Sonar's heart went out to Jag. The guy couldn't take praise without brushing it off as unwarranted. He reached across the table, placed his hand on top of Jag's free one, and squeezed. "To me, you're remarkable. Kind. Considerate. Caring. A damn great sniper and the best partner and lover I've ever had."

Jag dropped his chin, but peered up at Sonar from under his lashes. "You're good for my ego. I never say thank you enough. You stuck by me when any other man would have cut me loose and left."

Sonar offered up a soft smile. "I don't shirk my duty. Besides, I wanted to be at your side. Still do."

"Which was a damn dangerous and idiotic place to be." Jag scowled.

Sonar couldn't argue. They had been jet-setting around the world after a deranged madman turned serial killer with a bone to pick with Jag. Anywhere else probably would have been a safer place, even in the middle of a shootout. Still, Sonar couldn't turn his back on Jag then and knew he never would. "Not when you love the guy." Sonar nodded. "You're the one for me. I'd wait years if I had to. Love is worth fighting for, you know."

Tears started to pool in Jag's eyes. In a blink they were gone. But Sonar had seen them and they tugged at his heartstrings. Jag was one rock-hard man. For him to get emotional meant something touched him deep. Really deep.

"How did I get so lucky?"

"I'm the lucky one," Sonar answered truthfully.

Jag shook his head. "No way. I'm pretty sure anyone else would have long since kicked my ass or taken me out with friendly fire. You keep me on my toes, amused, and optimistic."

"Don't forget horny," Sonar added tongue-in-cheek. The resulting chuckle from Jag sent a cascade of happiness over Sonar.

"Horny is a given. You keep my motor running."

"It's only fair. Half the time I walk around with a hard-on, all because of you."

Jag snorted. "I hope it's for me. If you're getting turned on by Mac, it's time you took your turn with the counselor."

Sonar snickered. "Don't worry. I'm pretty sure it's your ass I'm ogling."

"Pretty sure?" Jag's eyebrows shot up.

"Yeah. Probably." Sonar took another bite and chewed while watching the sparkling of Jag's amber eyes. Happiness. Sexual heat. Amusement.

"Maybe you need another look just to be sure." Jag commenced eating.

"Wouldn't hurt. Besides, I'm always up for an inspection." He grinned saucily.

Jag chuckled. "What am I going to do with you?"

Sonar turned serious. "Love me."

"That, I already do. No question about it."

Epilogue

Six weeks later.

"TARGET DOWN."

Jag kept his gun in place, watching through the high-powered scope to verify the guy he had just shot didn't get up, morph into another being, or miraculously heal in a matter of seconds. Been there, done that, and paid for his assumption in a major way. They'd been sent to take out a particularly cruel and ambitious man who presently climbed the ladder of leadership through child slave trafficking. He'd landed on a high priority list for elimination. The military brass had called in the best—Jag.

Two minutes ticked by. Nothing happened. When the buzzards flew in and started to squawk over their newfound feast, he finally lowered his rifle. "Done."

Sonar nodded, releasing his binoculars to hang from the strap around his neck. "Finally."

After nearly a month tramping around the mountains of Kunar, Jag was more than ready to go home. Their person of interest eliminated, mission now complete, he could make the call that would fly them back to the states and headquarters.

Exhausted, dusty, and sweaty, he couldn't wait to find a shower, wash away days of grime, and feel human once more. He glanced over at Sonar and grinned. Maybe they would share a shower. Wash each other's back. And other parts.

Sonar turned and met Jag's gaze. He arched an eyebrow as his eyes lit up with mischief. "I've seen that look before. Don't tell me you're fantasizing about getting me naked again?"

Jag grinned. "Of course I am. You in the nude is damn sexy." Though they'd been paired up for this mission, they didn't dare strip down and have hot, hard-core sex in the caves where they hid for obvious reasons. Namely that distraction made for a direct line to getting shot. Secondly, they were professional. Nothing more than a kiss while they were on the trail of their man. Focus remained the name of the game.

With their task complete, they could return to the intimate side of their relationship, something Jag had been eagerly anticipating since they arrived in this hellhole.

"How are you holding up?" Sonar asked as he started packing up their belongings into the large rucks they carried.

"Tired, but good." Jag wiped at the perspiration dripping off his brow. His sweatband collected most of the moisture, but not quite all.

Sonar sat down on his rear, his backpack to his right. He stared intently at Jag. "No, I mean how are you really doing? You've not said a word about being back here. After everything you've been through in this damn place."

Jag drew in a deep breath. "Good."

Sonar tilted his head, his lips thinning as if in skepticism.

"Really. I'm not lying. You'd know if I was." He threw that out there knowing Sonar would find confidence in Jag's truthfulness. "I hated the thought of coming back here but knew it would happen. This is the hot spot right now. Besides, Mac wanted to test me. This is the place to do so."

"It has to be hard…."

"You're here. That helps immensely." Jag laid his rifle down and sat up in order to cup Sonar's face. "There will always be nightmares of this place, but I've moved on." He briefly brushed his lips over Sonar's. "With you beside me, I can get through anything."

He trailed his knuckles along Sonar's jaw. "You're a great man, Steel, and I've not said thank you enough."

"Your actions speak for themselves."

"When we get home, I'll thank you in other ways."

Sonar studied his face for a long moment before the tension began to ebb. "I guess that means you still love me?"

Jag smiled softly. "Yeah, I still love you, Bat Ears."

Sonar beamed and kissed Jag back. "Guess we need to call for a chopper pickup, then. I can't wait to get back home so you can show me… after you shower."

"Uh-huh. You're just as gritty as I am. And that damn sand gets into every nook and cranny. Nasty stuff."

"True. Guess that means we need to shower together. Just to make sure we don't miss a spot."

"There you go, reading my mind again."

Sonar's mouth dropped open in mock horror. "Fucking scary."

Jag smacked him lightly in the chest. "You're so bad."

"Well, yeah. What fun is being good?"

"Hmm. Good question." Jag settled his lips over Sonar's once more. A second later he pulled away with a frustrated growl. "Make that call. Let's get the hell out of Dodge."

"On it." Sonar dug his satellite phone out of the ruck and punched a button.

TWO DAYS later, they walked through headquarters after dropping their reports off in the main office. Too tired to cook, they opted to take advantage of the cafeteria before heading home to clean up and enjoy a couple days of downtime to themselves.

"Look what the cat dragged in." Howler slapped both men on the back. Turk did the same.

Jag offered up a tired grin. "Good to be home."

"I bet." Turk scratched his forehead. "At least you had this guy with you. I'm sure that helped alleviate the boredom."

"Uh-huh." Jag winked at Sonar.

Sonar rolled his eyes. "Afghanistan isn't what I'd call a prime vacation spot just ripe for horny adventures."

The two other guys laughed.

"True." Turk shouldered his backpack and walked to the door. "Welcome home."

"Ditto." Howler followed in Turk's footsteps. Soon they disappeared around a corner, presumably on their way to the training grounds.

Sonar plopped his ruck down on the floor beside a vacant seat. He pointed to the table next to them. "Look familiar?"

"Yep." Jag walked over to the fishbowl, brimming with brightly colored condoms. "Guess people around here don't use condoms. It's still full."

Sonar smirked. "I'm not sure what to make of that."

Jag shrugged. "We're shifters. Who knows?" He leaned down and read the latest piece of paper attached to the side of the glass. "Gentle when stroked—fierce when provoked."

"Who the hell uses that motto?" Sonar blinked at such an odd slogan.

"No idea, but I like it."

"You would."

Jag found a sticky note, scribbled on it, then added it to the growing number taped to the bowl.

Sonar leaned down. "Roll on?"

"Appropriate don't you think?" Jag smiled like the fabled Cheshire cat.

"Uh-huh."

"Got anything better?"

"As a matter of fact, I do." Sonar picked up a discarded pen and scribbled on the same piece of paper Jag had used.

"Rough riders." Jag threw his head back and laughed. "Now, that really fits."

Sonar beamed. "What can I say? I had inspiration."

"I think we've created a monster."

"Oh, yeah."

Jag read the happiness and amusement on Sonar's face. His heart buoyed in return. He knew he had something amazingly special. His heart beat with the tender emotion. Thankfully, Sonar seemed just as inclined. Good thing too. Jag wasn't the easiest guy to get along with. Without love to temper him, poor Sonar would have kicked him to the curb weeks ago.

That hadn't happened. Instead, they'd forged a bond so strong, nothing could separate them. Not now or ever. True love lasted forever or so Jag believed.

Mark still held a portion of Jag's heart. That would never change. But Sonar had taught him that a man had room for more than one person. The feelings might be different but just as deep and intense. A while back he would have scoffed at the idea. Today he embraced it.

He backtracked a few steps in order to plop his ruck down next to Sonar's and watched as Sonar headed to the buffet for some much-needed food. Jag started toward the front of the room but a discarded newspaper at his seat caught his eye. In particular, an ad. For a jewelry store.

Jag stilled for a moment, his gaze automatically landing on Sonar. *I'll be needing those services again before long.* He'd planned on proposing, just needed to find the right moment, preferably devoid of sand, insurgents, and bullets flying. Tonight could fit the bill. He'd play it by ear. One thing was for certain. If Sonar would have him, they'd be married before winter.

With a small smile, he strode to the serving line, a plan already beginning to form in his mind.

They'd almost finished eating when Mac strolled into the room. He smiled, patted them both on the back, and raked the table where two overloaded trays were down to just a few bites left. "Welcome back."

"Good to be home."

"You did a great job out there. Both of you." His gaze flicked from Jag to Sonar and back again. "Hold up okay?"

Jag nodded. "Sonar kept me focused. No problems at all."

Mac inclined his head. "I knew you could do it." He squeezed Sonar's shoulder. "He's a pain in the ass most of the time, but I get the impression you don't mind at all."

Sonar smirked.

Jag could read the double entendre that flashed through Sonar's mind, because it did his as well.

His eyes met Jag's. "No, sir. I don't mind in the least."

Mac snorted and shook his head. "Get going. I can smell the rutting hormones already."

"Yes, sir." Jag finished his drink in two large gulps.

Sonar shoveled in the last piece of pie, then wiped his face with the napkin. "Thank you, sir."

Mac waved his hand. "Don't come back until Monday." He turned and walked out, leaving the two of them alone.

Jag smiled widely. "Three whole days. Whatever will we do?"

Sonar squeezed Jag's thigh. "I'm sure we'll come up with something."

"We always do."

Sonar eyed him mischievously. "Unless you're tired of me already."

"Not even close." Jag tugged Sonar over for a brief yet meaningful kiss. "I'm keeping you for good."

"I'd like that. It's so hard to find a decent alpha these days." Sonar grinned wickedly.

Jag laughed. "Just don't forget it's *this* alpha that claims you."

"Why would I ever want another? You're all that I need." Sonar nuzzled Jag's cheek and offered up his lips for another quick meeting.

Jag's heart soared. They were home. Safe. And had been granted uninterrupted time to do as they pleased. Together. He couldn't hold back his joy or his excitement.

Not everyone got a second chance at love. He did.

Nothing like returning from a battle zone to put things into perspective.

"I love you, Bat Ears."

Sonar beamed. "Going to take me home and show me?"

Jag laughed. "Oh, yeah."

"Then bring it on. I'm hungry."

Insatiable Sonar might be, but Jag didn't mind in the least. One look from the guy sent blood shunting to his cock. Sonar had that much of an effect on him.

They left the cafeteria and walked out into the sunlight. Mac stood nearby chatting with Howler and Turk. Griz ambled over to join the group, as did Tracker and Misty. When the door shut, all eyes turned to Sonar and Jag.

"I've given them a few days' leave, so play nice," Mac warned.

Howler beamed. "You lovebirds forgot your condoms."

Jag flipped him off. "Bite me."

"I'd consider it, but something tells me Sonar might object."

"And you'd be right," Sonar growled. "We don't share."

"We?" Misty grinned mischievously.

No time like the present.

Jag spun around and eyed the small group. He quickly scanned Sonar's face, then decided that his question could no longer wait. They'd been secretive before. Now, Jag wanted their relationship, their love, out in the open for all to see. Immediately, he dropped to one knee. "I don't have a ring. Don't have much of anything. But I'll give you my heart and my love for all time if you'll just marry me."

Sonar's eyes grew misty. He blinked before a smile expanded on his face. Reaching down, he hauled Jag back to his feet and into his arms. "Yes. To all." He sealed the deal with a kiss full of promise.

Hoots and hollers carried over. Jag ignored them, too absorbed in Sonar's thrilling lip-lock.

He pulled back and beamed at his new fiancé. "I'll make sure you don't regret it."

Sonar laughed. "You don't have to worry about that. I love you more than I've ever loved anything else in my life."

Jag's heart filled with nearly overwhelming emotion. "I love you more than my own life." He pressed his lips against Sonar's for a brief caress, a hint at what would come as soon as they had some privacy and a long, hot bath to wash the piled-on grime away.

The others came over and patted them both on the shoulder. Congratulations were given from the whole crew, along with a bit of ribbing. Jag graciously thanked them, but only had eyes for Sonar. Their gazes met over the small crush. Jag read the twinkle, the supreme happiness, and knew their future loomed bright.

Sonar was an exceptional treasure and Jag vowed to spend the rest of his life showing him just how wonderful love could be.

Starting right now.

Amazing what had transpired in the last few months. From the ashes of destruction, violence, and absolute grief, he'd risen. With a little help, he'd managed to find a great partner in all senses of the word. Together, they could do anything, including rock the world with their love. He'd make sure of it.

CHEYENNE MEADOWS, while growing up in the Midwest, began reading romance novels in high school, immediately falling in love with the genre, to the point where she decided to write professionally for a career. However, that dream splattered against a brick wall, resulting in a quick death in her first writing class in college when the professor told her bluntly that she wasn't any good at it. She shifted gears quickly and left her writing dreams behind, eventually settling on becoming a nurse.

A few years back, she stumbled across a fan fiction writing site on a favorite author's webpage. She began to read stories others wrote, not only making some wonderful close friends from the experience, but also, really learning to write for the very first time. Here she was able to share short stories, practice her writing skills, and truly develop into a writer. More than that, the experience allowed her to revitalize her dream as she rediscovered joy in writing.

Now, she spends her days off with her characters, seeing how much trouble everyone can get into. When she's not working or writing, she enjoys playing in the garden, hanging out with her diva kitty, and using her backyard as a living canvas for her whimsical landscaping, and, of course, reading romance novels.

Facebook: www.facebook.com/cheyenne.meadows.10
Blog: cheyennemeadows.blogspot.com
E-mail: Cheyenne1.meadows@yahoo.com

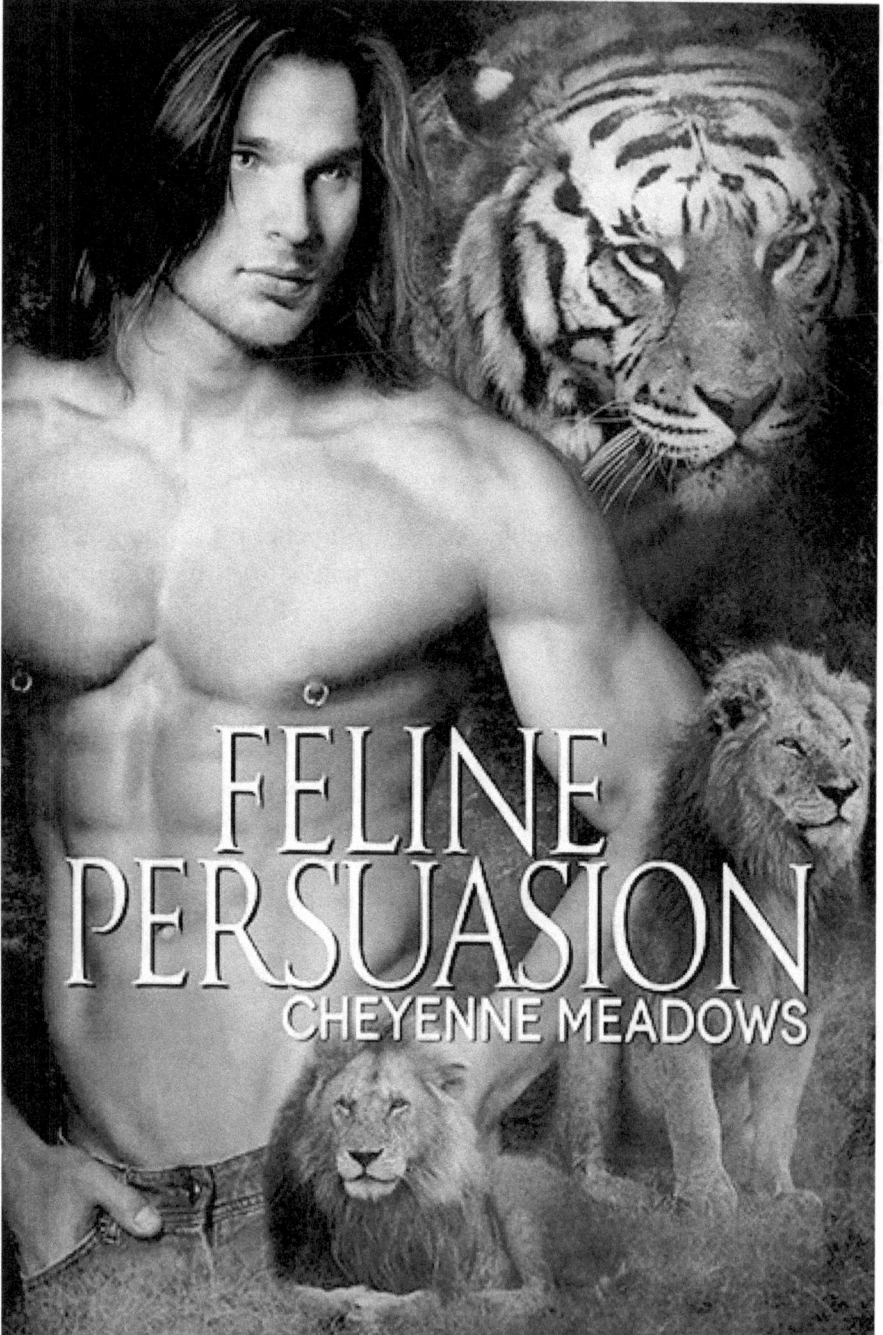

FELINE
PERSUASION

CHEYENNE MEADOWS

When tiger shifter Cade turns an oily owner of a consultation firm over to the FBI, he finds himself with a hit man on his heels. Chester was in possession of security-breaching national secrets, and even more concerning, evidence that shifters exist, and if it got out, trouble would follow for all shifters. So now Cade is on the run. He holes up in an isolated hideout where he doesn't expect anyone to find him--least of all a former one-night stand.

Alpha lion shifter Micah can't shake Cade from his mind. They spent one glorious night together before Cade ran off without leaving even a name. He's determined to find his runaway and protect what he's come to think as his despite Cade's one and done rule. He surprises Cade in his secret nest in the forest, learns the reason for Cade's self-imposed exile, and decides to call for help. This nets them Stone: a top-of-the-line bodyguard and the one man Micah can't stand. Stone isn't thrilled either. He can think of better things to do than spend days in the wilderness with the uppity alpha who stomps on his last nerve.

Despite their differences and history, they need to find a way to survive and expose the traitor in their midst. They also realize chances at love are fleeting unless you grab the opportunity between your teeth and hold on for one wild ride.

www.dreamspinnerpress.com

FRIENDS
WITH *Benefits*
CHEYENNE MEADOWS

Playboy wolf shifter Wiley can't duck out of his pack's biggest annual event, despite knowing his grandmother has possible suitors lined up and waiting. Wiley has no intention of settling down, and the situation dangles just above disaster. Thankfully, Wiley's best friend, lion shifter Ram, agrees to pose as Wiley's boyfriend for the weekend.

They find out fate has other plans when they kiss on a dare, and the passion erupts, so hot and intense they fear the couch may spontaneously combust beneath them. Neither man is able to push the small act of affection from his mind, but both struggle with uncertainty and the ramifications of following where their libidos lead.

If they can't outrun their feelings, they'll have to muster the courage to face their fears before they lose everything, including their friendship.

www.dreamspinnerpress.com

SHADOWING
Mace

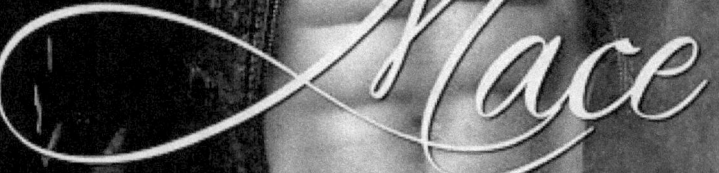

CHEYENNE MEADOWS

With his brother away at a conference, alpha wolf shifter Shadow finds himself paired with IT analyst Mace, the one man he can't stand. Stuck with the partnership due to his pack leader's order, Shadow can only count down the days until his life returns to normal. He's a loner. Period. No matter how much his inner beast protests.

Mace isn't thrilled either, but can't resist the temptation to push all the surly alpha's buttons, even as he fantasizes about what could be. Flirting with danger, he's determined to make the best of the situation, if he can only get Shadow to give in to both their desires.

Unfortunately, a twisted revenge-seeker has other plans. A series of events rocks the entire pack, leaving innocent people hurt and fear running rampant. Both men are thrust into the chaos, working tirelessly to track down the culprit before someone winds up dead. The pressure of trying to stay a jump ahead, with absolutely no clues, pushes them to the brink. Add in a burning hunger for each other, and their world begins to crumble around them. With no other choice, they have to trust and depend on one another in order to have a chance at solving the mystery and saving lives.

www.dreamspinnerpress.com

Also from Dreamspinner Press

Cardinal Sins

LISSA KASEY

www.dreamspinnerpress.com

Also from Dreamspinner Press

Portland Pack
CHRONICLES

PRICKLY
BY NATURE

PIPER VAUGHN
KENZIE CADE

www.dreamspinnerpress.com

FOR **MORE** OF THE **BEST GAY** ROMANCE